TURLY THOUGHT THOMAS
WOULD TRY TO FOLLOW HIM.

He knew it, could feel the blood running in the young man. He should not have gone to see him. But he could not avoid it, not knowing what waited for him at the torch. One last time, if it *were* the last time, he had wanted to see his son of the west, the son he had come to fear. But Thomas was *his* son. That meant something. He thought of Jeneen again as he walked rapidly to the meeting place with Dermot. Jeneen had tried to keep him from the flames' attraction; she had been able to hold him back the way Ellman had. To keep the burning hurt and pleasure from him. The fatal draw. They had been able to do that. No one else had. But now there was no Ellman, and no Jeneen.

"Are you ready, Turly?" asked Dermot.

"I am ready," sighed Turly, who realized that he was past ready, that he was ready for something beyond fire even. It scared him for a moment. But he told himself that it was part of his old search for a father whom he had never known. It was not death. He did not want that, and shivered as he wrapped his robe close around him.

"Then let us go to the torch on the mountain," said Dermot.

Books by William Barnwell

The Blessing Papers
Imram
The Sigma Curve

Published by TIMESCAPE/POCKET BOOKS

William Barnwell

THE SIGMA CURVE

VOLUME III OF
THE BLESSING TRILOGY

A TIMESCAPE BOOK
PUBLISHED BY POCKET BOOKS NEW YORK

Another *Original* publication of TIMESCAPE BOOKS

 A Timescape Book published by
POCKET BOOKS, a Simon & Schuster division of
GULF & WESTERN CORPORATION
1230 Avenue of the Americas, New York, N.Y. 10020

ISBN: 0-671-83451-7

First Timescape Books printing November, 1981

10 9 8 7 6 5 4 3 2 1

POCKET and colophon are trademarks of Simon & Schuster.

Use of the TIMESCAPE trademark under exclusive license from trademark owner.

Printed in the U.S.A.

FOR LOVELY ANNE,
WHO GOT THE LAST FIRST

A journey is always good. It allows men to find whatever it is they are after, even though the landscape of a journey is full of lies.

—from the *Diary* of John Vail

Chronology of
The Blessing Trilogy

2020—*The Falling and the Fires.*

2102—*Birth of Turly.*

2105—*The hiding of the Blessing Papers.*

2120—*Turly goes south for the first time. He finds the Blessing vault and the Box of the Papers.*

2121—*Turly joins the Ennis in the west of Imram and becomes their champion.*

2122—*Thomas, son of Turly, is born. The two return north to the Circle communities.*

2125—*The North Circle is formed and Turly is made its first Center.*

2139—*Turly goes south for the second time. His son Thomas, almost eighteen, goes with him.*

THE SIGMA
CURVE

Prologue

The silence was underpinned by a buzz rising, like the sound of a distant field of summer insects, from deep within the orbiting Home.

"Would you like more tea?" asked an old man, breaking the silence and running one aged hand up and through his thinning gray hair. In his other hand, balancing there, was a dark blue cup which he waved slowly and gently in a circle.

"No, no more," said Colleen. "The Blessing deadline makes me nervous enough."

The man and woman were standing at an oval window and the view was of the earth lying far beneath them, a huge arc of darkness beyond it. Vast stretches of cloud were torn at several points so that the tan of one continent could be seen. The blue shimmer enclosing the earth was like a tight mist and seemed to be only a centimeter deep at that height. The two watched the earth float, unturning.

"Yes, it *is* almost time," said Tain.

"I . . . hope the changes made when the Box was hidden did not affect the Plan greatly," said Colleen, her wrinkled hands shaking slightly, her large eyes squinting as if looking into light.

"We won't know *that* until the time comes," observed Tain. "But either the Plan will work, or it won't; either the curve starts again, or all sinks lower."

"Well, it must work," said Colleen anxiously, her strained voice an indication of her deep concern and hope for the vision of the future she held in her head.

"It depends on Blessing and his people now," said Tain. "We will see if he was *too* clever."

Colleen nodded her head. But she knew that events were in the saddle now, and all that remained was for those in the Home to watch their fruition. "You know," she said, "all the history we have studied makes me less and less sure that design of *any* king will ever work the way you want it to."

"I know what you think," said Tain.

"When the young Turly made his choice in the west of Imram, I said that there were two men of the past who seemed to symbolize the problem of free will colliding with the exacting demands of design. Augustine and Pelagius."

"Yes," said Tain. "Determinism, and submission to it, versus free will. The puppet versus the chooser. An imposed scheme, coupled with super-natural grace, versus a personal desire to do . . . what?"

"You remember well," said Colleen with restless attention.

"When something is brooded on long enough, it sets up home in the brain."

"Perhaps," said Colleen. "But have you ever tried to decide on the view you think is best?"

Silence again. Buzzing. The great blackness outside the orbiting steel womb, locked high in a position which allowed it to orbit the earth only once every ten years, seemed to reach inside the Home and instruct the gravity of its long silence.

"I don't know," said Tain. "The same history you speak of also seems to suggest that man needs a structure of *some* kind."

"You respect the long controversy."

"Do I?" said Tain, sipping the last of his tea.

"In Imram, centuries ago, there was a compromise about that. It was argued that the two things—super-natural design and human choice—could combine."

"And did the compromise work?" asked Tain, knowing he knew the answer.

"As a religious movement it was stamped out in the way compromises usually are. But the human impulses that formed the two views could not be so easily handled. They remained."

"Clearly," said Tain, watching the earth. After a moment he turned to Colleen. "And should *we* have chosen one view alone and eliminated the other?"

Colleen sighed. "I think the Blessing 'compromise' came as close as possible to a solution of our problem," she said, raising her chin.

"Choice and design," mused Tain. "So you still think the Blessing Plan is best?"

"Don't you, in spite of everything else?"

"Ah . . . yes," he said.

"And it will continue to do so to the end . . . unless the *Others* come back," said Colleen softly.

Tain paused at the mention of the Others. Choosing not to pursue the ambiguous matter at that moment, he walked to a metal cabinet, opened it and put his cup onto a rack. After pushing a button which caused the cup to be carried in a precise track to the kitchen on another level of the Home, he turned back to Colleen. "But will Blessing's Plan eventually be stamped out like the old compromise you spoke of? Will a new extremism evolve?"

"I'll tell you in a few weeks," said Colleen. "When the deadline for our contact is reached."

Both then stared out the window even harder as if looking for something miraculous. The moon was just coming up over the rim of the earth to the right side of the window, and they could also see the symbol of the orbiting Home printed on a small jut near the window. It was like a four-legged spider trying to gain purchase on a slippery marble, the Church of Spirit and Science symbol of a paradoxical universe conceived as both open and closed.

Colleen turned away and began pacing up and down in front of the window. Her old hands were twisting again at the small of her back, her tightly bound silver hair looking almost phosphorescent in the dim light. "The transmitter is still ready?" she asked, not facing Tain.

"It was ready before you were born, Colleen," said Tain in a tired voice, as if this were something he would have to put up with. "*If* final contact is made with the Box, we will be able to talk with Blessing constantly, without these long interruptions. It can begin again. The structure—whether man's or something else's, I don't know."

"And the storage tanks are ready to feed them?"

"It is all there, the history, the words of wisdom, all the material they will ever need to grow again. Like the milk of a good pap. If things go as Blessing—and the Home—wants them to go. And if they do, perhaps this time man can make a better choice of it and go on to a better end than *this*." The old man looked around the room which seemed to become barren even as he spoke.

"As director of the Home, you have always been hopeful," said Colleen. "But you did not think, when he was in the west country, that the boy Turly could so easily have turned his back on us."

Tain did not answer immediately but looked down at the glow of the earth which was like a colorful and rigid bubble. It was lovely, he thought, but the silence in the room was like a third companion.

"True," said Tain at last. "But his ability to choose was *one* of the things we were after."

"And his son?"

"That will be up to Blessing and . . ."

"I know," interrupted Colleen. "But Thomas must choose too, and the time is very near."

"Yes," nodded Tain, who tried to visualize the island of Imram on the other side of the earth. The distance and the silence which separated them from it was appalling. But there was nothing they could do until a permanent connection with the Blessing Box was made. Nothing at all, and Tain knew it.

"I want to see it again," said Colleen unexpectedly, her restlessness unabated.

"See what?"

"You know."

Tain looked closely at Colleen's wrinkled face. "You know what the Home thinks about that."

16

"I know," she said. "You come too."

"All right," he said, and followed her off down a corridor of shiny steel. Stopping at a covered niche in the wall, Colleen touched a strip of silver light. Tain watched as a panel rose slowly into the ceiling.

"Ah," said Colleen, staring at the bearded figure standing upright in the niche.

"Beautiful, isn't it?" said Tain. "Still, after all these years."

"Good—the best—even for its day," said Colleen with pride. It had been her great-grandfather's work.

The immobile machine, surrounded by a mist like that around the earth, was the exact duplicate of a human being. It wore only a loin cloth, and its hands and feet were marked with what looked like blood-crusted holes. The eyes were large and hooded by delicate eyelids which seemed almost to twitch under their gaze, as if waiting.

"The old holy man," said Colleen. "The reason for the Falling."

"The *intended* reason for the Falling," said Tain. "It has yet to be proved one way or the other that it was the *only* reason. The Others might have . . ."

"Perhaps," said Colleen, her eyes seeming to glitter in the light from the niche. "The old earth needed such men, and to lose them like it did—as it seemed it did—was more of a loss than could be easily repaired. The groundwork for the Falling was laid."

"Clever work," agreed Tain. "Your people were good at what they did. Machines indistinguishable from the real thing. But the Falling would not have proceeded so well if Blessing had not already placed such machines in other countries in preparation. It wasn't this one alone."

"True," said Colleen, thinking of the legends of the early times, immediately before and after the Falling.

"Nor if the Fires had not followed so soon. No one has been able to account fully for what Blessing called the 'lure of the old ghosts.'"

"That's what *he* says."

"Then you tell me what it was," said Tain, again roused by the old CSS arguments about the Falling.

"I can't," said Colleen, still staring at the shimmering figure in front of her. She mused on how the figure itself was unchanged, the same as when she had come to look at it when she was a child; she had changed greatly, and it had not. "I can't, unless it was original sin."

17

"What?"

"Or the work of the Others, as Blessing argues."

After a moment Tain sighed and reached forward to touch the light that lowered the panel into place. He and Colleen walked back to the window into night and looked down on the earth again.

"It would be nice to step on the earth just once before I die," she said. "I have had nothing but words and pictures of it all my life."

"Would that be salvation, even if it were possible?" said Tain gently.

"I don't know that either," she said. "But next time salvation must not be found *this* way, living in one lone Home waiting for a possible renewal of the race. Next time the heavens must be filled with men, and the earth must not be allowed to fill with toys dreaming of images only."

Tain seemed to frown. "Would *that* be salvation?"

Colleen renewed the nervous twitching of her hands behind her back. "You are right, of course," she said. "The old struggle goes on. And as I say, we will have an answer one way or another in a few weeks, but we will have to live with that answer forever."

"Yes," said Tain, glancing out at the old symbol, unblemished by time. "A few weeks."

Chapter 1

Turly, feeling the pain in his joints that early in the morning, put another log on the dying fire. Bright bits of light sprang out in a brief celebration as the log settled in amongst the others.

"I never in this life thought I would forsake truth," he said quietly to no one.

What truth? said another voice that seemed to be low and inside the Center's head. This voice, laid down years before, right after the leaving of the west of Imram, and given birth by his refusal of the old ghosts of his past which had prompted war and revenge instead of defense and understanding, had become almost a constant companion for Turly who now ran his fingers briskly through his thick hair, shadowed like a redbird in flight.

"I found the truth but it was not mine," he said.

What truth?

"I don't *know* anymore," said Turly, shivering beneath his heavy blanket.

Then come back to us. We will give you truth.

"No!" said Turly with irritation, as the fire momentarily crackled and popped like steps in a forest of dry leaves. He stared into the flames and thought that, once again, he could see various scenes from his past. They were of love and pride, or of his Ennis mate Jeneen in the west of Imram. And others, like the defeating of the hated Order of Zeno and their friends, the Gorts. The making safe of the Ennis in their new home by the sea. And then the scenes shifted abruptly to the last journey back to the northern Circles and the long and tiresome work of forming a new alliance of the many tiny communities into one larger whole that might better protect itself from any possible threat from the rebel-held south.

Turly remembered with agony the many hours of cajoling it had taken to form such a union. He had gone from Circle to Circle preaching, arguing, beating down the old fears, setting up new Circle doctrines, and instituting programs he thought necessary to the well-being of the Circlefolk, like the reading and writing of words. He was famous in the north of Imram, although he had come to hate the doing of it all. He was now the Center of the North Circle.

The flames in front of Turly shifted as if in a wind. His eyes glazed as they became one with their movement and the light moved in his eyes.

All those days, he thought with one deep part of his mind, *all of them.*

What had they been but to bring him to that moment of torment, to the mystery of the fire which still enthralled him, and to the memories of grief at what he had become without Jeneen? He gently rubbed the long winding scar on his right forearm. The hut was cold but for the spot of fire in the middle of it above which Turly huddled; it was almost morning. He groaned and felt as wretched as he had ever felt before, the cold creeping subtly into his painful joints. He knew there were some good memories, and he tried to hold on to them as he thought of his son Thomas.

Thomas, tall and thin and white like a reed blanched by winter. His odd head and body like the disfocus of sight: the body, when you looked at it, seemed to be three meters away; the head only two and a half away. He had long been accepted by the Circlefolk, after their initial praise and then amusement. But he had become a boy who wandered cold and alone and who had only a few friends. As far as Turly knew there were no women in Thomas's life. It was as if he did not care for the flesh at all. Turly wasn't sure why this was so, except that his own early distrust of the boy had bent him in a certain way that was hard to define, and this had made the rest of the members of the Inniscloe Circle, except Meriwether, reluctant to show an undue concern for the son of the Center.

"Why?" groaned Turly, wrapping himself tighter against the cold. There was no answer from the flames as they stood steady and calm at that moment as if listening to him.

Such an early distrust of Thomas, as if he were an extension of the Blessing Plan, had at first been an obsession and then a grief which he regretted but could not seem to undo or erase. A barrier had been raised between himself and his son, one erected by himself, and Thomas had kept his distance ever since, even to the point of living by himself as soon as he had turned fourteen and been able to build his own hut and care for himself. Their conversation had for several years been limited to the weather and Circle business.

"Guts of the beast," said Turly, spitting to one side.

The flames still remained calm. As Turly stared at them he told himself again that his own son *could not be* part of the dreaded Blessing Plan of the Others. *He could not be.* The love he and Jeneen had had could not have given rise to anything so vile. But then, at certain times, the old suspicions would creep back. A tangible wall remained between him and his son, and it was a clear wall that showed the boy growing away from him.

Turly thought he heard something in one corner of his large hut and he swiveled to see what it was. The shadows were murky in the early morning air filtering through the closed window slats but it seemed there was nothing there. The Center turned back to the fire, wrapping himself tighter in his heavy wool blanket. Thoughts of the past continued to plague him as the light danced in the fireplace. The perils from the south still existed, and had increased in frequency in just the last few months; it made Turly curse the Blessing Plan for the thousandth time.

"I will not let it win," he muttered to his blanket.

Win what? said the other voice.

"I don't know," said Turly, his mouth dry and tasting like iron.

21

The Center's eyes seemed to glaze as he stared at the again dying fire. The flames flickered and danced and swelled suddenly in a way they should not have been able to do given the amount of wood on the fire. Turly leaned forward as he thought he saw forms grow in the air. There were vast towers and rings of steel that seemed to float slowly in a graceful arc. He had seen them before. There seemed to be long needles that shot up into the darkness and were lost to themselves. There were forms of things Turly could not name. He started to reach for another log when he heard the sound again, like the scratching of a large rodent in the walls.

"What is it?" said Turly.

No answer.

Turly shrugged and knew that it was a part of a feeling he had had ever since leaving the west of Imram and coming home to the north. He had felt that something was always watching him. It was delusion on his part, he thought, but then he would recall what Thomas Blessing had told him on the Arid Islands almost seventeen years before. He had said: "In a way, the Blessing Box is still in your head, Turly." Turly did not know what 'way' that was, but he had fought it. Steeling himself, Turly watched the flames die as the sounds of the Circle coming to life began to drift in to him.

Chapter 2

Young Thomas rose, hearing loud noises outside his hut. He yawned and dressed slowly, his dun-white tunic almost matching the color of his hair. Moving easily to the door, he opened it, stood silent for a minute in thought, then left for the front gate where the commotion seemed to be.

Thomas saw a scout called Plaken talking animatedly with a number of men standing near the tall front gate. He walked slowly to the outer circle of men and listened as Plaken told of an attack on one of the Circles up the coast. It had been the Danae of the southeast. The scout's mouth, as he told them of it, seemed to move with some difficulty as if the strings of spit there were holding his dry lips together.

". . . and they were taking only one thing this time," he said.

"What?"

"Circle symbols," said the man, pointing to the east and making appropriate signs with his hands.

"Only the symbols?" said one man. "And nothing else?"

"That's all. No women and no food."

"Why?"

"I don't know," said Plaken, shrugging his shoulders. "I'm not the Center."

"Where is the Center?" said someone.

Several faces turned toward Thomas. No one said anything to him directly; he would tell his father, they thought, but there would be no use asking him to.

"Turly needs to know," said someone else in a loud whisper.

Thomas turned away and drifted slowly to the Central hut where his father lived. He agreed that someone ought to tell the Center what was happening, and that morning he didn't particularly care if he were the one to do it. The sun was coming up and Thomas knew that Turly would be waiting for it to warm him to life like a lizard. The hurt in the Center's bones could make him mean at times, Thomas knew, as he walked with an almost casual step toward the large hut.

Almost to the door of the hut, Thomas noticed that the tilt of a water screw on one of the nearby wells was wrong. He could feel its wrongness. Without thought he twisted the screw, corrected it, and made it work. He then moved on to his father's hut.

"Center?" shouted Thomas at the door. "Father?"

Turly stirred inside. Still wrapped in his thick wool blanket, he was reclining in the chair in front of the ashes of his fire, feeling heavy and drugged.

"What?" he shouted back after a moment.

"The men want you," said Thomas in a lower voice.

Turly said nothing and began to unwrap himself. He pulled off his nightshirt and stretched himself gingerly to find the needles of pain where they were hiding.

"Come in!" he shouted to the outside.

Thomas stepped into the half-darkness of his father's hut. He did not want to, but he saw his father's bare chest, which was still muscular and firm. And on it was the odd round scar with semi-circular marks carved inside it. "Father," he said, with all the respect he could muster, "did you sleep well?"

"No," said Turly. "And you know it."

"Yes," said Thomas.

"What do the men want?"

Thomas moved to one of the windows and looked outside. "The Danae have raided Bellsloe again, but this

24

time it looks as if they are staying and coming down this way near the coast."

"Well?" said Turly, his face in shadows.

"Something else."

"Yes?"

"It seems they are taking *only* Circle symbols."

"What?"

"They are taking only . . ."

"I heard you," said Turly with annoyance, turning back to the smoldering fire and ashes. He gazed into the remnants of heat for what seemed like hours to Thomas, who leaned back against the wall near the door and watched his father.

"Only the Circle symbols," muttered Turly at one point.

"That's all," said Thomas.

Turly looked over his shoulder at the young man. He pursed his lips and stood silent for a time. "All right," he said at last.

"All right what?" said Thomas, wary and insolent at the same time, wishing to show his independence but also fearful of the possible wrath of his father.

Turly turned and went to his bed, picked up his heavy brown tunic and slipped it over his head. He shook his reddish hair free as his head cleared the top of the tunic. "Nevermind," he said.

"What will I tell the men?" said Thomas, feeling an old hurt coming back. He remembered this part of his father well: the suspicion, the questions without answers, the innuendoes. He wanted no part of it and prepared to leave without a reply for the men.

"Where are you going, Thomas?" said Turly sharply.

"Outside."

"Tell the men to get their arms," said Turly slowly and with a hesitant deliberation. "We're going to have to find the Danae this time."

Thomas stood by the door and watched his father's face, which was still in shadows. "Yes," he said and looked back once before going out and closing the hut door.

Chapter 3

Turly sat down before pulling on his basu fighting gear and thought of two things: the Blessing Plan and the Danae. He wondered once again what part of mercenaries of the southeast coast of Imram might be playing in the Plan. As he puzzled it over, he noticed that beads of sweat had come to his upper lip. It was the worry of it, he thought.

An old worry. The Plan that might make every man in Imram less than a piece of sand in a desert, his aloneness violated, molded without consent into an alien design. Such design would make each man an unwilling cog in a vast toy structure, Turly thought, blend his flesh into an unchanging fabric.

The North Circle Center wiped his upper lip dry. He felt again the need to resist as strongly as he could the Plan's warping weave. He did not know if he could do it.

"It has been many years," he said aloud.

But he knew that he could at least deal with the Danae. Getting up, he slipped on his brown pants, tied on his heavy leather boots, and gathered his knife, spear, and the long graceful bow shaped like a sensuous curve.

26

Turly felt good as he handled these things and the blood began to rise in him. He believed that with the Danae moving openly in the northwest part of Iram he might have the chance to find answers to some of his questions about their role in the Plan. Laughing almost without thought, he stepped out of his hut.

The morning was cool and clear, the sky a watery smudge of blue that arched sharply downward in the foreshortened landscape of Imram. Good aromas were arising from the iron pots scattered around the inside of the Circle stockade. Turly studied briefly the nest of brown-and-white mushroom-shaped huts lying around the inside rim of the Inniscloe Circle. It was his home, he thought, as he began to stride briskly toward the front gate, and he loved it with the love of a last hope, in spite of his own troubles.

As he passed one of the near huts, he heard someone call out.

"Turly!"

Turly stopped and looked back at his Advisor Henley, who ran up beside him and waved his soft hands. "I hear the Danae are after Circle symbols," he said, his breath puffing. "Why?"

Turly glanced up at the Circle flag flapping on its usual pole. It was a brown circle on a field of red. Turly did not know why the Danae were after the flags or shields, although he guessed it had something to do with the Plan.

"I don't know," he said. "What do you think?"

"Well, why should they start taking them only now?"

"Why not?" said Turly.

"This is the first time," insisted Henley. "There must be a reason for it."

"Yes," said Turly, studying Henley's face, the right eyebrow of which was perched up higher than the left one, and thicker. This seemed to make furrows on the man's forehead that sloped from right to left. A heavy nest of dark hair, streaked through with white strands like cobwebs, lay tousled on top of his head and thin sideburns grew down to the rear of his chin. Turly thought Henley's eyes were like gray marbles, liquid and shining, and centered by a dash of black. He seemed at once intense and sleepy. If it weren't for his good wisdom at North Circle meetings, Turly would think him one of those half-stupid men who had been touched by the Shee, taken away and made mad by them.

"This might mean something is happening at last," said Henley.

"What?" said Turly, shaken out of his revery.

Henley flicked his head to one side. "Perhaps the Danae are at last forcing us to come south after them."

"I don't know what to think," lied Turly. "But I'm not going south. What I *am* going to do is go after the Danae who are up here."

"Let me go with you," said Henley.

"Why?" said Turly. "Look at you. You can't even walk fast around this Circle without breathing hard. How can you keep up with us on the way to the coast? Besides, I can maybe afford to lose a few fighters but not someone who has some sense."

"Yes," said Henley without pride. "But I'm not in *that* bad a shape. And I want to go to talk, not to fight. I am, after all, your Circle Advisor."

Turly looked at Henley for a while, at his determination, and then bobbed his head. "All right," he said. "Let's go."

The two men started off to the front gate in silence. When they reached it, Turly saw Thomas standing off to one side, his white hair shifting lazily in the morning breeze. The casual lift of his head, the way the face looked out absently through the open gates and over the surrounding plains, reminded Turly of the boy's mother, and he moaned inwardly.

"Center!" shouted Plaken, who was still spinning his tale. "The Danae seem to be staying this time."

"So," said Turly, looking around him at the gathered Circlefolk. His voice was raised and his shoulders pulled back at attention. He knew he had to *look* like a Center as well as be one. The face of the Center had to be worn in public. He thought that such a truth was sometimes as wearing as the morning pain in his joints.

"When will we go, Center?" said Plaken.

"It is a five-hour march to the coast," said Turly. "We might catch the Danae at the Ferry Junction by noon if we leave now."

There were cheers in the group as the men understood that, for the first time in many months, there would be action taken against the invading Danae.

"Where is Smith?" said Turly looking around.

"Still asleep, I think," said Thomas, who had walked up as Turly had been talking.

28

"Go get him," said Turly.

Thomas nodded and moved off to Smith's hut. Smith was known as a good trader and a good drinker, but he often slept later than most to recover. As he walked along, Thomas believed that he liked Smith most of all for his acceptance of a bad situation. It had not taken long for the young Thomas to hear the stories about Smith, Meriwether, and his father. There had been much bitterness. Thomas knew that Smith and Meriwether lived together, but did very little else, the old troubles still festering between them.

But Thomas liked Meriwether as well. She had tried to be like a mother to him in the early years. His *only* mother. Thomas did not know why, but he had liked it, had needed it.

There was something else he felt about Meriwether, but he couldn't name it at the time. He had been ten years old when something had happened; it had branded his memory and he thought of it again as he neared her hut.

He had been wandering all day in the Deep Wood between the Circle and the Inniscloe Lake, doing what came easy for him, watching animals at work, learning from them things he could never have gotten from the teachers in the Circle. Watching animals, he could tell how they worked. The tubes of blood, the deep liquids, the lines with sharp energy in them. He could do that with the simple machines and tools at the Circle, too, but it wasn't the same. It was all too clear to him why gadgets worked or did not work as they drew water, turned meat on a spit, or locked a chest. The watching and feeling of tools and animals was something he had always done, as long as he could remember. And there were times when he thought he could actually envision shapes there were no names for.

After such a day of wandering and watching, Thomas sneaked back to the Circle, full of faint light at dusk, and avoided his father's hut. He crept to Meriwether's hut and quietly peeked inside the one window to try and catch Meriwether's eye without Smith seeing him. Since the Circlefolk tried not to antagonize the Center by seeming to take his son's side, Thomas knew he had to be careful. He did not want pity. So he had to talk with his friends like Clare and Meriwether in secret.

No one but Meriwether was in the hut, and she was lying nude on the bed opposite the window. Thomas, surprised and strangely moved, thought his friend heavy around the hips and upper arms. He could barely see, visible in the dim light of the hut's interior, that her eyes were staring at the ceiling with what looked like an amused sadness. Ducking down lower by the window, Thomas thought her full hair was like golden wool. He remembered how many had said she was still beautiful, and he began to watch her with a new shade of interest as she suddenly rose from the bed and walked to a polished iron mirror in one corner.

What is beauty? he thought.

The older woman turned and posed in various ways in front of the mirror. Thomas strained to see all of her, especially the dark mystery where her thighs met, but he could not. The shadows in the hut were too thick. Breathing more rapidly, he focused on the line near the base of her throat where her work tunic had shaded the sun and below which were mounds of the softest flesh he had ever seen. In a way he was sorry that it was whiter than the rest of her; it seemed almost a flaw. But he could see that the mounds were tipped with a brilliant red-purple like holly berries.

Thomas had no words for what he came to feel.

"Cursed ice," he breathed to the windowsill. Looking back over his shoulder once, he noticed that the early evening sky was a deep purple with hollows of pink showing through. As he turned back to the window he saw that Meriwether was brushing one thigh upon another rhythmically, and he ached that the curve and angle of the mirror was such that he could not see her front. He wanted to do that very much. She seemed to be touching herself below the stomach, rubbing there. Thomas thought that she was moaning softly while doing so.

After a time Meriwether stopped, suddenly, as if she had made up her mind about something. She raised her hands to her face and Thomas nearly cried aloud. He thought her painted nails had blood on them.

Thomas reflected, as he neared the front of Smith's hut, that the woman who had been like a mother to him had then said his father's name over and over. He now thought he knew why, but it didn't matter to him.

Smith was standing by the door, buckling up his tunic.

He looked up at Thomas and smiled calmly. His thinning brown hair was curly and unbrushed and his head looked fat, but his face was still handsome. The flesh under his rounded chin shook slightly as he nodded his head.

"Hello, Thomas," he said. "I heard about the Danae from Clare."

"The Center wants you, Smith," said Thomas.

"Yes, I suppose so. Well, here, let's go."

Before they could leave, Meriwether stepped out into the cool morning air. "Hello, Thomas," she said, reaching to him and hugging him lightly.

"Meriwether," said Thomas, not returning the hug, but not refusing it either.

"Will you be going with the others, should they go?" she said, with some concern in her eyes, for memory's sake.

"They're going and so am I," said Thomas.

"Let's go on then, Thomas," said Smith, who began to leave without saying anything to Meriwether. After a few steps he paused and looked back at her. "I will just be a few moments," he said.

Meriwether nodded her head but said nothing. Thomas joined Smith and the two walked quickly to the front gate. The morning air was clear, and through the cooking smoke, through the sunlight coming down clean, came the sound of dogs barking. Smith had nothing to say to Thomas, and Thomas nothing to Smith.

About fifty Circlemen had gathered near the gate and were arranging themselves in rows of three with a fourth man every fifth row as a group leader to keep order and rank intact. They were all dressed in basic Circle brown with an individual design stitched or painted on the front of each tunic.

Thomas saw his father going through the men checking them for their tunic designs. He knew his father was adamant about the designs; each Circle member had to have a separate mark, a different symbol from all others. Some had bright slashes of light, others had the heads of various animals, or pictures of the Inniscloe landscape; some had odd shapes without any apparent meaning.

Right before he and Smith got there, Thomas saw Turly throw his hands up in the air as one man began to run off toward his hut. Thomas thought the man probably didn't have on his design tunic. The Center's own tunic had a simple red circle to denote his status. But

31

Thomas knew where the real design was: the scar on his father's chest, which was also a circle whose circumference stretched from just below his navel to just above the collarbone. Inside this carved circle was an odd marking: two half-circles touching at an angle. When Thomas had been younger, Turly had been proud of it in a way; as he had aged, however, he had stopped referring to it. So had Thomas, who thought his father carried it like a weight. Once he had heard him say that his blood did not want to circulate there.

"Ah, Smith," yelled Turly from the front of the group, beckoning toward the two with one hand.

Smith waved back and then tucked in the rest of his tunic. Thomas held back somewhat as the two men met.

"Smith," said Turly. "We have got to check the Danae this time. It could be more than a raiding party. Have you heard what they've been doing?"

Smith nodded.

"I have got to check it," said Turly.

"Yes, Turly, you do," said Smith.

"What?"

"You are the Center of the North Circle."

"Yes," said Turly. "But while I'm gone, I want you in charge of the Inniscloe Circle here. Close it and keep it closed until we return. Possibly three or four days. Keep outposts. You will have the women left to hold off an attack on a closed Circle."

Smith looked around at the walls. "I think so," he said without conviction.

"If we get to Melnor Circle, and we find a sufficiency of men, I'll send some back."

"Good," said Smith.

"Let's go, Thomas," said Turly, after clapping Smith lightly on the back. "You take the last group behind Clare."

"I hope you find it," said Smith.

"It?" said Turly.

"What you are after."

"We'll find them," said Turly after a pause. "It has been too long without a fight."

"Yes," said Smith, smiling.

Turly turned and went to the front of the line of men. Moving to the outside, he felt good. His morning pain was gone, although he knew he might pay later for it. Look-

32

ing back once, he saw Smith standing near the rear of the column.

Thomas assumed his rear position and then tried to get his old friend Clare's attention up ahead.

"Clare!" he shouted.

Clare swiveled his blunt head toward Thomas and lifted his eyebrows. His hair, the color of stale Circle brew, lay straight forward over his arched nose, almost covering his eyes. Ringlets of that hair were brushed haphazardly forward over and around his ears and joined with a thin mustache and beard trying to hide his face. Thomas often thought the effect was that of a turtle with pieces of wet straw clapped over his head and face by mischievous boys.

"Thomas," rumbled Clare. "We fight."

Thomas remembered the times he and Clare had argued about basu fighting. It had seemed, when he was younger, that Clare would never be fast enough to fight well. He seemed to hunch forward at a steady pace that was good only for carrying mud and sticks. But in practice Clare had proved to be something more. His slowness concealed a deceptive speed which could confuse an opponent into a move he would not otherwise have made, and Clare would win.

Clare looked back at Thomas stoically while keeping himself in step with the others. His eyes were as glazed as they ever were and seemed not to allow for Thomas's existence. No one could tell exactly where Clare was looking at any given moment.

"You're ready, Clare?" yelled Thomas.

Clare nodded his head as if he had just done something he was very proud of, skilled in, but had to acknowledge its doing in modest terms.

"Good!" yelled Thomas. "We'll talk later!"

Clare swiveled his head back to the front, nodding all the while in the same slow rhythm.

The line of men moved out of the Circle area, its floor of red mud beaten down from long use. The weathered gray-brown logs of the enclosure picked up the growing warmth and light of the cloudless day and gave a solidity to the wood which it did not always seem to possess. For a while people stood in the gate and waved to the vanishing men, and then they moved back inside and slowly swung the heavy gates outward to complete its exact circle.

Its life went on.

Chapter 4

The east coast, which could be seen in the distance, was brown and rounded like a slug as it seemed to inch along through the moving water, its humped back just visible at spots above the waves.

The group from the Inniscloe Circle had collected a full complement of men from the Circle at Melnor and, after dividing out a few to go back to Inniscloe, had proceeded as quickly and smoothly as possible to the coastline near where the Danae had last been spotted. The day was gray-white, the thick lumpy clouds making the sky seem like unstirred pudding.

Turly had been walking for hours and he still felt good. From time to time he massaged the old sword wound on his left shoulder, its small flower of healed flesh a constant reminder to him of his youth, of his days in the south, and of the struggle he had had with Oliver at Clonnoise Abbey.

All behind me, he thought. *I will have other struggles perhaps, but never again in the south.*

"Turly?" whispered Henley, as he scurried up to the Center.

"Yes?"

"The scouts tell me we've found their exact location. They have about twice our number."

"Good," said Turly. "A truth awaits us."

"What?"

"Nevermind," replied Turly. "I want to see Garrett."

One of the men at Turly's elbow turned and ran to the middle of the column. He poked at one of the column leaders and then took his place as the man looked forward at Turly, nodded his head, and walked quickly to him.

"Center," said Garrett.

"Garrett, we have a problem which we ought to talk about."

"Yes?" Garrett narrowed his pale brown eyes and cocked his head to one side toward Turly. His greasy brown hair, like thin mud, was bald in the middle of his head but full on the sides, sweeping down and around his ears. He was a few years younger than Turly, but his face showed the same marks of age as Turly's. Lines ran through his face as if to underline the furrows he had been born with. His short blunt nose made him appear at odd moments as if he were skeletal, but his body was trim and tight. It had the memories of the years before when he had traveled south with Turly. The battles at Straiten and later at Hastings Hall had left him pricked for life.

"Garrett, we have found the Danae. But they have a larger party than we do. Rather like the time at Boulder Gap. Unfortunately, we do not have Sean with us. What do you suggest?"

Garrett stared at Turly and then at Henley. He put down his water bag, slung by a rope over his neck. Scratching through his fine brown hair, some of the threads of which seemed to lean out with lives of their own, Garrett half closed his eyes. He remembered Turly had done this to him before. Called on him knowing that he knew less than Turly about what to do. Turly seemed to put an inordinate value on him because of the past, he thought. But he knew he was a follower, not a leader. He did not know what to do, although he had suggestions.

"What do you think, Turly?" he said. "Cut them in two? Beat each side?"

Turly smiled as if satisfied. "Good, Garrett," he said.

"You have the best advice always. I'm glad you returned from the south safely too. I would have missed you, as I miss Kelleher, Harve, and Bulfin."

Men dead years ago, thought Garrett. *Turly lives in the past.*

"Yes," said Turly. "This time, though, we want a live body. A full attack would be to their advantage. You are right, Garrett. We must bait and lure. Wait our chance to isolate some of them. Garrett, take your place again and pass the word to the scouts. Watch and wait."

The Circle column began to wind its way to the fringes of the coast, the sea wind blowing across them its salty mist, the light colors of the island heightened and made brisk by the dark smooth rocks of the coast and the opaque sky.

In about an hour the scouts returned to Turly and indicated that the Danae were camped in a line near the water, waiting for their ships from the south to come in. Turly immediately motioned to his column leaders. They all came in a trot, Thomas bringing up the rear. They huddled around Turly as he squatted on the ground.

"The Danae are here," said Turly, while drawing on the sand with his knife. "We are here. I want the column to break into three sections. One will loop up above the Danae. The second one will continue straight to the coast. The third will loop down here to the bottom below the Danae, who will be caught in a three-way trap. They will have no way of knowing exactly how many of us are involved in the attack. They will know only that three groups are coming at them."

"Where are the ships?" asked Henley, his voice seeming to merge with the distant sound of the constant waves breaking on the shore.

Turly glanced up at him. "The ships are not far off the coast. I want them to be there. I was *hoping* they would be there. I want most of the Danae to have a way to escape. I don't want to trap them entirely, like rats in a hole. Otherwise they might all stand and fight."

"True," said Henley.

Turly turned toward Thomas and saw the wind blow his white hair like surf. "Thomas, you . . . stay here with my column. We are the middle group. Garrett, you take the top group, and Clare the lower one. Are there any questions?"

"Which group will hit first?" asked Garrett.

"I will give a signal," said Turly. "Garrett and Clare, you watch for me here at the center. Groups one and three will make themselves known first, together. Then the middle group will move in to isolate and put the final discouragement on them. They should panic and run for the ships. But a few brave stragglers should give us what we need. A live body."

"Father," said Thomas, "what if they do not run, but stay and fight?"

"We have never seen them do that yet, have we?" said Turly. "And if they do, then *we* fight to the end. But I would like at least one live Danae to be taken back to Inniscloe. Whoever first gets the opportunity to do so, make the capture and get him to the rear. I have never talked to a Danae and I want to. And besides, this is our part of the island and we have the right."

"The right to do what?" asked Thomas, running his fingers absently through his hair.

"To kill them all if necessary. All but one," said Turly with conviction.

"Thomas, your father is right," said Henley. "If we can't fight and beat the Danae openly, the north of Imram is then subject to any kind of attack. So far there have been only small raids, as you know. But stealing only symbols is like a slap in the face. They have to be punished. The Danae might come in even bigger groups and raze the Circle."

Thomas said nothing. His mind was moving beyond the island into what seemed like a large vacuum. Whenever the question of the North Circle's fate came up, his mind would blank like that into something close to nothingness. It seemed to him that he could neither miss nor dismiss Imram in any of its separate parts. The island as island was not of great concern to him. And he did not know why, unless it was his father's long harangues about it that had turned him bitter and cold. He thought at times like that that his mind lived somewhere else.

"Ready? Let's go," said Turly, clapping his hands.

Garrett took seventy men and marched up the coast. Turly pointed down the coast and asked Clare if he was ready.

"Yes, Center," said Clare, while nodding and bobbing his head in rhythm. His deliberate motion reassured Turly. He knew that Clare would do whatever he was told to do, and do it well, with a solid intensity. Turly

37

wished his son had half the intensity of Clare. If Jeneen were alive, he thought, he would have. But it was *his* fault that Thomas was the way he was.

Turly shrugged once, then gathered his group and set off. They walked in silence for about fifteen minutes while the scouts splayed out into the countryside. The sky had cleared somewhat and pale patches of blue could be glimpsed occasionally through the gray-white wool of the sky.

The Danae camp by the sea was not as large as the scouts had thought. Turly scanned the coast thinking it might constitute a trap for *them*. He could see nothing that would suggest an ambush, only the clear congealed green of seaweed bobbing slowly in the sea. He knew both of his groups were in place and waiting for him to signal, and it was time. The sea was running at high tide; the Danae could get to their ships easily. The fine curved ships shifted lazily from side to side, their sails of different colors, maroon, yellow, and dirty white.

Turly stood and raised his sword. The light in the sky was sufficient to shatter across the uplifted blade and so dart up and down the coast. The two Circle groups, one above Turly and one below, began to move inward as if they were one. Turly watched them as they advanced. Another minute or two and the fight would be on. He turned to his own men and looked at them closely, trying to see each one as a separate grain of sand, with separate drives and fears that could yet be driven, without harm, into a singularity of purpose, like this one of facing the Danae and winning an answer to a complex question. He wasn't sure how they would do. But if they had not thought about such things as he had, or as deeply, yet their fighting skills were good; he had seen to that. They could fight as good as they could read, better perhaps.

Thomas was cradling his sword like a toy. Turly watched him and knew that he did not want the boy killed on the beach, but he knew with a sudden vibration of thought that he did not want him to continue as he was either, cold and aloof. What, then, did he want his son to be?

A stupid question, thought Turly. *As if I had control of anything.*

There was a growing murmur on the coast line where the Danae were. Turly's group had been standing behind a dune of sand which was sufficient to hide them from the

38

Danae's sight. Turly fell to the ground, scrambled up a ridge, and lay with his eyes just above the crest of the dune. He could see that the Danae had spotted the Circlemen up and down the coast, and several of them were running back to the main group waving their arms. The beach was as tan as an old pair of Circle pants, and it seemed to Turly that the Danae were moving to defend themselves against the Circlemen. It was time to begin the assault in the middle.

"Now!" shouted Turly, who rose and began to run down and around the smaller dunes and beach rocks without looking back to see if he was being followed. It seemed to him that there was now only the raw, unexperienced adventure to come. And that would require no contact with the body at all; the body would take care of itself. There would be no chance anyway of thinking about it, or there would be second thoughts and then defeat.

Turly heard the shouting and cursing coming from the Danae. They had seen all three groups and were now doing what Turly had thought they might do. Most of them were running for the ships, their legs throwing up spray as they plunged into the shallow water.

But some were holding their ground, waiting for the Circlemen to come. Good, thought Turly, speaking to himself as if from a distance as he ran faster with drawn sword. Twenty meters, ten, five. The first Danae was clumsy; Turly feinted easily and struck in, striking blood, and he wheeled in joy: The blood lust of killing was on him. Two more Danae fell by his blade before he reached the center of the temporary camp where they had stored the Circle symbols. The sight of the brown circles scattered amidst red banners stung Turly into a new fury as he swung sharp iron into raw flesh.

The main body of the Danae was already in the boats which were pushing farther off from shore and out of reach. The rest of the Danae were mostly on the ground, their blood staining the sand a watery black. The three Circle groups had linked up and were systematically adding to the pile. Turly's eyes bulged as a small eye of calm surrounded him momentarily. Through this calm he saw Thomas in lone battle with a single Danae, who was clearly a seasoned fighter. But Turly, amazed, could see that the man could not touch Thomas. His huge sword would swing in a sure arc, its speed and edge inevitable, but Thomas would not be there when it arrived. The young man moved without hesitation and there was no emotion on his face at all. Although he was being attacked by a real sword, swung in real wrath and not basu practice, Thomas's own sword seemed like a walking stick only, something to balance with, for he made no attempt to use it as a weapon. The Danae could have been killed several times by the boy, but Thomas moved like a dancer, carefully, gracefully, in precise balance.

Turly knew part of it was basu training. But there was another part that was not. Thomas seemed to be able to know what the Danae would do and so dance out of harm's way with the cold arrogance of a good player who knew what to do immediately after his cue had been given, or just immediately before.

It was disconcerting to Turly. Thomas did not want to kill the Danae, that much was clear. But why the cold play? Turly, out of anger, was prepared to rush the man and finish him. But then, as Turly was about to act, Thomas seemed to pause briefly. The Danae raised his sword with both hands over his head. Thomas made a single leap into the air and popped the Danae violently in the chest with both feet. The air gone from his lungs, the Danae stumbled and fell, a look of wild confusion on his face, his lips gasping like those of a beached fish. Turly let go his bad thoughts of Thomas, his questions, why he had done what he had done. He knew that the Circle now had at least one live prisoner.

"Get him up and back, Thomas!" shouted Turly to his son.

Thomas nodded, sheathed his sword, and picked the man up from the rear, being careful first to remove all weapons from him. The Danae was like a rag doll and was no problem.

Turly looked around the beach. Seeing the frenzy ebbing, he sheathed his own sword and counted the number of Circle dead. There were not near as many as Danae dead. Out at sea the Danae ships were like colorful insects floating serenely unconcerned. A few shouts wafted across the water, but in no great amount.

"Well, Henley," said Turly to the old Advisor who had come down quickly after the fight had ended, "there was no fight to speak of. The Danae were not prepared to see the North Circle protected by Circlemen."

40

"That, or they are naturally cowards who can raid only when they know the odds are in their favor."

"Perhaps," said Turly.

In a moment Clare came with his hunching walk. He was sweating and the artery at his neck was jumping.

"Thomas has a talker, I think," he said. "Although the man won't say directly *why* they were taking only Circle symbols."

"Bring him over here," said Turly.

"Turly," mumured Henley after Clare had left, "how will you broach the subject? If they had a good reason for taking the symbols, they will have been told to say nothing, don't you think? Perhaps we should take an indirect approach to this matter."

"You want to question him, right, Henley? If I didn't know better, I'd think you wanted my job. And I . . ." Here Turly stopped. He did not want anyone to know that he no longer wanted to be Center.

"Yes?"

"You can try," said Turly at last.

"I thought merely that I might learn from the Danae what we need to know without his knowing we know," said Henley, the deep furrows in his brow slanting in their journey from left to right above his calmly attentive eyes.

Convincing enough, thought Turly. "Question him then, Henley. Pretend you are Center for now."

Henley nodded as the Danae was brought up. There was a cut on the man's left arm and blood was smeared around the edges of the cut. The man, whose face was white and strained, was holding the crook of his arm tightly to prevent the loss of any more blood. He kept opening and closing his eyes suddenly as if trying to ward off sleep. Thomas and Clare stood behind him to listen.

"You are a Danae," said Henley solemnly.

The man looked pained. "Yes, of course."

"Why 'of course'?" said Henley.

"Why not?" said the man.

Turly bristled. He did not like the way the man was not groveling, and he could not hold his tongue.

"What are you doing up *here?*" said Turly abruptly, pointing toward the coast with his chin.

"In north Imram?"

"Yes."

"Raiding."

41

"You have taken odd things this time, Danae. Flags and gate ornaments. Why?"

"We have never been asked to do that before," said the man.

"Asked? By whom?" said Henley.

"Yes, by whom?" interrupted Turly, waving Henley back now, wanting to take over himself.

The man looked at Turly and smiled. It was an infuriating smile as if the man knew his answer would startle him.

"Who asked you to steal Circle symbols?" repeated Turly, fingering his sword.

"Lord Hastings of the south."

"What?" said Turly and Henley together. The beach seemed suddenly silent save for the occasional lonely cry of a seagull wheeling and holding itself still in the moist air. Over the sea the sun had broken through the clouds and laid down spikes of light as if to walk with them slowly and carefully over the water.

"*Lord Hastings?*" said Turly. "Lord Hastings of Straiten asked the Danae to steal Circle symbols?"

"Well, he *paid* us to do it. We don't do things like that just to be doing them. That's what we do: Things for pay. If we steal other things at the same time, we get paid more. We were to be paid a good deal for all this," he said, pointing with his finger to the pile of Circle flags taken back from the Danae. "It didn't work out this time."

"Wait a minute," said Turly. "Are you *sure* it was Hastings, and not one of his men?"

"A big man, red curly hair, balding on top, huge arms and legs, stomach to match?"

"Yes," said Turly.

"That's the man," said the Danae.

"White-boned demon," muttered Turly, the engraved sign on his chest seeming to burn. "But he lost power *years* ago. He was supposed to be *dead*.

The Danae grimaced. "Well, if he was dead, he is now risen and back in power, the best I can tell."

"He has regained his old territory?"

Nodding, the prisoner gripped his arm in pain. "He has, I think, declared himself once again ruler of most of the south, with the exception of my home."

"The Danae home?"

42

"Yes," said the man, who was growing whiter with loss of blood. "That's why he has to *pay* us."

Turly pondered the sky. The past was rushing back to him now, like a dream deferred. He knew the political consequences of Hastings' return to power; it could have far-ranging effects on the north. Raising one hand to his head, Turly thought an old splinter had re-entered it.

"Turly?" said Henley. "What shall we do with him?"

"Hastings?"

"No, the Danae."

"Bind his wounds and give him food. He has told me all I need to know."

"I don't think so," said the prisoner.

Turly glanced at the man who had strange slanted eyes, bloodshot but intelligent, his brown hair cut in a sloppy bowl shape. "No?" he said.

"I know *where* we were to take the stolen symbols, and it was not Straiten or Hastings Hall."

Turly was stunned again. This was more than he had expected; more than he had wanted even. Hastings was alive and well, risen from the ashes of defeat, and here was a man who seemed willing to tell him what this was all about. His eyes, which had almost become accustomed to the frozen glaze of despair, began to come alive again.

"Turly, the man needs care," said Henley.

"Yes, take him and dress his wounds. We'll talk later," said Turly, gesturing toward the Danae with a certain kind of bare happiness.

Chapter 5

Tents had been erected near the beach and Circle guards posted against any possible return of the Danae. The prisoner's wounds had been treated, and he was tied to a log in the middle of the camp. All was calm.

After supper, Turly returned to his tent alone. The night smelled of salt and sea air. But the skies were crystal clear and Turly could see the fine brilliance of the stars, their diamond and ruby points shimmering to each other their quiet messages.

"They are a mystery to me," said Turly softly to his own shadow wavering against the tent wall, which billowed with the light wind.

"Ellman once told me," said Turly to the same shadow, scratching its head as well, as if it were trying to remember if it had forgotten something important, "that the stars cared whether I lived or died. That I had come from the heart of a star once long before anything else and would return to it many years hence. He said—and this is amazing to me now that I think of it—that we actually remember the light from the middle of that star, ourselves as part of the light, and that is what we dream of at night, what we remember most when we yearn for either the past or the future. Do you think that is so?"

The heavy shadow moved its head ambiguously as the sea wind rippled along the side of the tent.

"Ellman was a good man," said Turly. "I wish he were here to tell me what to do now. He was good at that."

Turly shook his head and so did the shadow. Feeling tired, his shoulder beginning to hurt, Turly stepped into his tent. He walked to his field desk and took out a sheet of paper to write out his thoughts. Dipping a quill into a small bottle of red ink, he scratched on the surface of the paper until he thought of the sound of rats' feet.

Something crackled a twig outside the tent.

"Who is it?" said Turly, without looking up.

Nothing.

Turly placed the end of the quill on his chin.

"Where were we?" he said softly, sitting back comfortably in his three-legged chair. "Ah, Ellman."

"Father?" said Thomas from outside.

Turly shook his head. The present, he thought. *The present is always here.*

"Yes, come in," he said.

The flap folded back like the petal of a flower and Thomas stuck his head in, his thin nose gathering darkness from the light of the candle on the desk.

"Father, can you talk, or are you about to sleep?"

"No, no, come in, Thomas. I was thinking of . . . something else."

"I can see you tomorrow if you like."

"Come in, Thomas, and close the flap. It's getting cold out."

"Yes, it is," said Thomas.

Waving his son to a pile of rugs near him, Turly got up to wrap himself in another blanket. If he didn't, he knew the morning terrors would come later. All those sparkles of pain. "Well?" he said to Thomas.

"I have been talking to Henley about the prisoner. He said you were excited and wanted to go south."

"I did not *say* that."

"He said that is what you would do."

"Henley is perceptive, but I have not made up my mind."

"But if Hastings is alive? I remember your telling me about him. His power in the south; the things from the

45

past we no longer have; all the killing weapons. If he is back, he has to be dealt with, doesn't he?"

Turly stared at Thomas. He had not heard Thomas talk like that before. His son had never shown interest in his past to that degree. But now he did. "That is true what you say, Thomas. *If* he is alive. We have only a Danae's word for it. Besides, Hastings has always kept to the south; he has never come this far north in force."

"What if he will now?"

"Why should he? I've been back here more than fifteen years and have done nothing more than bind together a few Circles into some kind of unity for our own protection. Hastings would have no fear of me."

"Perhaps he has something else in mind," said Thomas.

"What, my young son, what?" said Turly.

"To break the Blessing Plan, as you wish to do?"

Turly released his breath in a long downhill rush. He had not thought of that possibility. Hastings *would* wish to thwart any plan that was not his own. That would mean that he, Turly Vail, was a natural ally of Hastings of the south. They might have to meet. It was an appalling thought and Turly shivered somewhat as the wind sent a snapping rhythm through the tent's fabric, moving it like a tan membrane.

"What else?" said Turly after a moment.

"I don't know," said Thomas. "But we can go south and try to find out. We can find Hastings and ask him."

"Thomas, you don't know this, although I've told you many times, but it is dangerous to travel in the south. I did it years ago, but made it only because I had help of sorts. And that kind of help I no longer think I can get, even if I wanted it."

"But father," said Thomas, "this is not something we can ignore, is it? The whole North Circle may be in trouble. The south may be about to move north. What would we do then? Shall we sit up here and wait for it to come, or do we go down there and perhaps work out something with Hastings?"

The boy makes sense, thought Turly. *He makes sense.*

For this reason, although he knew Thomas to be as smart as anyone in the Circle, Turly grew suspicious again. He reached over to his desk and grabbed the quill pen and a sheet of paper. He thrust them toward Thomas, his face dark.

"Write it down, Thomas," he said. "The song."

Thomas's face reddened. "Why?"

"Because I tell you to."

Sullen, resentful, Thomas took the quill and paper. He smoothed out the thick paper with both hands on his knees. Dipping the pen in the ink on Turly's desk, Thomas began to write. When he finished, he drew something in the bottom corner and then handed the sheet back to Turly, who scrutinized it carefully. It said:

> Upon A Knee
> A Nothing Sings
> And When It Does
> It Gives Us Wings

"Good," said Turly. "There is nothing wrong with your memory or your skill in writing. But this I don't like," he said, pointing to the drawing in the corner. It was a Circle demon, with tiny wings at the shoulder sprouting up into the air and dragging at the heels on the ground. Its huge round eyes leered out at the viewer.

"Why do you do this?"

"The verse says 'a nothing sings' and 'gives us wings.' That is what rises in my head when I hear it."

"Which are *you*, Thomas, wings or demon?"

"If I were part of the Plan," said Thomas, knowing what his father thought, "would I be urging you to find yet another man who was against me?"

Turly thought about this in silence for several minutes. He tried to visualize the Circle community as a place of motion, a spinning mist of energy in a single place; to this he countered the tapestry of the Blessing Plan, which he saw as a crystalline structure of harmonized parts, without any motion at all.

"Father?" said Thomas with a touch of impatience. "Will we go south or not?"

"I don't know yet," said Turly slowly. "I don't know, but I will tell you when I do."

"Will you?"

Turly stood up, his fists on the table top, leaning toward Thomas who sat with a noncommittal look on his face. "Now get out," said Turly.

"I'm going," said Thomas, rising and moving to the tent flap. "But the problem won't go away, you know. It won't, and it will grow. Soon you will have to decide what to do about Hastings, the Plan and," he added softly,

47

"about me." Thomas ducked through the flap and was gone.

Turly sat back down with a light thud. He was tired and disgusted with himself. He remembered vividly the day when Thomas was five. He had taken apart and put back together again an old Circle puzzle that not even Turly could completely solve. That had been one of the first things that had set him off. The episode had completed a pattern of suspicion, born of loss and frustration, that had begun years before. The discovery of the well-laid plan of the Others, guided by the ancient Thomas Blessing, the early birth of the son who was somehow different, the death of Jeneen. The journey back to the northeast and the founding of the North Circle had sapped Turly's ability to worry about all that for a while. In the early years he had blocked out the fears, accepted his son, loved him. Old Fionna, before she had died, had been Thomas's nurse and had loved him well, although Turly doubted that Thomas could remember her.

The suspicions had grown later. Was Thomas part of the Blessing Plan? Part of that intricate plot to subvert and destroy not only Turly but everybody else on the island? It was a fear that had changed shapes over the years, and had seemed to grow bulbous and scaly in his mind. Attaching to his son the fears he had of the Plan, and of the alien Others about whom he knew absolutely nothing, he had made the boy a virtual outcast in his own home. Turly had come to hate that, too, but he hated the Plan more. It had killed many people and would kill more if it could. According to Blessing, it had helped destroy the larger world that he, Turly, still knew little about; and it had mapped out his future and Jeneen's, or thought it had—the death of Jeneen had stopped that.

The tent flap rustled again. Turly looked up expecting to see Thomas again.

"Turly?" said Henley.

Disappointed but relieved, Turly sat back in his chair and told Henley to come in.

"Turly, we must talk," said the Circle Advisor, his furrowed brow grooved deeply.

"Talk," said Turly wearily. The night cold was coming in, and a night bird sang one sad tone.

"I heard you arguing with Thomas," said Henley in a level voice.

But Turly could tell the Advisor was unnaturally nerv-

48

ous. His tongue licked his lips every so often. "Did you, Henley?" he asked. "And what did you think? That I am a bad father?"

"What? Well, not exactly."

"It is none of your business. It is between Thomas and me."

"I don't think so," said Henley.

"Oh?"

"The argument this time involves more than two men. It involves the future of the North Circle, of which I am one of the Chief Advisors who are responsible for such things. Thomas is right. You have got to decide *now* what to do about Lord Hastings, but not simply because he might be *against* the Blessing Plan as you are. He may also be *for* it."

"What are you talking about, Henley?"

"You have to think of the Circlefolk as well as yourself in this matter," said Henley. "If the Danae prisoner is right, we could all be in danger of an attack from the south, or worse. If what *you* have been saying is true, the Blessing Plan could well be on the move again—and with Hastings' *help*. In either case, as Center you have to take defensive action. Do we do that by sitting up here and building bigger stockades, or do we try to go and find out who or what has been pulling the Danae's strings?"

Turly looked at Henley sharply. "Have you been talking to the prisoner again?"

"Yes."

"And what did he say about the Plan?"

"For one thing, that the symbols were not to be taken to Hastings Hall as we thought, but to the Lower Mountains and the caves of the Order of Zeno."

Turly jerked forward in his seat. "What! The Order of Zeno? To *whom* in the Order of Zeno?"

"Barry would not say."

"Barry?"

"The name of the prisoner."

"Oh."

"Turly, he also told me that the Order has linked with Hastings in some way. And he thought it had something to do with the Blessing Papers."

Turly stayed rigid, the words sinking in. With dismay he opened his mouth and tried to speak, but could not.

"Are you all right, Turly?" said Henley with concern.

49

Licking his lips, Turly nodded. "The Danae knew about the Box?"

"He evidently knew about the Papers."

"There are no Papers."

"He said there were."

"He wasn't there," said Turly, growing angry. "He could not know."

"Nevertheless, that's what he said. And you know the legends all say 'Papers.' "

Turly stared at Henley's calm face. "I say there are no Papers."

Henley held up the palms of his hands. "I am only telling you what the Danae said."

"All right," said Turly. "Now, the Danae says that the symbols are supposed to go to the Order and that the Blessing Plan might be involved. How can we trust him?"

"I don't know," said Henley. "What has he got to lose?"

"What?" said Turly, pulling back from his thoughts about the Papers. He knew he didn't really know if there were any Papers in the Box he had found, since he had never had the chance to open it. But he found it difficult to admit the possibility after all those years of saying there weren't any Papers. It was another problem which he had hoped never to face again.

"Turly?" said Henley with insistence, knowing that the Center was dreaming at an important point.

"Oh . . . I said, can we trust him?"

Henley shook his head. "Why shouldn't he take up with us now? He needs to eat. There would be no profit in holding anything back from us, or promise something he can't deliver. As long as we have a good rope around his neck, so to speak. He may well be able to lead us south to the source of our problem."

Turly brooded for a moment. He had thought never to go south again. And now this. What could he do? "Henley, I want to die in the Circle walls, not anywhere else. Do you understand?"

"Yes, I want that, too. But this may be too important to think of that."

Turly knew that as well. And there was a part of him that had recently begun to itch, to want to move again, but it was a pain.

"You know what Hastings can do, and what the Order can do," he said at last.

"Yes."

"Well?"

"I am older than you, Turly," replied Henley, "I still feel something in me that wants to know about the mystery of Imram, the stillness that seems to be under everything, the waiting of it, the oddness that exists at its edges. I want to know why we are here *in this place, at this time*."

"Do you?" said Turly, wondering why the Advisor had not said anything like that before. Perhaps there was something in Henley he had not seen until that moment. He thought then that they were more brothers than he had suspected.

"Yes," said Henley. "And when I left Bellsloe to join you at Inniscloe in the early days, I did so for those reasons. I had heard your stories and admired your courage and your insistence on learning what we could as men of choice."

Turly nodded.

"I was saddened over the years as these things seemed to drain from you. It bothered me that you neglected your own son, but that was a province of the heart and there was nothing I could—or should—do about that. But now these matters touch the North Circle and threaten all those things you had earlier loved. As your Circle Advisor I must tell you that this business of Hastings and the Order is something we cannot ignore. If we do, we are finished. I feel it."

This saddened Turly as he thought of it. Had he changed that much? He leaned back into his chair and gripped the arms of his chair. "And what would you do should I choose *not* to pursue this?"

Henley's brow furrowed into a new depth, as if what he thought and worried about had made even the bone in his skull respond. His lips barely moved as he spoke. "I would then have to leave your service, Center, and I would have to recommend to the Center Council that you be relieved of your position. I'm sorry, but that is something you allowed us to do."

Turly nodded again, hearing it but not believing it.

"This may require more skill than you now possess," added Henley.

"Perhaps," said Turly, who thought Henley might be right. He felt very tired.

Henley saw the look of despair on the face of the man

51

who, in spite of all else, was the hero of the legendary trip south and the man who was the founder of the North Circle. Sitting forward, he lay one hand on Turly's desk. "I might not have to do that, Turly, if you will consider this. You see, you are the *only* man who knows where the Blessing vault is. You have told no one, as far as I know," he said. "And the Blessing Papers *may not* after all be the real enemy. What if Hastings and the Order are cleverer than we think? What if the Box is *for* us, and they are not? What then? Should anyone else go south and find that out, what will he do? How would he find the vault should he need to? What if we finally *need* the Blessing Box, Turly? No. *You* are the only one who can help us should it come to that. You are the only one who knows where the Box is."

I am not, thought Turly. *Thomas knows. I have told him in the same way my father told me. In the riddles and songs I passed on to him in his first years of life. He knows them by heart. He cannot erase them should he wish to. They would serve him as they served me. But he is not the man I was. He cannot go south alone. He cannot do it succssfully or find the means to get to the Box. He hasn't the will or desire. I cannot let Thomas or anyone else go south alone. That means that—with all against me—I must go south again. All these years of forgetting are to be for nothing. I, who despise the Blessing Plan; I, who would see Imram cleansed of it for good, as well as cleansed of Hastings and the Order, as I cleansed the North Circlefolk of their fear of themselves; I must go south again.*

"Turly?"

Turly looked up at Henley from the depths of a great dream. He studied the Advisor's furrowed face and tried to think back to his youth, to how he felt right before he had gone south the first time. "Henley," he said after a time. "Tell me, are you a member of the Mythic Sequence Church?"

"What?"

"Are you?"

"It is against your New Circle Doctrine to be a member."

"I know. Are you still a member?"

"How shall I answer?"

"With the truth. Tell me by what you live."

52

Henley looked at the floor and then back up. "Yes, I am still a member."

"I thought as much," said Turly. "You are forgiven. You gave me a truth. I needed a truth."

"What will you do?"

"I outlawed the Sequence for reasons that, it seems, are no longer so pressing. I wanted to save the North."

"Ah."

"Henley?" said Turly after another long silence.

"Yes?"

"We will go south. But we must return to Inniscloe first. There is something I have to do. I must go through the Framing again."

Turly turned from Henley then and Henley could not see the odd look of resignation on his face.

Chapter 6

A few days after the fight on the coast, and back in his hut in the Inniscloe Circle, Turly pulled out an old manuscript copy of his *New Circle Doctrine*. It was bound in black sheepskin and contained almost a dozen pages setting up the order that was meant to replace the then outlawed Universal Mythic Sequence Church.

Turly flipped to page five. At the top it said: NEW DOGMA. Listed in numerical order were ten steps Turly had wanted all Circlefolk to understand and try to follow. He ran one finger down the list. It was a good set of rules, he thought. Reasoned, protective of each individual's rights, urging the openness of each member's singularity, and demanding the ability to read. He stopped at the admonitory last steps:

8. The North Circle is not all there is. Act as if it were your temporary home.

9. Each stone in the road is a new world. Pick it up and look at it.

10. Avoid the need to live forever.

Turly sighed and lowered the manuscript. He had written those words almost ten years before, shortly after the North Circle had become a reality. The words had seemed good to him back then, and they still did. He had wanted to make the Circlefolk impervious to any attempt by the Blessing Plan to make them over into a prearranged mold. And he had outlawed Sequence framing to prevent any repetition of the poetic ambition of Reynolds John, a good man, a good Framer and poet, who had gone terribly wrong because of his need to be the *best* poet in Imram.

He now saw the contradiction in his New Circle Doctrine. He had simply set up his own mold, and had laid the groundwork for another kind of ambition. But his wish for independence had succeeded in part, for there were members of the Circle who were determined to go their own way in spite of Turly, and the Mythic Sequence Church had survived in secret.

The sun was going down and Turly could see thin gray slats coming through the cracks in his hut window. He placed the book of doctrine back into the polished wood chest at the foot of his bed, stretched his arms, and walked out into the Circle compound.

Times had changed. The Center had always known that merely to outlaw something was not to kill it. It simply went underground. The Mythic Sequence ritual had gone underground, and it had flourished. Turly had guessed that, but could not acknowledge its presence as such. To do so would have been to recognize its value, and his lack of power in such matters. He had thought it best to let it lie, to let its adherents, old and new, meet in secret and continue to frame the reality they evidently needed.

Now, thinking of his youth and of Ellman, Turly felt the need himself to return to the ocre table, the ritual cloth, the tub of beaca, and the fleshing out of the dreams that could not be found in nature.

He would have to do it in secret. Henley had agreed to help in the deception; it was a condition Turly had demanded for the trip south. The night was cool and Turly waited under the eaves of his hut, a quiet rain drizzling its soft mist onto the thatched roof with the sound of a tiny army marching forever.

Henley came out of the darkness and waved to Turly. "Are you ready?" he said.

"I am," said Turly. "I told you I *may* lift the ban on

the Sequence. I thought the discrete Circle dogma would help my people. It did help, I think, but clearly it has not given them all they need."

"No," said Henley.

"Need is strange, Henley. What will suffice?"

"If I knew . . ." said Henley, then stopped with no answer. Both men shook their heads as if discussing the vagaries of the weather.

"I have to see the Framing again, Henley, in order to make up my mind. It has been so long," said Turly.

"It has," said Henley.

There was a quiet moment between the two as Henley tried to feel out the voice of the Center who had originally outlawed the Sequence and now wanted to know its adherents. Turly tried to sense the depths of Henley's distrust and thus the distrust of all the Sequence believers.

"Do you fear the Framing, Turly?" asked Henley at last.

"What? Oh no, I was thinking of something else. There are things I fear, but the Sequence is not one of them. It is, in fact, an old friend. I do not fear what I can see, or know. I know the Sequence conjurings. It is the unknown that chills the heart."

"Only the unknown?"

"And old ghosts," said Turly.

"Ghosts?"

"Old ghosts. The memories of men which are phantoms one cannot always banish. They can work strange things, force strange thoughts and events."

"Is that why Hastings, and the memory of him, is so bad?"

"It is one reason," said Turly, caught in his revery. "But let's go on to the Sequence meeting."

"Your disguise?"

Turly turned and re-entered his hut. He emerged a minute later wearing an old beige tunic stained and tattered from years of storage. He flipped up the hood and cast his face into darkness.

"Good," said Henley. "Now follow me and say nothing throughout the service. The people would be hurt to know you were there without notice, that I let you see them in an unlawful act."

"I understand," said Turly. "I'll be quiet."

The two men moved off into the Circle gloom, silent after a full day of celebration for the successful return of the Circle men from the coast. Turly wondered how many of the huts were empty; how many of the Inniscloe folk had sneaked off to the Mythic Sequence meeting. He thought that the Sequence must still give the old Circle-folk, and some of the new ones too, perhaps, that deep sense of a life-giving reality which he thought he had found years before in the caves of the Ennis.

The life of the Ennis Stone. The whirls of the Stone which seemed to inspire a man, through his own thoughts, to carve out of the hard nothing of life a pleasing space in which to live. The beautiful and the ordinary combined.

The night air was still and slightly muggy. Turly could see none of the moon's light through the heavy overcast. Only spots of occasional light like dim stars shone through open flaps in the Circle huts as the two passed by them. They reached the gates and went through. Turly had not been out of the Circle at night in a long time. The cold and the pain in his body prevented his wanting to do that, and he felt as if he were passing through a boundary into a different country. He began to follow Henley like a thief.

"Quiet now, Turly," whispered Henley.

Pulled by Henley off the usual path leading to the water holes, Turly could see a glen not far from the Circle, its trees a clump of thick darkness. Turly knew the glen was well-hidden by natural design, with heavy thorn bushes prohibiting an easy entrance. It was a hard place to get to for the casual traveler and so often bypassed. It was a good place to store Circle grain as a result; the chance of the grain being stolen by raiders was lessened. There were huge piles of wheat stacked under rough wooden sheds. Walking toward one, Turly could see a glimmer of light, like a thin edge of dying fire, running up one side of the pile.

Henley motioned Turly to one side as he pushed open a grassy flap and stepped inside the structure. Turly held his tunic tightly at the throat to keep his hood on and so joined Henley. He could tell, by glancing around the inside of the secret place, that there were about twenty-five people sitting on rude benches. In front of them, lying squat and solid, was the long ritual table covered by the yellow cloth of the Sequence steps. Sitting upon it was the beaca bowl, a dark brown mound of beaca rising above it like a small mountain peak. The colorful frames of the

57

Sequence, seven in all, ran the horizontal length of the Ritual cloth. Turly nearly blinked when he saw the demon woven into one of the final frames. He had met that demon in the fight with Oliver at Clonnoise Abbey more than eighteen years before. Turly knew he had killed Oliver, but not the demon. He wondered again, as he had many times, what the presence of the demon on that cloth meant.

Turly knew everyone there, but he held his breath like the tight string of a bow when he saw who was to be the Framer that night. Wrapped in the traditional stiff circular collar of the Framer was his son Thomas, who stood quietly in front, calm and cold, waiting for all who would come.

Why is Thomas a member of the Mythic Sequence Church? thought Turly, disturbed. *He is too cold for it.*

Thomas's large head and loose white hair seemed less disproportionate inside the billowy Framer tunic. Arms folded behind him, he had the poised look of a man about to execute a precise dance. Turly knew that was deceptive, only a necessary part of being a Framer, who had to put himself in the proper mind in order to find the right words, to start the words coming, the images moving, to be ready to state the details of what he saw marshalled in his eyes. Perhaps that was why Thomas was there, thought Turly. Because he has only to observe and report but not be involved directly, as the people had to be.

Even as Turly held his breath, Thomas began the Mythic Sequence steps, his voice low but firm as he spoke the traditional words:

We are here and many, for us, for the dead and the unborn.

Turly bent his head and remembered the joy he had once felt as a Framer. His mind twisted and turned in its remembered agony as the words came to smooth and soothe that agony.

As Framer I must give you oneness.

Turly thought of the Stone in the west and the oneness it had brought, the sense of the ordinary and the beautiful made one thing. The insistence of the everyday being made part of dreams. That had seemed an advance over the Circle's ascent into the dreams of another time, another place, another life. Beaca dreams.

And I will do so.

58

Which was right, the dream apart or the dream in life? The dream one could attain only at Myth Time, or the tattered dream one could meet around any corner, but which could also grow—as Turly knew—dim and haggard?

As Framer tonight I must lead you through the Sequence.

Turly accepted the beaca bowl as it was passed to him, and he took the small white pipe Henley slipped him. He filled the pipe with the shredded beaca weed and put a spot of fire to it. Beaca fumes were rising throughout the cramped room delicately like an undersea plant wavering serenely in its dense water. The air grew heavy and mucous as other pipes were lit and puffed.

I believe in the birth of me and the miraculous signs.

It all came back in a flood of goodness. Tears came to Turly's eyes as he heard the words of so long ago.

In the true memories of youth.

The hypnotic words came slowly and with emphasis. Thomas was pacing the early words more slowly than Turly would have done, drawing out the standard entry into the Sequence for effect. It was good. Turly wondered which of the seven monomythic steps the young Thomas would choose to elaborate.

I see the desert and the inward terror.

Turly knew he had seen the real desert of life and the real inward terror. He thought Thomas's words were of dreams of terror and not the terror itself. Terror could not be dreamed. It had to be lived through or died of. That had changed him, he thought, past anything he had ever wanted to be. He had been changed in the Leeve Desert in the west and had never been the same.

The journey to come, the multiple struggles.

I have seen all those things as well, thought Turly, the tiny pipe clutched in his lips.

I will see the death of me and the coming to despair.

Indeed, thought Turly, as it will come to all of us. The thing which walks steadily and comes on without pause ever. Turly bunched his eyes and with his thumb and forefinger rubbed them into light.

But the rebirth of me from the Circle itself.

No rebirth from what he had seen, from what had come to him in the night and whispered in his ear. Not even the Ennis Stone had promised that kind of endless life. There were only two things in life. And death was one of them. What rebirth, thought Turly, where? Into what? But the tears came.

The final breathing and the going to the higher One. Turly knew he had believed *that* once. It sounded good, filled the mind. *The higher One.* What was it? He had never seen it, nor had ever experienced it. Only the *craving* for it. Such a lifting oneness had not come to him even in the Leeve Desert when he had needed it most. It had seemed to remain secret and without substance. Turly thought that, in all the work of men, it had no place. It had been for that reason, among others, that he had outlawed the Mythic Sequence Church. He had wanted another way to live other than to look for a oneness that did not exist.

As he thought this, the formal opening ended. The audience had followed the seven steps of the mythic sequence by quietly murmuring them in repetition. That was a change, thought Turly, who remembered that the old meetings had been loud and full of response to the Framer's words. Perhaps the new stillness was a natural result of its illegality, mused Turly, who was even then beginning to feel the effects of the beaca weed as it worked on his mind. He felt that he was moving slowly on his chair, that the air was thicker, and that the light was broadening into a pathway to the truth.

Thomas paused briefly after the last line of the beginning of the sequence and leaned forward against the great table while he seemed to prepare his vision. Turly watched him closely; but when the hooded eyes opened again, he thought they were looking directly at him, knowing who he was, and Turly felt the guilt of intrusion.

But Thomas spoke, his voice low at first:

> "The clear darkness like a lover's touch
> Smooths his worry.
> The hunger is come again, but pulled clean
> Into a warmth that does not fail.
> He feels rocked into a sleep without fear
> Until the rocking grows into a vast roar,
> Pushes the shore to him,
> Blunt rocks of dim light striking,
> Cramping, telling him it is time
> To come forth,
> The red star telling him it is time

> In lights without candles,
> Without time or end."

The people were already caught up in it. It was the first step: the memory of birth. Turly had not forgotten when Ellman had once done that step; it had stirred him to dreams that seemed to go beyond Myth Time, but really did not. A young boy, he had wandered for days and nights thereafter in the woods and marshes around Inniscloe Lake and had tried to read the signs he thought he had found all around him. It had been a good time, a time of discovery. But Turly had nearly cried when none of the signs had spoken to him.

> "The tunnel breaks,
> A hand descends and moves with gesture
> To him, pulls him into the greater light,
> Greets him in this life
> Which promises him greatness,
> An exploding star leaping into the night
> Drawing a trail of fullness
> Thick as milk,
> A saying of his coming
> Into the Circle that would have him,
> And would need him."

Turly was loving it again. No matter the contradictions. The reality of his life was being framed for him, and he loved it, knew he *needed* it. The words moved him and flowed around him in promise of something else in life, something extra that could lift him up if he let it, give him sufficient reason he had never had before, reason to go on; to continue, to find an answer to his life.

Thomas was good at this, thought Turly in a separate part of his mind. How long had he been doing it? The Center of the North Circle noticed that Thomas himself seemed strangely moved by his own words. It must run in the blood, mused the other Turly, *in Vail blood*, although Thomas seemed to retain the studied calm he had always had.

> "The man had lived in a bubble,
> Like a skin covering his mouth
> So he could not scream,
> His life thin and tasteless,

The savor gone
So that he spat it out
And cursed it with his breath
Till it shriveled.
His eyes clouded,
He could no longer see,
His chest like ice,
The light removed from his eyes,
A hurt deep within him
Like a sin remembered."

Turly snapped his head up, his feelings made taut by
the separate side of him. Thomas was not speaking to
him directly, but the words were. Turly felt the touch of
the words on him, words that peeled back his hurt and
laid it open to the sun where it seemed to squirm and
grow well. He felt a surge in himself, a surge of rebirth.
He had not expected this. It was almost as if Thomas had
known he would be there.

"But a word came and nestled close,
Telling him its sign had been found
And it was his and he lived
In a truth
Which would not fail.
A hovering fire pulled him
Into the absence of all that he hated,
Pulled him into life
And a full house of joy.
Promised long before he knew there was a house,
Or joy."

Turly's heart was lifted up. Those were the words that
came to him: lifted up. He said to himself: *lifted up.*
What it meant he did not know. He knew there was never
a way to fully fathom the words of a framed reality. They
were things to be accepted and believed in, things that
could allow a man to travel his lifetime in expectation of
the miraculous signs which had accompanied his birth
into a world he could never truly understand except in
terms of the frames he made of it.

Thomas continued with a controlled emphasis. He
lacked the fervor of Turly, the fervor Turly had once had,
and he lacked the sense of design Ellman had had. But
the boy knew the value and force of the words he used;

he knew the steps of the Sequence and what could be spun around them; and he did it well, the spinning and the Framing. His voice, low and soothing, spun more:

"Into the hard brilliance,
The higher One which no man knows,
He would now go. . . ."

Before Thomas could finish, harsh sounds erupted outside the meeting place, near the Circle itself. Turly, shaking off the effects of the beaca and the words, rose slowly to his feet. He cocked his ear and heard the shouts of many men.

"Turly," whispered Henley. "Turly!"

As his hood fell away, Turly placed one hand on Henley's shoulder to calm him. Thomas had stopped at the first sounds of trouble. His face was poking into the veils of smoke in the room, but his eyes did not show surprise or concern that his father was standing in the midst of the meeting. The other members did show surprise, but it was surprise muted by the effects of the ceremony. Turly thought he could feel, through his sharp attention to the outside noise, their collective emotions of fear wafting like the smoke itself.

The sounds were growing louder. It was more than men shouting. There was also the sound of swords clashing with metallic clacks, and the soft thunk of spears.

"All of you," shouted Turly to the now startled Circle-folk. "You are all forgiven! The day of the Mythic Sequence is back. You need no longer sneak into the forest to do what you wish to do. But there is something else now. You hear it. I will talk to you all later," he said. "Stay here until I call for you."

Stepping to the door, Turly raised the flap carefully as if he were looking into a beehive. Motioning to Henley, he spoke in a low voice. "Henley, come with me."

The two men slipped out into the night, leaving behind the candle-flooded room. The night remained night, bleak and covered. Branches whipped into Turly's face as he rushed out of the secluded glade toward his Circle. He could hear the shouting at the front gate. As he and Henley rounded the near arc of the Circle walls, tall and thick, they saw torch light coming out in a square shaft through the open gate. In the heart of the dusty glow, flickering and malevolent, Turly could see riders milling

63

about as if trying to control their mounts. But he also saw Circle men running amidst the riders.

"Ah, benighted!" shouted Turly. "More Danae? I didn't think they would be back so soon!"

"The Danae don't usually ride horses, Turly," said Henley with harsh breath. "I think I recognize these men from many years ago, in raids on Bellsloe Circle."

Before Henley said it, Turly also remembered the green Riders. Squinting in the half-light, stepping carefully on the night ground, he saw what he feared. A large H, dull in the reflected light, rode floating on what seemed a deep velvet green.

Hastings had come north.

Chapter 7

Meriwether wrung her left wrist as if it were the stubborn arm of an ill-mannered child. Smith had just left for a business meeting near the front gate; his last words had stung hard.

"If he still lives in your dreams, let him live with you in the flesh, too. He does not want you, though, and you know it."

The only response to that had been silence. She had not known that she had talked in her sleep all those years. Meriwether rubbed her long fingers through her dark blonde hair, streaks of silver in it; she moved her fingers angrily at first, and then fanned the hair out and back. The rankling memory of her unintentional betrayal of Turly to Hastings many years before in the south was a burning sore that still wounded her. When Turly had returned to the Inniscloe Circle more than a year after he had left them all at Boulder Gap, it had seemed like a dream come true.

Turly's hair, when she had first caught sight of him, was red-white as if stained by the setting sun; it brushed his shoulders, which were thinner than they had ever been. He carried an infant on his back; at his heels was an odd little woman who had lived with them long enough to see Turly's son Thomas accepted by the Circle as a true Inniscloe man. But Fionna had died before the next winter was out, and her last words had been to her, to Meriwether: *Save him,* she had said; *he has died in the west. Bring him back to life here.*

A clear ache had shot through Meriwether's breast. She would have given all that she had, or would have, to jump through time and be Turly's again. But she could not. After their tortured return to Inniscloe Circle, after the fight at Boulder Gap, she and Smith had made the link called for in Circle lore and it had bound them for life. She had chosen Smith thinking all the while that Turly was to die and, even if he didn't, that what he offered was not what she wanted. The hurt had been real when she saw him again. She had mistaken her heart and the hurt had grown into a strain. She had hungered for Turly many times since, but there was little she could say or do. And Turly had never encouraged her.

"Turly, I loved you, even when I gave you to Hastings," murmured Meriwether to herself in the deserted hut. Those were words she had wanted to say to Turly many times but never could. She cried softly, knowing the stupidity of her despair, the continual desire for something that could never be. The vivid image of their meeting at the front gate of the Circle then returned to her.

She had been carrying a child in her belly when Turly came through the gate. In the strange joy of seeing him again, Meriwether had run to him awkwardly, and thrown herself against his chest.

But Turly had pulled away, his eyes strangely calm, looking at her swelling belly and then over at Smith whose face was both relieved and appalled that Turly had returned.

In the weeks and months that followed Turly's return, there had been little opportunity for Meriwether to talk to her youthful lover. Many plans had been set up by Turly. Plans to combine all the disparate Circles into one union to be set against the rest of Imram. Representatives had been sent out, and charters drawn up. Smith had been one of the representatives sent to Bellsloe. During his absence Meriwether had steeled herself to approach Turly in his hut one night. The words spoken then, and the meeting itself, were burned into her memory. The bleak night hovered over the roof of her hut as she remembered it, and the light in that hut seemed to flood into holes at the side of her head, holes which sucked light into darkness.

"Turly?" she had said.

"Yes?" he said, looking up from his desk, seeing it was her, his glance grazing the top of her skull.

"May we talk?"

"Of course," said Turly, with an air of abstraction. Meriwether had rubbed her cheek with one hand and tried hard not to cry.

"I wanted to tell you about the time at Hastings Hall," she said.

"There is no need," replied Turly quickly. "That is over."

"No, it is not over, Turly," said Meriwether with warmth, with a smooth flow of understanding of how he must feel. This had irritated Turly.

"Meriwether, I gave you up then, after the escape, in the swamp below Hastings Hall. I gave you up to what it was you wanted: Smith and what Smith could give you. That is what you wanted and it is what you got. There is no need to explain anything to me. I forgave you for being what you were: Yourself."

Meriwether's face had crimsoned and turned dark with that knowledge. "But I did not know then what it was I really felt or needed, Turly. I still loved you, I know, and wanted to be with you in one part of me. I did what I did to save both of us. They would have killed you, Turly, without me to persuade them that you *did* know something they wanted. They were then willing to give you the time which you needed to help us all escape, and I . . ."

"You *nothing*," said Turly with a sharp violence of expression, his jaw clenching, its muscles fanning up into his face. "Nothing," he repeated.

"Turly . . ." The flesh of Meriwether's mouth drooped.

There had been a pause in the room as Turly looked at Meriwether from head to toe. "You carry Smith's child, Meriwether. *Smith's!* You *chose!* And that is the way it should be. Even if I did not feel the way I do, we could do nothing now."

"How *do* you feel now, Turly? You have said little to me."

"I would say nothing to you if I could," said Turly,

67

standing up. "I loved you once, and then I thought you had betrayed me. I lost you and nearly my life, but forgave you."

"Yes," said Meriwether.

"And then there was someone who came after you who saved that life and me and everything else that I came to care about."

"Thomas's mother?"

"Thomas's mother," said Turly.

"You met her . . ."

"In the west. She was an Ennis, a woman who held me cleanly from the one thing I had always been drawn to, and feared. Fire. I did not need the flames with Jeneen. She held me back," he added, his eyes glazing with good memory. "I loved her. I forgot you. I will never forget Jeneen. Never. I will always love her. Part of me is still back with her now, buried in the rocks. I don't care for you or your needs. Why did you come here? What is it you want? The past is done."

"But, Turly, I . . ."

"Should you ever come here again in the dark of night like an old game we used to play, I will tell Smith and accept the consequences. Do you understand?"

Meriwether had understood. It meant that Turly was willing to die rather than have any kind of relationship with her. She knew it then, and she remembered it now, and was consumed with shame and guilt. Shame for herself, and guilt for what she had done to Turly. For a while she had been resentful of this, of his turning his back on her like that, but she knew most of that turning was in her mind only. Knowing this, and accepting what had happened, she had watched his son Thomas grow and had secretly loved him as a child that might have been hers, for she had eventually lost her own child near the end of her term. After that, it had seemed only right to her. Her role of foster mother to an odd young boy would have to do. But the pain of it all remained down deep within her.

Smith had sensed this pain and it seemed to seep into him as well, after a time. He had known of the *cupla* between Turly and Meriwether when they had been young, and before she had chosen him. That had been their right. He had felt a certain pity for Turly that he did not know that Meriwether had wanted all the things Turly could not, or would not give her. Furs, copper bracelets, pots from Bellsloe and Harven, good relations with the other members of the Circle. Smith could give her that and did: wealth and security. Circle property. Turly had been much too adventuresome for that, too alone in himself and his quest to want or need a firm position in Circle life. Turly had, however, been very good at certain parts of that life—the Myth Framing times—but for the rest of it he had seemed to care little.

Smith had given the young Meriwether everything she had wanted, and he had thought his love was returned for it. But he had heard, for too many years, the cries coming from Meriwether's lips, in her sleep. He knew that she and Turly had not taken up the *cupla* after Turly's return, and therefore there was no way to protest her feelings. Turly, for his part, seemed permanently linked to the woman in the west, Thomas's mother, who was dead. He had never given even a hint that he was again interested in his youthful love. But, nevertheless, the relationship of Smith and Meriwether had become one of a qualified unhappiness, and it had turned Smith sour to a certain degree, and to drink.

When the North Circle had been officially formed, Smith thought his old friend was sure of himself at last, a man who had finally found himself. The journeys to places like Cliffharkey, Lufnal, Bellsloe, Marrot, and Clellnear had seemed to invigorate Turly and lend him new purpose after his tragedy in the west. There had been a fierce determination in the young man's eyes which, Smith knew, had dimmed through the long years after the North Circle was in place.

What will happen now? he thought often. *What now? A man withdrawn and alone. A man and a son who were legend, but still men.*

The problem with his son Thomas was symptomatic of the trouble boiling inside Turly, it seemed to Smith. The young boy had had to be brought up by other members of the Circle, his own mate for a while. Turly had seemed to turn away from the boy as if rejecting his past, or perhaps trying to avoid its losses: The strange young man with the large forehead, who had irises so dark the holes in the middle of his eyes seemed bigger than normal and seemed to be able to see into you and through you, *knowing* you as they did so.

Thomas and Meriwether had grown to be secret friends —although Smith had known of it always—and had played together often in the fields and marshes around the Inniscloe Lake, bringing back to the Circle small objects of interest, a broken bird, a rock with odd markings on it, or perhaps a plant no one else could recognize. Turly also knew of it but had said nothing, as he had said nothing of the groups which still framed reality in the outlawed Mythic Sequence. He simply ignored it all and brooded alone in his Center hut, only occasionally settling a dispute that might have unsettled the Circle. Thus he had allowed his son to grow as he could, and Smith knew that the boy needed the friendships he could get as something to hold on to, as if it were perpetually night and there were few candles. And, in the early days, Smith had given a certain surreptitious support to the relationship of his mate and the son of the Center of the North Circle.

Meriwether remembered all this as she stared at the top of the hut, its small chimney hole allowing the gauzy wisps of late supper cooking to wander up and out into the night.

The sounds of struggle at the front gate reached Meriwether through a great buffer of dreams. She sat up and almost shook her head to clear it. What was it out there? She thought he knew about the underground, but believed Turly would not punish them with such vigor. Even with his old hurt he wouldn't do that.

The night was damp and was now charged with a slight tingle of danger. Meriwether put her head out of the hut door and looked to the sounds. She could see swirling dust and mingled figures moving in and out of the gates; the huge fire in the middle of the Circle threw shadows backward into that area. Staked at the edge of the fire there in the center was the Danae prisoner. Meriwether could see that he was squirming at his bonds, trying to get away. Meriwether knew that if the Danae got away, a valuable source of information would be lost. She could not let that happen. Stepping back into the hut quickly, she seized a blut blade and headed for the man, feeling her own shame and anger burn.

The Danae was indeed trying to free himself. He pulled and picked at the ropes holding his wrists together; they were loose. But his eyes were cast at the front gates and were covered by the orange color of the flickering fire. His face looked as if it were on fire itself, an incandescent mask of pitted flesh.

"Don't move again," said Meriwether as she placed the blut at the man's throat.

"Who is it?" he said.

"Meriwether."

"Meriwether?"

"Yes. A Circle woman. Don't move again," she said.

The man stopped struggling against his ropes and leaned his head back against the pole to which he was tied.

"What is your name?" said Meriwether, looking toward the fight at the front gate.

"Barry. I am a Danae.'"

"I know," said Meriwether. "That is why you will not move again or I will clean you."

"Clean me?"

"Cut your throat and open your bowels."

"I see," said Barry.

The two stood still, as if in a painting. The ground, however, in the dancing light and shadows, seemed to be moving like a ship at sea. The utterly black late winter shadows were harsh, and jumped and leaped with a glacial solidity as the fire ate at the wind.

"May I tell you *why* I wanted to be free?" said Barry after a moment.

"I *know* why you want to be free," said Meriwether, holding the knife rigid at his throat.

"No. I mean, there is another reason."

"What?" said Meriwether. She noticed that in the fiery glow his brown eyes looked like wet mud. He could not grin very well, but she could tell that his teeth were at least straight and level, which wasn't always the case with the teeth of Circlefolk.

"There are green Riders out there," said Barry. "From the south. They want me. If they get in here, they will kill me."

"Why?"

"They do not want me to say what I have already said."

"About Hastings?"

"Yes. And more."

"They will kill you?"

"They have killed men whom they thought dangerous to them."

"Are you dangerous to them?"

"As soon as I was captured alive I was dangerous to

them," he said. "They knew Barry would not hold his tongue for long. He likes to work it too much for profit. The southmen dislike the Danae anyway, unless they need them, *especially* when they need them."

"You like your safety too?"

"Of course," he said.

"I see," said Meriwether, dropping the knife and cutting loose the bonds holding the man. "That makes sense."

Barry then rubbed his wrists and thanked her. After a moment he asked her if she really would have cleaned him.

"Yes," she said, brushing back her hair.

"I need a place to hide in now," said Barry.

"My hut," said Meriwether, after considering it. "Follow me." She had a small shivering sense of newness, of something that was totally unexpected and therefore to be thankful for.

"Gladly and without remorse," said Barry.

"What?"

"Nothing," said Barry, who then fell to following Meriwether like an infant its mother, falling and tripping but as close almost as flesh. Behind them the noise and fighting were continuing. Meriwether wondered why the front gate hadn't been closed. She also vaguely wondered if Smith was in the middle of all that. If he was, she thought, he might not come out alive, as he was sorely out of basu practice.

"This is it?" asked Barry, interrupting Meriwether's thought.

"Yes. Now you get in the big chest against the far wall. Crawl in and cover yourself with sheepskins. Unless you make noise, no one can find you until it is over. I assume you intend to stay here with us for a while."

"Nothing less," said Barry as he lifted the lid of the chest and put one foot inside. "I am a man without a country now. A man who takes money for an act loses more than the money when he does not act."

"That sounds true," allowed Meriwether. "Get in the chest."

"In the chest," said Barry.

Meriwether closed the chest carefully and then went out to the blackness which circled the inside of the huge timber walls of the Circle. She inched slowly around to the front gate hoping to learn who the attackers were. There was no other way out of the Circle except through the front gate, so she was not worried about the Danae prisoner escaping unnoticed. She *was* worried about Smith. She knew the Mythic people had planned a meeting outside that night, and that Thomas was to be the Framer; she thought *they* might be safe enough in the Sequence's hidden meeting place, but Smith's safety was a different matter. In spite of their troubles, she felt deeply for Smith, and knew she would miss him in many ways if anything should happen to him.

The sounds just outside the gate were like the sounds on pig-killing day at the Circle. The odor of blood came to her in memory; the sight of red fluid steaming in the cold air of killing time.

It is life, thought Meriwether with melancholy. Such quick and casual death had always been the fate of Circle life for as long as she could remember. Even Turly's warnings about "old ghosts" and their revenge had not lessened the killing that much. Pigs and men. It would never stop, she thought. Just as life never stops, or birth.

The light sloped out into the night through the gates. Meriwether could barely see, as if through a dust storm, that there were horses and men with green uniforms who were swinging large swords and catching the Circlefolk who were not quick enough to elude them. The defenders on foot were leaping at the horsemen from behind, knocking them off, and then killing them on the ground. Meriwether, watching, muttered a phrase from the Sequence: "Move us from the inward terror."

She could see neither Smith nor Turly. Thomas was not to be seen either. Conjuring her worst fears, Meriwether pressed her soft body firmly back against the rough-hewn wood of the walls, closed her eyes, and cried for herself, her own lost child, and her love almost forgotten. When she opened them, a man was standing in front of her. Through the prism distortion of her tears she could not tell who it was. It could have been the demon on the Circle tapestry for all she could tell, and she almost wished it were. It would deliver her from her torment.

"Meriwether! What are you doing here near the gates? Unarmed women should be in their huts."

"Turly? Is it you?"

"Yes. Have you been hurt?"

"No," she said after a pause. "I was . . . looking for

Smith. He was outside. And Thomas was going to the . . ."

"The Sequence meeting? I know. I was there."

"You?"

"Me. It is all right," he said.

"But Smith?"

"I saw only Thomas there," said Turly, his image still distorted through Meriwether's tears. "He is all right, as far as I know. I do not know about Smith."

Meriwether was seized by an emotion she could not name. Turly was lost; Thomas was growing and almost lost. She did not want to lose Smith, too. "Smith!" she screamed in a floating wail that seemed to move through the wood of the Circle and out into the alien world and beyond.

"Meriwether," said Turly, putting one hand on her shoulder, "we will check on Smith in a moment. There will be time later to cry for him if necessary. The basu fighters are winning now, but the gates have to be closed. I want you to go back to your hut for safety. Come, I'll take you," he said, pulling her arm while looking back out the gate.

"Turly," said Meriwether as the two reached her hut.

"Yes?"

"Barry is in the hut."

"Barry? The Danae captive? What is he doing in your hut?" Turly had already noticed the stake was empty. He had assumed that Hastings' men had gotten him, that being the reason they had come.

"He did not want to be captured by them. I cut him free and hid him in my hut."

"Does Smith know?" Turly was incredulous. The act seemed to be something done by the old Meriwether who could not clearly discern what was for the best.

"Smith left before I did it," she said.

"Well, the man is gone now," said Turly. "You are lucky you weren't killed."

"He seemed genuinely afraid of the riders. He said they would kill him if they got him."

"Oh?"

"He said they knew he would tell you about the existence of Hastings and his plan of invasion or whatever."

Turly flung open the hut door, his sword perched at an angle to his lower body, ready for the killing thrust. He could see no one in the hut; the black and white

74

wool wall coverings fluttered briefly in the door's draft.

"He is gone," said Turly.

"He was in the chest," said Meriwether, pointing to it.

Turly walked carefully over to the glistening chest, so polished that even in the dimness of the hut there seemed to be a light hidden in the wood itself. Turly spoke to the chest.

"Danae? Are you in there?"

"Who is it?" asked a small voice inside.

"The Center of the North Circle."

The top of the chest flew open and a brown head was poked out. "Ah," he said.

"Get out of the chest, Danae," said Turly. "I am to exchange you to the men out front."

"What . . . ?" breathed Meriwether.

"For what in exchange am I worth?" asked Danae.

"You tell me," said Turly, his sword leveled at him.

"I have already told you about Hastings. And your Advisor about the Order, and the Papers. Hastings' men will kill me whether they know that or not. Either way they don't care. They know Barry is not one to die to keep from telling his enemies for the moment about his employers at the moment."

"But you haven't told anyone to *whom* in the Order you are to give the symbols," said Turly. "You could still be lying."

"Yes, well, you know now that the symbols are to go to the Order, but should I tell you to *whom* in the Order, you would have no more need for me. I want to keep my skin. I will take you to the place where we arranged to meet the Order, and more or less on time, then you will know . . ."

"Do we trust you?" asked Turly.

"Why not?" said Barry. "The green Riders will eventually come back with more men, if you stop them now, or not trade me. They will level the Circle. They have some marvelous weapons, as you probably know. And then you won't care one way or the other about trusting me, will you? But if you go with me now, we may be able to stop that and allow you to find out whatever it is you want to know."

"You make shrewd sense, like my son at times," said Turly, his sword dropping to his side.

"I'd like to meet your son," said Barry.

Turly looked up at him. "You did. He was the one who captured you."

"Oh. The one with the large head, and white hair?"

"Yes."

"Indeed, I have met him. A good-looking boy nevertheless."

"There is nothing wrong with him," said Turly.

"I did not say there was. *You* did," said the man, patting his clothes and straightening his tunic sleeves.

"Do you want to live?" asked Turly, suddenly afraid for his son and knowing it, but not saying it.

"I see your point. I like you *and* your son. Provided I am free once I take you to the Lower Mountains, I will continue to like you both."

"Well," said Turly, "I . . ."

Behind the three the door flung open and Smith staggered in holding his right shoulder, his hand stained a light red. Meriwether moved to him with a halting motion.

"Turly? In my hut?" said Smith, breathing hard. "You honor me. It has been a long time." His face was a deep white and his flabby body seemed to be flowing off him.

"Smith," exclaimed Turly. "You were in the fight?"

"No, not really," he said. "I had gone out to check on some of the stores for spring planting. On the way back I saw you and Henley coming through the woods. I waited and you went into one of the Sequence hay bins. I followed to see what you would do. I was never as curious as you, Turly, but it was puzzling. Then the attack started. You and Henley came out; but I was unarmed and so hid while watching the fight. As some of the men on horseback were turning to leave, they spotted me and took one swing apiece at me on their way past. I think they got me in more than this place," he said, gesturing with his chin toward his shoulder. His face, still handsome as in his youth, hung in the air, his nostrils flaring with quick breath.

Turly felt an old pang of friendship and sorrow. "Meriwether, get the Healer. Danae, come here and help me cut his tunic off."

Smith sank to the floor of the hut, groaning. Turly caught him up in his arms and carried him to his bed. He remembered the time, when he was much younger, when Smith had saved his life by coming to warn Ellman of the approach of the green Riders who had asked for the boy with white hair. Would he lose Smith now because of the same group, but without the same bond between them as there once was?

Turly knew, as he placed the limp Smith onto his gray bed, that he would be going south much sooner than he had thought. He shivered and was afraid, wishing he could feel as fearless as he had once felt. Something was after him, he thought; the net was tightening. And it would not stop until it had him. The bed and the man on it seemed to narrow into a fine focus that allowed Turly to see every line, every wound, every point of human pain that was there.

Chapter 8

The day was unusually warm for late fall, and the clear sky was polished by a variety of small fluffy clouds like cotton rags.

Turly was both uncertain and firm as he prepared to set out. He was afraid of the journey south but ready again to find his answers there. This time he knew it wasn't Meriwether and his parents he was after, but answers to the uncertain questions raised by Hastings and the Order of Zeno. Being Center, however, he was careful not to show his lack of total conviction about it. His army of basu fighters had been marshalled with the help of Henley and Clare. All had their finest tunics on, beige with stripes of red at the shoulders, and with their individual designs emblazoned in front.

At noon the group was ready to move. The women of Inniscloe Circle were dressed in bright clothes, pink and ochre and light tortoise-shell green, like a choice of spring flowers. They all waved gaily as the men marched out the front gate.

Smith, being too injured to go, was left in charge of the

Circle while Turly was gone. Turly had been sad to leave him, but he felt there would be time later perhaps to mend the wounds which had festered between them for too long. Also, Smith was no longer the fighter he once was, his paunch of commerce too evident. Turly knew he would need fighters, especially when they neared Straiten, should they have to go that far south.

Henley was coming with them for the same reason he had gone to the coast after the Danae: to talk and persuade if events called for such action. As a special Circle Advisor, he insisted on it and Turly saw no reason to deny him. Lord Hastings, as he recalled, was a difficult man to talk with. He would need all the help he could get.

Thomas had been eager to go, had in fact insisted that Turly be sure that he was included in the final draft. Turly wasn't sure why Thomas had become so anxious about Circle affairs, since he had rarely done so before, and he felt that the boy did not himself truly know why he wanted to make the trip. Turly was reluctant to press him on the matter, not really wanting him to go, or not go. He knew that Thomas might be needed there in the Circle to take his place, if he were capable of taking it, and if the people wanted him. But Turly also reflected that he himself had not fully grown to manhood until his own trip south. Perhaps that might be true for his son as well. Perhaps, he thought, as he watched the men march out of their home Circle.

The gates were soon closed behind the men. The ears of their horses were bending backward and forward in a variety of positions and attitudes like those of the men themselves. The noon sun was raising the temperature and the unusual activity had caused a sweat on the skin not often found at that time of year. The night's rain had been a long one, but the trees along the way hung out their last remaining leaves as if to dry them for good.

The goodbye cries of the Circlefolk retreated in the wind, and the column wound south toward the Lower Mountains. Turly had Barry and Henley ride beside him at the front of the line.

"You are sure, Danae," said Turly after riding silently for a while, "that it was someone in the Order of Zeno who gave the order to steal only the Circle symbols?"

"Yes. But Hastings approved the deal."

"Why didn't *he* pay you?"

79

"Just to steal old flags and banners? He pays for better things."

"Like what?"

"Well, to steal bodies from cemeteries, for one thing."

"What?"

"Steal bodies."

"*Any* bodies?" asked Turly, his memory stirring him.

"No, no. In specific places and under specific stones. We would have lists to go by, to have something to measure our success by. We would check off the names of the bodies as we got them," said Barry casually.

"Did you always find the right bones on the list?"

Barry shrugged. "You mean, did we ever dig up a body just to have a body to show Hastings? In some way—and somebody did try it once—Hastings knew if the bodies and the names matched."

"What did he do with the bodies?"

"Skeletons mainly," said Barry. "Some of the graves were very old. There would be very little left. What he did with them, I don't know, nor do I care. I was paid for it and had marvelous times in Straiten. That was enough for me."

Turly glanced at the man riding beside him whose dark eyes seemed to lack any white. Turly thought him to be much too articulate to be a graverobber. He bore watching, thought Turly, or his cunning might change sides again in an instant. But Turly was also pondering the reason for Hastings searching out old bones. Could it have to do with the search for certain men who had lived during the time of the Falling, as Dermot had tried to do? Could Hastings be closer to discovering the clues that Dermot had wanted so badly? Perhaps discovering the secret of the Blessing Box itself?

"Probably so," said Barry.

"What?" said Turly, startled.

"The bodies were probably being used to trace Hastings' dubious claim to lordship of the whole island, no doubt."

Turly rode quietly for a while, aware that the Danae could not read his mind, but not certain what the man did know. Picking up on the nature of the graverobbing, Turly once again tried to probe the problem he confronted. "What were some of the names of the bodies you did collect?" he said.

80

Barry brushed his hair to one side and sniffed a few times. "Oh, names like Crosby, Estes, Faldoon."

"And you know of no connection between the names?"

"No, and looked for none. As I said, the pay was always good."

"Tell me, Barry," said Turly after a moment's silence. "Did you ever dig in the southwest of Imram?"

"Near where?"

Turly thought for a moment before answering. "Near the Clonnoise Abbey."

"Clonnoise Abbey? Clonnoise Abbey. No. In fact, I don't even know that I've ever heard of it. Clonnoise Abbey?"

The man seemed genuinely puzzled and so Turly did not press him. It was good to know that the grave of his mother in the Clonnoise graveyard had not been disturbed. He was not worried that Hastings or his men could find the entrance to the underground vault of the Blessing Papers. Hastings had gone over the grounds many times. Turly did not think that the Box had been hidden in order to be easily found.

"Henley," said Turly, pulling away from Barry and turning to his Advisor. "What do you think of the practice of violating the rest of the dead?"

"Stealing bodies?"

"Yes," said Turly, patting his horse, Deep Thought, on the rump.

Henley's dark hair and face wrinkled in meditation. His words then moved liquid and smooth, touched with the profundity which he could affect when he was trying for the truth of things.

"I think it is something this island needs. A past recovered."

Turly frowned. "I know, Henley, I know. The past was withered for us. But can it be found in death only?"

"Why not? You have told me several times about the images the Blessing Box gave you. Of the thing called the Rising Machine."

"But there is no longer a Rising Machine," said Turly, hiding his alarm at the thought. "All that was destroyed in the Falling."

"Was it? We don't know that. And you yourself have remarked on the magical things you saw on your journeys to the south and west. Why couldn't other such miracles have survived?"

Turly wasn't surprised; he had thought of that long before, and he had reached no answer. He was at least certain that there were *some* of the old machines which had survived, but he had not seen all of them. The ones he had seen in Hastings' museum were awesome enough; and he had seen other things in the little picture cube he had gotten at Blessing's cave home on the Arid Islands. He had shown no one that cube, the nature of which he could not explain even to himself, who had seen so much. One day, exasperated with knowledge of such impotence, he had hurled the small cube into the Inniscloe Lake and never tried to retrieve it.

"Are we looking for magic again?" asked Henley.

Turly shook his head. "What we are looking for is evidence of Hastings' ambitions on this island."

"But should anything else come our way, we will not refuse to investigate, will we?" said Henley, riding with an awkward grace.

"No," said Turly. "Of course not."

Henley looked around as if surveying the landscape for magic. The mane of his horse Shoreline had several loops holding iron rings of an ornamental design. Against the mare's pitch-black fur, the design was almost lost, and Turly watched the rings bob as they rode. He wondered where Henley had gotten the rings, but didn't get a chance to ask before the Advisor spoke up again. "This is my first trip south," he said.

"I know, Henley. You are not alone. There have been few Circle men of Imram who have gone south and returned. I don't blame you for it, if that is what you mean."

"Smith told me what he knew of the south way back when I first moved to Inniscloe as your Advisor. It was strange and compelling to hear that such legends were real. The same with your stories of the Blessing Box. Almost like an accident in the fields. We run to it to see the blood and wring our hands and exult in our hearts that it was not us, and yet we are unable to turn our eyes from it," said Henley.

"You may see it now," said Turly.

"And if I die in the south?" asked Henley after a moment's thought.

"Then you will die in the south," said Turly, knowing he meant himself as well.

"This is true," sighed Henley. "But I want to go. I may

be of some little use, although not as a fighter. There are some things in the world that are bigger than comfort."

"It is not as bad down there as either of you are saying," pointed out Barry, who had pulled up to them and caught the last few sentences.

Turly pursed his lips as he tried to figure out how familiar the Danae was with Straiten. He let it go as he knew too little of him. Time would, as Ellman had said, lay open the truth of the matter as one might peel a plum or crack an acorn. The freshness, or the decay, would eventually spill out.

"I wonder why Thomas wanted to come," said Turly to the open air.

"Thomas?" said Barry. "He spent most of last night talking with me about the south and asked some peculiar questions."

"Did he?" said Turly.

"I was going to say, Turly," observed Henley, "that Thomas has been spending more time recently in seeking the past, showing more interest in such things, than you seem to have imagined him to."

"Has he spoken to you, Henley?"

"Oh, yes, and always with an air of already knowing about what he asked. Disconcerting sometimes," he added.

"Odd," said Turly.

"Well, he remembers much of what you told him when he was a child. Did you know that?"

Turly thought about the hours of singing and reading with Thomas before things had gone wrong.

"I did it for a reason," said Turly.

"He remembers your story about the last fight you had in the west, with the Order, and with its Head, Dermot. But he asked me something I had no answer for."

"What was it?"

"He wanted to know about the 'torch on the mountain.'"

Turly jerked his head toward Henley and held his breath. Those had been almost the last words of Dermot, Head of the Order of Zeno after Oliver's death, the man who had been responsible for the death of Jeneen. Turly had hated him for it, and had swung blindly at his neck just after the explosion which had sent Jeneen into as many pieces as Imram. Dermot had told him of the "torch on the mountain" in the Order caves; he had said he would show it to Turly and tell him its secret if he would join with the Order and follow in his father's footsteps as eventual Head of the Order. He had refused Dermot, and he had never learned the meaning of the phrase.

"Why did he want to know about that?" asked Turly, suddenly, remembering that he, long ago, had in fact told the much younger Thomas about it.

"I don't know," said Henley. "I didn't know what the torch thing was. Thomas did not seem disturbed, however."

"Thomas is calm about everything," replied Turly.

"Well, yes," said Henley in his conciliatory tone. "But I thought it unusual. You might talk with him about it when you have a chance."

Turly leaned back in Deep Thought's saddle and tried to catch sight of Thomas to the rear. He thought he saw, at the end of the line of men, the deep blue tunic the boy had worn that morning. "Thomas and I don't talk much anymore," he said.

"That is your problem," allowed Henley. "But we may need Thomas before the journey is over. He may be an important part of this group. He is your son and the logical heir to your legacy of security for the north."

Turly nodded several times. He brooded on the problem of Thomas for a while, dismissed it, then turned his attention to the flat land stretching in front of him. It would be a hard two days travel to the Lower Mountains. But the observation of natural beauty, and the recognition of old landmarks, was something even the cynical Center of the north could still enjoy.

Chapter 9

On the way to the Lower Mountains, Turly guided his
men as best he could down the distorted corridors of his
memory. Trees and bushes had grown and changed a
path here and a path there that he once might have
known. But the shapes of rock remained and they enabled the Center to find the entrance to the caves of the
Order of Zeno.

Near the north slope of the mountain range, Turly
found the strange arms of quartzite which seemed to lie
open like a pair of arms. The defaced sign of the Others
was still over the entrance, and his chest scar tingled
slightly as he saw it. Motioning the group to follow, he
spurred Deep Thought on into the dark. Once inside he
rode silently, watching for first sight of the huge door
which would look tiny at a distance and then grow to
mammoth proportions.

Turly thought the door might be the best way into the
caves. Not knowing the current state of mind of the Order,
he wanted to catch them by surprise if possible. But they
were cunning, he knew that. Nevertheless, he was hopeful

and felt a sense of wonder return as the dark space stretched before him. And there it was.

The giant door of bronze.

"Turly," said an awed Henley over the clattering sound of the horses. "That was not made by men."

"I don't know who made it, Henley," replied Turly, also having to speak above the echoing hooves. "I can tell you who the Blessing Box said made it."

"The Others?"

"Yes."

"Do you believe that?"

"I believe it for lack of anything else to believe. You see the door now. Wait until you are nearer. Wait, if ever, until you touch the Box and feel the images in you. Then *you* decide the truth of things."

"Then why do you not want to believe any longer?"

"I went through other things, Henley," said Turly, not wishing to dredge up again all that he had gone through.

The two men rode on in silence, watching the door grow larger and larger, changing color from a shiny orange to a metallic bronze. The huge bolts and vast crossbars dwarfed the mind of Henley as they drew closer. Turly was watching for the smaller door in one corner near the ground. When he saw it, he threw up one arm to slow the horsemen to a walk.

"Do you think the Order is the same as when you were here?" asked Henley, as if he wanted to hear a human voice speak. The massive door was looming over them and they still had not reached its base. The column of men was like a straggling line of ants at the base of the Circle gate.

"We will find out, Henley. Men do change. But change also brings new passions, and new fears." Turly knew this to be true in his own changes.

Turly heard Barry speak from behind him, but his voice was not as awed as Henley's. "Does this move you, Turly?"

"Maybe," said Turly.

"I think it moves you, Center," said Barry. "Your son told me that there has been no *Circleman* who has ever tried to build anything so big as this. Why not?"

Turly did not want to talk about it. His dim view of human experience, growing through the years, had so jaded him that any grand contrast to that dark view was not interesting to him anymore.

Henley started to speak but stopped when he saw, as did Turly, a disturbance at the base of the giant door. Touches of orange appeared and moved to form a line that stretched from one end of the door to the other. Turly knew what it was.

"Order monks," he said quietly.

"How did they know?" whispered Henley as if they could hear, or that it could matter that they could hear.

"They would know," said Turly with a sigh. He raised his hand in the semi-dark and stopped the men riding behind him. He motioned for Barry to pull up beside him, and then waved back to Thomas who spurred his horse into a trot.

"Yes, Father," said Thomas, who felt strangely excited by the spectacle in spite of himself.

"We meet the monks," Turly said, pointing at the door. "We are going to ride up to them and see who is now Head. You wait here with the men. Should there be trouble, bring them on. Should the Order be contrary, I want you ready."

"Yes, Father," said Thomas, who felt the responsibility keenly. This was the first time in many years that he felt good about his father, and he ran his fingers briskly through his white hair.

Turly beckoned to Henley and Barry and they rode on together to the base of the bronze door. As they approached the line of monks, one stepped out to meet them. He was about Turly's age, his mouth oddly fishlike, rounded and bunched, but he was not ugly. Silver hair, close cropped in a thin fuzz, covered his skull. His eyes were hooded by heavy lids that drooped at different angles, giving him a humorous look as if he were almost asleep. The nose was wide and flared out onto the cheeks; ears were pressed close to the head. As Turly stopped in front of him, the monk pulled one hand out of the deep sleeves of his Order robe and raised it almost in salute.

"You've come again," said the man simply.

Turly was not surprised. "Yes," he said, "it seems I had to."

"Probably so," said the man, standing absolutely still. He looked back at the waiting cluster of men. "We can give all of you accommodations as long as you need them. Please stable your horses out here. My men will take care of them."

"And you are . . . ?" said Turly.

87

"Excuse me," he said. "I am Percy, current Head of the Order of Zeno."

"Percy," repeated Turly, thinking of why he was there. "We must talk, you and I. In a friendly manner, I hope."

"I assure you, Turly, legend of the Order, son of our founder, that we are *not* the Order of either Oliver or Dermot. We have returned to the original Order created by John *Vail. We believe in One Being; all else is illusion. Therefore there is no need to interfere in the practical affairs of Imram. We no longer care about the Blessing Papers *or* your current activities. Does that answer you?"

"It does," said Turly, relieved that there would be no bloodshed. "For now I suppose."

"Good," said Percy. "And your companions here?" he said, pointing to Henley and Barry.

"This man is my Chief Advisor, Henley of the North Circle. The other is a Danae named Barry. We brought him as a guide to help find out certain things."

"Henley, welcome to the Lower Mountains, home of the Order of Zeno. I hope your stay will be rewarding for you." The monk then nodded curtly at the Danae, a slight smile on his face. Turly caught Barry's eyes and silently asked if Percy was the man to whom the Circle symbols were to be given. Barry shook his head. It was not.

"Thank you, Percy," said Henley, whose furrowed brow had been bunched in concentration while taking in everything the monk had said and reflecting on it, his eyes blinking.

"Please dismount if you will and follow me," said Percy. "We have food waiting. It is of course only humble fare, but nourishing. The Order does *not* believe in extinction."

Turly and Henley chuckled at the first evident humor in the situation. Turly waved back to Thomas to bring the men on. When all had arrived, warily, Turly had them dismount and turn their horses over to the silent monks. Turly felt in his bones that the monks were harmless now; he seemed to be able to feel, once again, the emotions of those around him. This frightened him vaguely, an image of the black Blessing Box riding in his mind, the bubble on its side a milky-white. But Turly pushed the image down, and he felt confident that this

88

time at least he could enter the Order caves and not find torture or riddles in wait for him.

And there were none. There was only good wine, simple cheeses and bread laid out on great flat tables with a cluster of chairs beside them. The grain of their old wooden planks ran in long looping whorls of gray. The monks sat with the Circlemen and began to laugh and talk as they raised their glasses of deep red wine together. The monks, when they extended their arms, could be seen to be white as slugs; their lips were red as the wine, and their closely cut hair was dense like the soft fur of mice. Turly could see no malice in any eye. The candles that lit the interior of the dining hall burned smoothly and with no flicker of discontent.

"Percy, you knew Oliver?" asked Turly after filling his stomach, the wine loosening his tongue. He had listened to Percy's conversation long enough to believe that he knew what his reaction would be.

"I knew him," said Percy.

"How well did you know him?"

Percy looked at Turly with an amusement that had never left his face. His cheeks pulled in and the words came out with a rounded accent on the vowels, like liquid rhythm, the words connected as a slow string of sounds. "He was not a close friend of mine," he said. "In fact there was a faction of the Order that had always opposed his need to meddle in Imramian affairs. I was unofficial head of that unofficial faction."

"Did Oliver know of the faction?" asked Henley.

Percy turned his head slowly to Henley and nodded. "Oh, he knew, and he had several of us killed. Accidents, of course. He knew *we* knew that the original directive of the Order had been violated. He wanted no opposition. He believed what he believed. But it was not Order belief.".

"You know his fate?" said Turly at last.

Percy looked directly into Turly's eyes, brilliantly green and stirred as they were by harsh memory.

"We know."

"You do not care?"

"Oliver had violated Order belief, as I have said. As far as we care now, he was a man on his own work that day at Clonnoise Abbey. Yours was not a blow against the Order."

Turly mused on that for a while. "But then why was

Dermot made Head after Oliver, if there was dissension against Oliver?"

Percy moved involuntarily for the first time. He held his lips pressed tightly together for a moment.

"Percy?" said Turly.

"Dermot was . . . a special case. When word of Oliver's death came back to us here, the faction that supported him had to turn to someone who was familiar with the doctrinal direction Oliver had taken. Who better than the scholar who had done all the research which had in so many ways guided Oliver?"

"And *your* faction?"

"Too weak then to mount much opposition; too weak as yet to support the changes that would come later, after Dermot was no longer Head."

"So it came," said Turly, "after the battle in the west?"

"Yes, oh, yes, that battle wiped out many of the Oliver-Dermot monks. When the remnant returned in rags, it was made clear to them that the Order was no longer the Order of Oliver, but the Order of Zeno. They accepted that."

"Where is Dermot *buried?*" asked Turly quietly.

Percy looked down at the piece of white cheese on his platter and said nothing. Barry looked up with a curious expression on his face.

"Percy, where is Dermot buried?" said Turly with an edge to his voice.

"He is not yet buried anywhere," said Percy quietly.

Turly stood up from the table and pushed back his chair. His hands gripped the solid wood as if he could give it pain.

"Dermot is alive?"

"He is alive," said Percy slowly. "But he is not well."

"Percy, is he *here?* Is Dermot *here?*"

Percy nodded. "Dermot is an old man stricken by his past and his wounds. He can barely walk, his legs are like sticks of near useless wood. He is a cripple, Turly. How he managed to live after the battle, we don't know. He lay for months in a stupor. When he regained consciousness, he did not know where he was. He still does not know fully."

"He is *here,*" repeated Turly coldly, "here in the Order caves?"

"Yes, Turly, he is."

"Turly," said Barry. "He was the one."

Turly bunched his shoulders in anger, dread and fear. The memory of the man who had killed Jeneen was alive within him again. He forgot the cynical acceptance of human strife he had encrusted himself with over the years; the past had returned in the flesh.

"He is here, Turly," said Percy. "But I must repeat that he is utterly helpless. He has no followers at all, no reason for going on, and evidently no memory of anything except some of his old researches, which he carries on when he can. We allow him to work in the library of the Order, doing things no one else wants to do."

"I want to see him," said Turly, his breath coming quickly as if he had run up a flight of stairs.

Percy stood to face Turly; his face no longer seemed amused. "You will see him, but not now. You and I have things to discuss first, as you noted. But I must tell you, Turly Vail, that while you are here with us, you will not be allowed to touch Dermot. There will be no more violence in the caves of the Order."

Turly slowed his breathing to gain control of himself. Percy was indeed the host here, and so far a good one. Turly knew the doctrine of the original Order, and he knew its rule against violence. Percy was not lying about that. Turly ground his teeth; he would see Dermot, but he would have to let the man live. It tore at his heart. As he sank back into his chair, he was overcome by emotion. *Dermot was alive.*

The meal ended and Percy rose to direct Turly and Henley to their rooms, told them to rest for a time, and then to come to his main study in the top level of the caves. Any of the monks could tell them the way, he said. The two entered their tiny cell and sat down upon the cots put there for them.

"Well, Henley," said Turly. "Welcome to the south of Imram."

"It is certainly different from what I had expected," said Henley, looking around the cell in the dim light, its stone floor reflecting nothing.

"It is, so far, much different from what it was," replied Turly. "The first time I was here, I was tricked, burned and almost hanged," said Turly, who still felt vaguely discomfited.

"Percy seemed to be a rather level-headed man," offered Henley. "And you know, Turly, he reminds me somewhat of the old man in Bellsloe who recommended you to me. The old fellow I told you about. I forget his name. He had the same liquid accent—you noticed it, didn't you—and the same amused look as if he knows something worth knowing, something that gives him an inner peace nothing can disturb."

"Yes, it *seems* that way. But the world is full of deceivers."

"Oh, I don't think Percy is one of those, Turly. If he were, it would violate all that I think good about man."

"Henley, Henley," said Turly. "If you had seen what I have seen, heard what I have heard, you would know that deception is the way of man. You think blind belief is what is good. How far has that gotten *you*, Henley? I mean past Circle life itself? How many men have you killed? How many women have you coupled with who have taken you to a different place than all this and then were lost to you for good? Eh? Tell me."

"I am limited, Turly. I know that. I admit it. But I think in my years I have been able to discern the surface of things and know something about what is beneath it. My experience in the matters of Circle politics has taught me both the currents and the undercurrents of thought, and what they might mean."

Turly watched Henley's dark hair float in the light of the candles they had lit in the room. The pale, sincere reflection from his rugged half-brow almost made Turly believe him. But there were too many things milling in Turly's mind to allow him to enter into a full-scale debate on Henley's beliefs.

"Let's rest a while, Henley," said Turly wearily. "Then we'll see Percy and have more than surprise to deal with."

"You're right, Turly," allowed Henley. "We'll need our wits about us."

The two men curled up on their cots and drifted into a light slumber. It was interrupted by the sound of a tiny bell echoing through the passageway outside. Turly shook his groggy head and listened. It was a chiming of the hour. He looked over to Henley's cot and saw that it was empty. Turly sat up and planted his feet on the stone floor, feeling points of pain in his shoulder. He rubbed his temples with his fingers and tried to wake up, to remember: He was in the caves of the Order; and Dermot was still alive.

Turly stumbled out into the still corridor and shuffled until he saw an orange robe. He went to the monk who was scratching something on a pad. As the monk turned toward him, Turly thought it was someone he knew.

"Tell me," said Turly, "where Percy's study is."

"Yes," said the monk. "Take the walk to the right and go about fifty meters. There will be stairs. Go up until you reach a door marked with orange lines. Go in and down to the left three doors. There will be a door with an arrow on it. That will be Percy's study."

"Thank you," said Turly, still thinking he knew the man from somewhere.

"You are welcome," replied the monk, turning back to his solitary work.

Turly followed the directions to the letter. Upon reaching the door emblazoned with a green arrow, he stopped and listened. He heard voices inside. Knowing one voice, Turly knocked and then pushed open the door.

"Ah, Turly," said Henley. "You are awake. I did not want to disturb you and so came on up here alone. Percy and I have been having a good discussion of the differences between Circle and Zeno lore. Join us."

"I will," said Turly.

"Some wine, Turly?" asked Percy, waving his hand at a shiny container sitting on his cluttered desk. There were three glasses beside it.

"No, thank you," said Turly. "I think the glasses of wine at the table made me groggy enough."

Percy's room was a natural cavern made livable by the furniture which had been built inside the cave itself. On the bare planks and rough-hewn lumber were signs of the Order. On one wall hung a banner woven of orange cloth picturing a green turtle.

"Percy, you have told us that the Order has returned to my father's teachings."

"This is true."

"You know I do not believe them."

"The teachings?"

"Yes."

"It does not matter."

"I did not know my father's mind," said Turly.

"We know that as well. I am sorry."

"I agreed with him about the nature of the Blessing Papers, if there are any, until I discovered the Plan behind them."

"The Papers' intentions, true or otherwise, are not our concern either," replied Percy calmly.

This startled Turly somewhat. "Then what *is* your concern?"

Percy cleared his throat, his fist cupped at his mouth. "Your father thought that man was lost and alone, that he was enveloped by an absurd nothingness which bid fair to drown him."

"I remember Order Doctrine," said Turly.

"He also knew that something was necessary after the Falling to bring man back to himself, to a sense of purpose about himself and his ways before he could begin again. The Order was the way he chose."

"Until the Blessing Papers?"

"Even after that," said Percy, "in some ways."

"And the Order's paradoxes? What of them?"

"Yes, the paradoxes," said Percy, making a steeple of his hands. "Nothing really exists, but everything exists. Everything is closed, but everything is open. Things can both be and not be. Thus the turtle and arrow symbols, as you know. The Zeno paradox of motion."

"Yes," said Turly, glancing ironically at the banner on the wall.

"Your father believed that there is an absolute Being which does not let us go into life alone. No matter what has happened in human history, man remains in this Being: always remains, therefore, the essence of what he is. No matter the different states of life and death as such. All remains. Nothing that you can do, and nothing that happens to you, can really change you fundamentally. Thus, while all is closed to you by remaining in Pure Being, all is open to you for lack of limits of any kind."

"Maybe," said Turly, who was remembering what Dermot had told him years before about the absurdity of any action at all. "But . . ."

"All exists in Being and all remains there still. It goes on. There is finally only *now*."

"And what of the demon?" said Turly quietly, feeling tired.

"What?"

"The demon, the *demon*," said Turly.

"He means the demon on Mythic Sequence Ritual Cloths," said Henley.

"Oh, well," said Percy. "There will always be demons too, won't there?"

"Indeed there will be," said Turly, "whether it is in your beliefs or in mine."

94

Percy said nothing but looked at Turly with something between pity and pride. Henley felt uncomfortable as he realized the tension in the conversation.

"Ah, but Percy," he said, "we in the Sequence believe there is a ground to Being, but that the *motion* involved in that Being is of the greatest importance. We do believe in the value of the motion that takes us from birth to death and beyond. We believe that is real and true."

"I realize that," said Percy. "And it is good that the Sequence recognizes an end in view. But the Order believes that a man never leaves the ground of Being and that all else is illusion. You believe in a loop of motion; we believe that the beginning and the end are the same. We are even now in the bosom of Being, still and calm and without care if we would only see it that way."

"And what of people like Oliver!" said Turly. "What do you say of the evil in men like him? Is that not real? He was of the Order."

"It is as real as error," replied Percy with an almost solid calm which irritated Turly, who was feeling as if the bottom of his wooden chair was made of hot iron. "We cannot as men see what is error, and what is not. We cannot explain all things, nor should we pretend to. Oliver was only a shadow which flickered in the depths of Being. If we accept such men and such actions as shadows which may have other meanings than the ones we give them, then there is no real problem."

"So men have no say in the doings of Pure Being?" said Turly, with an edge to his voice. He was beginning to think that he liked the Order's plan of Pure Being even less than the Blessing Plan.

"How can we?" said Percy, spreading out his hands as if to give thanks for a meal. "We are not mere actors in a drama to which we may or may not give assent. We flicker for a moment and then we are gone. But the flickering is an illusion. Understand that, and you fear nothing."

"I think I understand your peace now," said Henley, looking from Percy to Turly and back again.

"Ah, and would you like to share in it, Henley of the north?" said Percy.

Henley held his tongue and looked at Turly. Looking back at Percy, he scratched one eyebrow. "I think I already have the beginning of such peace," he said. "But it

95

is predicated on something else, a different way of seeing." Henley's eyes squinted as he talked.

"The Sequence way?" said Percy.

"Yes, the Sequence and something else."

Percy's eyes remained calm and unchanged as they stayed on Henley's face, the eyes full and dark as an evening coming on fast.

"I think," interrupted Turly, "that this has turned into a feast of fools. I want no part of it."

"You understand, do you not, Turly, that the Order no longer wants a hand in the external affairs of Imram, that the only worthwhile thing we have to offer is just what I have offered Henley?" said Percy. "Peace. Confidence. Assurance."

"That seems clear, Percy, and it is a good change. But I don't need it. And I'm still tired from the trip down. We can talk later about the words of our Danae prisoner, and the stealing of certain of our Circle symbols."

"Yes," said Henley. "I will see you back in the room, Turly. Meanwhile, Percy and I must continue our talk about peace for a while."

Turly smiled, one corner of his mouth rising toward his left ear. Not really concerned now about Circle or Order symbols, thinking that there probably *was* a good explanation for everything and that Percy would be gracious enough to unweave the tale for him, he nodded goodbye and returned to the corridor leading to his room. The air was musty, still and close. For all Turly could tell, it was twenty years before and he was running through the same halls with Sean, seeking escape. The cool dampness of the caves filled Turly with a sense of the heaviness of time. He walked on through a sea of memories, pushing his way in the murky, candle-lit currents.

When he found his room, he moved into it sleepily. The place was almost pitch-black inside, the candle having long gone out. Lying down on his cot, feeling his way, he closed his eyes and placed one arm over his face.

"Hello, Turly," said a voice that was scratchy and slow as if coming through a narrow hole.

Turly sat bolt upright, his sleep forgotten. "Dermot?"

Chapter 10

Turly sprang from his bed in a blind and savage rage. Fumbling with the flint he found beside the candles in their niche, he lit one candle, his fingers trembling. The flame guttered weakly and then steadied itself, making all things in the room rise up as if from a great depth.

"It has been a long time," said the strangely hollow voice. "I'm glad you came. I thought stealing your Circle symbols and things would stir your curiosity. I wanted to talk to you once before I die."

"You!" said Turly, staring at the limp form half lying on the other bed in the room. "It was you!"

"Yes, it was me, with help from some old friends," said the crippled monk without moving. The cropped hair, the dirty orange robe, the large ears fanning out abruptly to both sides, the long unwieldy nose which looked as if it were bending to touch the chin, the fish eyes which glittered at Turly, the face stretched into a deathly white.

"Dermot!" breathed Turly.

"Yes, Turly," said the harsh voice. "Or what is left of him."

Turly carried the candle aloft and looked closer at the monk, whose head was bent at an odd angle as if he were trying hard to listen to something in the distance. Turly saw with a gasp the wide scar bumpy like an earthworm crawling the width of one side of his neck. The rest of him was thin like a scarecrow in a Circle field. All bone and tendon. Only the eyes seemed alive.

"I should kill you *now,* Dermot," hissed Turly in a tightly held anger.

"I wish you would," said Dermot weakly. "I have looked for death for many years now, but it does not come to me, the dying. Why is that, Turly? We look for life, and we do not find it; we look for death, and we do not find that either. What do we do? We look and look and for nothing we can find."

"You'll find it," said Turly.

Dermot coughed and it seemed like a dry laugh. "Yes, I will find it, I suppose. After all these years, I meet you again. Perhaps now I can find it." Dermot shifted his body, using the weight of his upper arms to change position awkwardly. Turly could see that even so he could barely move his arms. The long robe concealed the shape of the monk's legs, but his large feet stuck out in their dark sandals and they seemed as lifeless as rotten wood in a forest.

"You got what you deserved," said Turly bluntly.

Dermot was silent for a while. He did not move.

"Dermot?" said Turly, whispering and feeling feverish.

"Oh, I haven't left yet, Turly. I was merely thinking of our last meeting."

"I should have stayed and made sure of your passing," said Turly.

"You should have."

"I may yet."

"You may. But first I must tell you of my regret that your mate died and you did not. What I really wanted, as I told you before the fight, was for you to join me and help rule the island through the dictates of the Order. You refused, called the charge, triggered the thing we had rigged the night before on Reynolds John's advice. I must say that I was as surprised as you that the thing went off at all. Amazing things, machines. It was something we had salvaged from Hastings' museum."

"You justify yourself," said Turly bitterly.

"Of course. But I learned only later of your loss. By

98

then I was contrite; I do not like to kill innocent people."

"Who is guilty?"

"Who is not, for that matter," returned Dermot. "But this is not why I am here."

Turly settled down on his cot, his muscles rigid. There seemed to be no physical danger from the old monk, worn by time. But Turly wished there were so that he could have an excuse to throttle him, watch the color come to the face, and the tongue stretch out in death agony. But he could not do it now. He was beginning to like the idea of the monk having to live as he was, a hopeless cripple who had to live remorsefully with the knowledge of chances forever lost.

"You remember the last words we had at the slope leading up to your camp?" asked Dermot slowly and deliberately. The candle light lay in the room like a yellow skin.

Turly nodded his head.

"I told you about the 'torch on the mountain.' Do you remember?"

"I would just as soon forget," said Turly, who thought the room had developed an undertow that could suck both of them into the deep rock of the mountain.

"I told you about it to entice you to join me."

"I know."

"You did not believe it, I think," sighed Dermot, who still did not move as he spoke.

"I had no time to either believe or disbelieve."

"True. But think now, Turly, believe. The 'torch on the mountain.' It is a good phrase, mouth-filling, don't you think?" Dermot's face seemed flushed in the light now, less drained.

It *was* a good phrase and Turly turned it over in his mind as if he were tasting a new dish, or an old favorite redone with new sauces to test the tongue.

"What is the 'torch'?" asked Turly.

"Think, Turly. What is the one thing in this life you have been most drawn to? What is it that has been the greatest mystery to you? What is it that you have had to hide yourself from most?"

There was no need to think about it at all. Turly knew.

"Fire, Turly, fire. It is your good and your evil. Your sin and your salvation. It is both of those things to you, Turly. Fire is the one thing that might lead you to good, and the one thing that might lead you to your doom. Do you know which it would be?"

Turly passed into a new dimension of wonder. He suddenly felt his brain bubble within itself, popping and burning along lines of blood in his skull. Fire. The one constant draw of his life. Dermot had spoken the truth, a truth Turly had not been unaware of. Fire had always been his hope and his fear; a source of unfulfilled dreams for himself and the island; a source of dread and renewal; it was self-destruction and resurrection.

"It waits for you, Turly. And whether you want to believe it or not, I want to help you. It waits now."

"What?" said Turly.

"The final fire. The torch on the mountain. The one left by your father."

"Left by my father? For what purpose?" Turly was stunned. He also thought briefly of what Thomas Blessing had told him years before, about a "final secret" of the Blessing Papers.

"He was *your* father, Turly, not mine. He founded this Order and then left it. But he did not change his mind about the fate of the torch. It was to remain and was to be regarded as the innermost secret of the Order of Zeno. Until the right hour arrived."

"Right hour for what?"

"Who knows? The Order was not told. But I think the right hour is now. I think the torch is for *you*."

Turly's eyes glazed. The thought sent him into a floating world of mystery that seemed to move around him in tempting guise as if on a birthday immediately before presents were to be given, and his mind was trying to probe the boxes to discover their contents before his hands could open them. But Turly pulled back, not yet wholly absorbed into that landscape.

"I think you would like to see me dead, Dermot, as much as I would like to kill you," said Turly, his mouth dry.

Dermot snorted. "This may seem true, Turly, but such sentiment finally has little to do with the affair of you and the torch."

"Why should I believe that?"

"You will also remember that I told you we had found the remains of your father."

"That is right," blurted Turly in a rush of memory. "Where is he?"

"He is *in* the torch, Turly. Waiting."

"Waiting? In the torch?" The room vibrated slightly as Turly rocked forward.

"In the torch. But unconsumed by it."

"Where did you find the remains?" asked Turly, trying to slow down time.

"*You* uncovered him, Turly," said Dermot, coughing. "At the Ennis graveyard east of the Ennis caves. You broke into an old tomb and found a strange figure there, a skeleton sitting beside a large globe embedded in the earth."

"Yes, yes," muttered Turly excitedly, who also remembered that it was Jeneen who had been with him and who helped uncover the bones. And it had been Jeneen who had insisted that they leave the mystery of the bones alone and return to the Ennis caves. He had since given the bones little thought.

"We found the skeleton too, Turly, with your help. You had been followed. It was the remains of your father, John Vail. And the globe with him, if handled rightly, tells more of the tale of his life and of the creation of the Order. It tells other things as well, but I can make little of it."

"You lie," said Turly.

"You can see for yourself," said Dermot with the least suggestion of a shrug.

"The torch can be reached from here?"

"It can," allowed Dermot, as he shook his hands like rattling bones.

"I must see it," said Turly, the form of Dermot blurring and being replaced in his eyes with the old skeleton poised in flames. Turly seemed to float on the burning images rising from his thoughts. He had never known from what source dreams came; perhaps he would know now. He distrusted Dermot, but he had to see these things for himself.

"Can you go there now?" asked Dermot slyly, knowing he had caught Turly's attention.

Turly thought for a minute. The expedition south had to be considered. There was still the threat of Hastings and the possible threat of the Blessing Papers. Should anything happen to him, his son Thomas would have to carry on. He was of the line of Vails, whatever else he was.

"In one hour, Dermot. I must see someone first."

"Tell no one about this, Turly," hissed Dermot, "or I will not take you to the torch. It is a high secret for the Order. I am not sure I can get you there as it is. No one else must know what we will do."

"No one will know, Dermot. But if this is a trick of any kind, I will kill you, cripple or not. Do you understand?"

"I have understood many things for a long time, Turly. Killing is one of the things I understand well." Dermot wiggled to one side and, as if he were an awkward toy, he pushed his legs and arms forward into a hunched position. He reached for a stick Turly had not noticed before and slowly raised himself up on it.

"Meet me at the orange-striped door in an hour," he said. "Let no one see you."

Turly nodded and Dermot took one blunt step after another out into the corridor. The sound of his stick hitting the floor at each step lasted long after Dermot had gone.

Chapter 11

Turly looked down at the sleeping form of his son whose face was still and composed in its sleep like a child's. Turly knew that that was what Thomas was. A child. Still a child. But beneath the child Turly thought he had long before seen something else. An awareness, a quickness that was surprising and frightening at times. It was almost sensual. The boy could look at something, feel it, and he would almost immediately know what the thing was, and how it worked. Turly shuddered.

Thomas's dark eyes blinked awake and stared up at his father.

"Thomas, Thomas," said Turly softly. "We must talk."

Thomas gathered himself up slowly and held his arms around his knees. His hair was curly in the damp of the caves, and he looked like a fatigued man who had had too little sleep to understand anything at all. But he did. "I know, Father," he said in his youthful voice, its tone cracking with the changes of age.

"Thomas, you and I have not been close for some time. It is not of your doing, nor of mine wholly. It is of both, and of the doing of this island." As he spoke, Turly felt the history of the island Imram, as he knew it, swirl about his ankles like a fog. "For this I apologize."

Thomas remained silent. He arched his large head forward to catch his father's soft words which struck memories of the early years when he had been taught to read and to write and to sing the old songs of his father's father. A time when the living had been good and full; when life was not a thing to hide from, or to find escape from, or to make holes for. He wondered why his father was bringing all this up now.

"I must do something, Thomas, that I think I have waited all my life to do. But before that, I want to remind you of some things. And I want to tell you that, as a son of mine and of Jeneen, your mother, I love you. You are of my blood and that makes love always possible. It will come to you, too. I could not tell you this earlier because I feared you and what you might be. But that does not matter to me now."

Thomas wondered what his father meant. What was this talk of love and fear? But he felt the urgency of the moment.

"What are you going to do, Father?" asked Thomas, his head tilted to one side as if listening to a faraway bird.

Turly continued to look down at Thomas and he felt from a great depth his pity reach up through roots of anger and hurt, up through the density of time and into the free and burning air of the present. He did not himself know what he was going to do, and so he did not immediately answer.

"I have an old question to ask of something," said Turly at last. "And I must do it alone. It is, I think, one of the reasons I have come here again. What that reason is I don't fully know." The gloom of the cave did not hide the clammy white of Turly's face.

"Why did you wake me then?" asked Thomas, suspicious.

"I wanted to tell you what I might do, and find if you have remembered all the things I once taught you."

"The songs and the map?"

"Yes, and where you must go to use them."

"I know the way," said Thomas.

"To the Abbey at Clonnoise," said Turly.

"Yes, I remember."

"Repeat the short song," said Turly. "The third stanza."

"All right," said Thomas, who did not move, but cocked his head to the other side and crooned rapidly:

> "High above the scene is set,
> All remains and all is changed;
> What have I to do with this, O,
> Who live and love and die below?
> *Fol de rol de rolly o.*"

"Good," said Turly. "Keep all those things in your mind."

"Until when?" asked Thomas.

"You will know. When the time comes and should the need be there, I think you will know."

"I do not have the coins you said I would need to go with the map and the songs," said Thomas, thinking of the many times his father had described the coins to him.

"True," said Turly. "But I think they, too, will come to you when the need arises. You already have most of the keys, but not the lock."

"What is the lock?"

"I have told you that the lock will find *you*."

Thomas smiled. The whole question of his youthful drills rose again. It had been something he had found fun to do, and easy. His mind had immediately focused on the map and locked it in his memory, as it had all else he had ever come across. And now the lock would find him?

"Yes," he said.

Turly stood rigid as if holding his breath. "Thomas," he said. "You have a secret no one else on this island has. It is a secret which you have in your head only. *It is the location of the Blessing Box.*"

"The Blessing Box? I don't . . . ."

"You know—as my grandfather once told me—but you don't think you know. The songs."

Is that what all that was for? thought Thomas.

"Keep these things in your mind should you need them," said Turly. "Remember."

When will I need them?

"Go to the Abbey. You know where that is. I told you."

Yes. I remember the stories.

"You may need what is there one day."

"I thought we were only going to Straiten to find Lord Hastings, and maybe on to Hastings Hall if that is where he is," said Thomas, suspicious now.

"We are," said Turly. "But, Thomas, should anything at all . . . happen to me, I do not want the location of the Blessing vault lost for good. Henley is right about that."

"But . . ."

"I am no longer so sure if the Plan of the Box is any worse than mine. I thought it was, but that was before I knew of Hastings' revival."

"Why is that different?" asked Thomas, warming to the occasion.

Turly seemed to sway where he stood. "If there is going to be *some* plan at work in Imram, I want it to be the best one," he said.

"The best one?"

"The one we want to follow," said Turly. *Grandeur and servitude.*

"How will we know that?"

"Thomas, we don't have the time to discuss that now. Perhaps tomorrow," said Turly, impatient to meet Dermot.

Thomas nodded, but he did not understand and did not know if he ever would. He thought he did not care for the Box, but only because he had seen what the fear of it had done to his father. Better to let it lie where it was, he thought. His worry was for the north.

"One other thing, Thomas," said Turly.

"Yes?"

"Should you find yourself in Straiten alone, there is someone there who may be able to help you should you need it, if she is still there. It is the woman of an old friend of mine, a man who helped me once. Her name is Derva and she lived at streets 65 and 70. The northwest corner. You may have to look for her. You may not need to, but I want you to know."

"You talk as if you won't be there," said Thomas, raising one eyebrow.

"I will be there," said Turly.

The two looked at each other in the gloom. Thomas felt a dread rise in him. He had always lived in Turly's shadow, and he had come to expect it. The thought of the possible loss of his father was a jarring pain. He began to think he could not do anything without his father there as

106

a foil. All his youthful confidence and daring, his talk of a different fate reserved for him alone, seemed threatened.

"You must keep in mind, as well, the nature of the North Circle," said Turly, with a certain tenderness in his voice. "Remember that I never intended for it to remain as I set it up. It is temporary, the North Circle, something in transition. It can be made better, given the circumstances. It may be up to you to help in the changes. But you must work to keep it intact and running so that no man is tied to all other men. There must always be good friendship, an openness to new things, but there must never be a total tying together into one thing. It would kill your spirit and that of every man living."

"I am of the Sequence, Father, as you now know," said Thomas. "The Sequence tells us that all men are on the same path."

"I know, and it does not matter. I know that the Sequence uses words to frame reality and that is good. My grandfather Ellman liked words, and so do I. The Sequence does not at least tie things together forever. That keeps hope and difference alive. The reality you frame is useful for that. Words allow a man to know things within himself alone. The feeling they make may reach all men, but the lone man can know a reality for himself in such a way. And that is good. The Sequence may stay. It is needed."

Thomas was silent as he absorbed this. The need for such choice was not a major change in his father. He had heard him talk—preach—of this in the early years. He had known also that his father had been considered one of the best young Framers of his time. Did he mean this change to last? Was this a real thing or a joke? He did not know and rubbed his head.

"Goodbye for now, Thomas," said Turly. "Go back to sleep if you can. I will see you at morning light. We leave for Straiten early." Turly touched Thomas's forearm and then held his fingers in the air above him.

"Yes, yes, I will," said Thomas, without conviction.

Turly nodded as if he would say the same thing in the same way, then he turned and moved out into the corridor and was gone. Thomas lay for several minutes, thinking. He quickly flung aside the covers and placed his white feet on the cold gray stone, rose and dressed.

Turly thought Thomas would try to follow him. He knew it, could feel the blood running in the young man.

He should not have gone to see him. But he could not avoid it, not knowing what waited for him at the torch. One last time, if it *were* the last time, he had wanted to see his son of the west, the son he had come to fear. But Thomas was *his* son. That meant something. He thought of Jeneen again as he walked rapidly to the meeting place with Dermot. As he walked, he reflected that Jeneen had always tried to keep him from the flames' attraction; she had been able to hold him back the way Ellman had, when Ellman had been alive. To keep the burning hurt and pleasure from him. The fatal draw. They had been able to do that. No one else had. But now there was no Ellman, and no Jeneen.

"Turly," whispered Dermot from the shadows.

"Here, Dermot," said Turly, who saw a dull orange robe pull away from the wall and move toward him, as if floating. Turly could hear the arhythmic thump of the monk's sandals; it was like a heart gone wrong.

"Are you ready, Turly?" asked Dermot. "Are you ready?" Dermot's voice was level and serious as if he were checking a book reference before a final copy was made.

"I am ready," sighed Turly, who realized that he was past ready, that he was ready for something beyond fire even and it scared him for a moment. But he told himself that it was part of his old search for a father whom he had never known. It was simply time to find the right answer. It was not death; he did not want that, but shivered as he wrapped his robe closer about him.

"Then let us go to the mountain," said Dermot.

They walked away through the opened door, avoiding the other doors, one of which led into Percy's study. Further down the corridor Dermot fumbled among the rocks. He found what he was looking for, and a deep square of blackness opened wide enough for a man to slip through. Turly followed Dermot and entered a stairwell of flat carved stones. There was utter dark then and Turly responded by grabbing a handful of Dermot's robe to be guided by. The two wound slowly upward. Stepping carefully on the night stone, Turly thought he was moving through sleep, the phantom lights in his eyes the only visible things.

"Stop a moment," said Dermot, who was breathing heavily and painfully.

Turly was also breathing deeply. The air seemed thinner than before. "What is it?" he asked.

"I've got to find the right exit now," said Dermot, panting. "Hold your eyes."

Turly shut his eyes tight. There was a sudden flare behind his closed lids and a puff of air rushed against his face, cooling the damp sweat on it. There was the smell of a room which had been closed for a long time.

"Through here now, Turly," said Dermot. "We are almost there, if I can make it."

Turly opened his eyes to a slit and saw things on a knife-edge. The darkness receded and a long passage stretched in front of his feet; it seemed sprinkled with glittering points of light, the dust glowing within itself. At the end of the passage was a turn to the left and a bright glow came through the passage which made the objects in it look clean and clear. Turly turned his face toward Dermot without actually looking at him.

"Dermot?"

"It is there, Turly, beyond the turn."

"And to get there?"

"You have only to walk to it. It waits as it always has."

"Will you come too?" said Turly, preoccupied with the glow ahead.

"It is not for me, Turly. It is for you. It is that which you have sought since birth. You have told me that. The fire which promises so much. What has it promised you, Turly, that you can now reject?"

Turly stared at the opening ahead, at the light which settled in his eyes like a friend he had not seen in a long time and one with which he had parted on unfriendly terms and so wondered what the greeting would be like. He half muttered to himself. Moisture sprang out on his brow; his tunic showed triangles of sweat at the armpits.

"It tells me I will not have to worry ever again," said Turly. "It promises me peace from all that troubles me. It promises me an answer to all things that come in the night. Is that not enough?"

"What?" asked Dermot, who had not heard him.

"Nothing, Dermot," said Turly, watching the dancing glow ahead. He took one tentative step toward it and then stopped.

"What, Turly, do you stop so close?" whispered Dermot. "You have journeyed all your life to this point. Would you stop now?"

"No, I won't," breathed Turly. "No." And he stepped again toward the torch on the mountain, moving slowly like a puppet to the bend in the corridor, his feet feeling like blocks of wood as they rose and fell on the gritty floor.

"Goodbye, Turly," whispered Dermot. "Goodbye."

Turly did not hear him as the soft roar in the corridor grew to fill his ears with its song and time seemed to bulge and shift. He was young again and lying in his father's arms being sung to; he was sitting at Ellman's feet being taught to read and memorize; he was with Meriwether as she gave up to him the mysteries of woman; he was again in the south of Imram and alone; he was in the Abbey at Clonnoise facing the Blessing Box, his hand reaching out to it, and then gaining its story in the almost incoherent images which had given him little time to decipher them; he was reaching toward the torch and gaining peace.

"Father!" shouted a voice behind him.

Turly did not know whose voice it was. He knew *he* was not a father. He was young again and searching for something he needed. There was no one else. And the search was about to end. He rounded the bend in the corridor and faced the torch which he saw was huge, and it wavered, bent, and held strong in a large square outline of white metal. On its bottom line Turly could see Order words carved: "All motion is an illusion." The words were meaningless to him, for within the turgid yellow flames Turly saw something vastly more intriguing. He saw the bones of the skeleton he and Jeneen had found in the tombs to the west and they shimmered in waves of heat.

The bones of my father, thought Turly. And they seemed to beckon to him, wave gently to him from inside the torch, their shape vague but recognizable.

"Father!" came the voice behind him. Turly did not answer, nor had he heard anything to answer. There were other things to hear, and they were in front of him. A moment he hesitated, then stepped into the flames, turned to shadow, and was gone.

Chapter **12**

Thomas followed his father. The light in the stone corridor was dim enough to allow that. He kept his distance and stayed close to the wall. When Turly met an old cripple, Thomas was surprised but still kept his distance. His father was a man who had always gotten his way, and he did not lightly tolerate fools or interference. But Thomas thought something was oddly different now. He seemed possessed of a secret that Thomas thought destructive. He, Thomas, could sense it. But he thought that this secret was something he could finally take apart and understand, given the time. It was a thing that was good and bad. His father wanted it badly, whatever it was, but it could tear him to nothing. Thomas wanted to be sure that it did not do that.

The corridor was tricky and deceptive. Thomas held back to avoid detection by either Turly or the monk, but he would lose the track easily and find only empty space in front of him. He would run ahead then and look wildly through the air like it was dirty water. Then he would see the two and fall back, thinking that the slumping cripple might have seen him. This happened several times. When an orange-striped door was opened, Thomas knew they had gone through it; he followed softly and saw them disappear through another door farther down. They slipped into the cool space beyond and were gone. But when Thomas reached the space, he could not find a door.

Thomas was frantic. His father might be walking to his doom, and he could do nothing about it; Thomas had the feeling that he alone could cause the defeat of the monk. If only he could be by his father's side, he could save him, think for him. His fingers flew around the perimeter of the rock where the men had gone. There were no latches, no bolts, and no ordinary springs that he could find. He leaned against the rock and swore. Sweat sprang out on his forehead and his breath came quickly. His thighs strained against the unmoveable flatness that mocked his human strength.

Not his fingers, but his head found it first. A coiling width in the enter of the door. A bolt of metal was licking out like a tongue into a carved slot in the wall, inside the bulk of the wall. It would move only when the coil was tightened. Thomas could see how it worked, as if the instructions were written in his mind, and he made it work. The space fell into a crack and Thomas pushed it the rest of the way inward and open. There was a long darkness slanting upward. He could not see the two men, and he half-ran up the blind thickness to find them. Although he did not know the right way, he could feel his father's presence ahead and hurried up the path until he was certain that he was nearer. He stumbled on, only to stop and press his head to the wall at various places.

Another square of empty space, a flight of stairs. Thomas mounted them rapidly, feeling he was losing rather than gaining ground. He threw his thoughts into the top of the mountain to find the father he sought. He knew he was up there. And he felt something in himself. Something nearer to love than he had ever known. Was it an indifferent love that he sensed, a love that would have the same effect as hate? Whichever it was, it held him in a severe grip that demanded much, but promised much. This he thought as he continued to climb upward.

Thomas reached the last exit. He stopped, wheeled to the wall, and probed it with his thoughts. There it was, the coiled spring. The wall sprang open to reveal a long narrow path of glittering dust stretching in the distance to a turn in the corridor highlighted by a furious glow of light coming from something around the bend. Outlined in that glow, right at the turn, were Turly and the old monk. The monk was shuffling and pointing ahead with one long arm; Turly, straight and proud, was looking ahead. Thomas did not know what was around the bend, but he feared it. The angry, flickering light said fire.

Fire, thought Thomas. *Fire.*

And Thomas remembered all the times in his youth when Turly would sit for hours in front of the flames after dinner, watching them, talking to them. Thomas remembered the numerous times he had had to ask his father why he had put his hand into the fire and later have to salve the burn with goat butter and wrap it with rags. He had never gotten an answer from Turly. It was just something Turly did, and such actions had acquired the force of a ritual for Thomas, a ritual of fascination and fear. He himself could not do it; he had tried it once but he had not understood its lure. He had stayed away from fire and had grown to hate it except as a necessity for heating and cooking. But for his father it had been ritual and Thomas knew its power for him. He could tell, in the brief instant he first saw the flames, that they had Turly now.

"Father!" hollered Thomas in the soft roar of the enclosed corridor. No answer. Thomas then saw the monk glance back at him in astonishment, turn back to Turly and say something to him. Turly continued on around the bend without seeming to recognize Thomas's presence. Thomas sprinted to catch Turly before it was too late, reaching the turn in the corridor and holding up his hands to shield his eyes from the bright glare. He could see a huge column of flame shifting only slightly as if a man were occasionally adjusting a long robe. It was inside a large square of dull white metal. Thomas could see nothing in the flames but destruction, and his father was walking directly toward it, his back rigid, his hands lifted to it, his head erect and attentive.

"Father!" yelled Thomas again, running to Turly. He would tackle him, he thought as he ran, and take him home to the Circle; they would learn to live together and be father and son again. He would not burn, would not be ash.

As Thomas sprinted past the monk, the ungainly figure,

with surprising agility, shot a foot out into the boy's path. Thomas could not sidestep it and could only throw his hands wide to protect his fall. He rolled over and saw, through his half-closed eyes stinging with dust, his father entering the flames and disappearing in a dark shimmer which swallowed him as if it were greeting and enfolding a long-lost son.

"No!" shouted Thomas in a despair that brought tears to his dirty face. He knew then that it *was* love he felt for his father, not hate, and he did not know what he would do without him. But there was then only the level roaring of the fire, the upward column of heat continuing without interruption, and Thomas hated it for doing so. He lay quietly for a moment with his eyes playing tricks with his sight, the tears there turning everything larger than life, distorting and rippling them. When he wiped the tears away, he wiped away the distortion with them. Standing up gingerly, he remembered the old monk and whipped around in fury to see the monk lying against one wall, a smile on his broken face. Thomas rushed to him and for the first time in his life wanted to kill something. He understood then the act of killing: The hate that bypasses the desire not to kill.

"Old monk," cried Thomas, "you did this, you led my father to this." Thomas gripped the upper edges of the old man's robe, the orange cloth smeared with age, and pulled them tight around his neck. But the monk showed no sign of fear.

"I did, yes, I did," he said. "I really did it."

Thomas stared at the great loose eyes hanging in the ravaged face. "Why," he sobbed, "why did you do it?"

Dermot at last looked the boy full in the face. His eyes were bloodshot in their glassy indifference, but they seemed to sparkle in a dying light, in the satisfaction of a goal realized. "You don't know why I did it?" he asked almost casually.

"No," cried Thomas, tightening his grip on the monk's robe.

The two stared at each other without speaking, a static tension between them. There was a flickering motion in Dermot's face as if he had just thought of something disturbing and he moved his arms slowly to Thomas's. "Wait," he said. "You said 'father,' young man. You said 'father.' "

"That was my father, monk," said Thomas, pointing to the fire.

"You are Turly's *son?*"

"Yes, I am," he said, reaching for his blut blade.

"Wait, wait," said Dermot, struggling now.

There is now living in Imram one person who knows the whereabouts of the Blessing Papers. A man with hair like the silver of the moon.

The words flooded back to Dermot. They were *his* words, written by him years before in his researches. But that person was *Turly,* he thought in amazement. Turly, the man who had just entered the torch on the mountain at last, the man who was *prophesied* to enter the torch, the man with white hair, silver like the moon.

"What is it, monk?" asked Thomas, noticing the perturbed look on the man's face. "Do you fear death?"

But this boy's hair is also silver and he is the son of Vail!

"Do you know who I am, young man?" asked Dermot, shaken.

"You are a monk who sent my father to his death," said Thomas grimly, but wondered at the question.

"I am Dermot of the Order," he said.

Thomas almost dropped Dermot's robe, his eyes widening with recognition at an old name his father had often used as a curse word.

"Dermot?" breathed Thomas.

"Yes," nodded Dermot.

"No!" said Thomas. "I knew my father hated you. *I* hated you. You killed my *mother,"* said Thomas, realizing a truth he thought he had long forgotten. He repeated it to believe it. *"You* killed my mother, and now my *father!"*

"I deserve the hate," said Dermot slowly. "The hate was deserved. I did not want to kill your mother. I deserved the hurt that followed when I lost command of the Order, when I was a cripple and banished back to the libraries."

"You deserved death—that is what you deserved," said Thomas, inching the blut closer to Dermot's throat.

"Probably," said Dermot softly. "But it did not come. I am alive and burdened for what remains of my life with the agony of the past. That is something, young man, which you will know one day. The agony of the past. Not

115

of mine, but of yours. Yes, you will find it too, and then you will think of me."

"And of my father," said Thomas quickly, to avoid being caught up in the monk's pity.

"Of course," said Dermot.

"Why did you send my father to the flames if you so regretted the past?" said Thomas, wanting an answer before death was given to Dermot.

"I knew the riddle of the torch before I went to get your father in the west. I had found it in the Diary of John Vail, your grandfather, founder of this Order." Here Dermot coughed and slumped against the wall. Thomas straightened him back up and shook him roughly by the neck. He wanted to kill the man, would kill him, but not before finding out why he had sent his father to his death.

"What Diary, where?" he said.

"In the library downstairs," said Dermot faintly. "Go read it if you like. It will tell you much that should interest you." Dermot looked up and half smiled, although the ragged, scarred face did not seem to allow a clear-cut act of any kind.

"You still hated my father and wanted to kill him!" shouted Thomas, thinking the man was trying to change the subject.

Dermot looked startled again. "No, no, that is not why I showed him the torch on the mountain," he said. "That is not it at all."

"What?"

"No. I didn't get him here by stealing your symbols just to *kill* him," said Dermot, coughing.

"But . . ." said Thomas, while waving with one hand toward the flames.

"No," said Dermot dreamily, one glittering eye looking at the torch. "He is not dead. He has *risen* now. It was something he was fated for. To enter the flames at last and become something else. It is all in the Vail Diary. Don't you see?" Dermot coughed and lay still as Thomas released him, backed away, then turned toward the torch. He edged toward it but could not get to within five meters of it as the great heat seemed to roast his flesh. There was nothing to be seen within the blue-yellow barrier of flames and he turned back to Dermot with disgust.

"You're a liar, monk!" shouted Thomas. "You lied! Nothing could live in that thing!"

116

Dermot did not respond, nor did he move at all. After a pause, Thomas walked to where the man was propped up against the wall; he touched him with one foot and, like the dry shell of an insect, the body of Dermot fell lightly to one side. Thomas bent and felt the monk's neck.

Alone. I am alone now, thought Thomas, who straightened up, looked back once at the torch, and then left.

The path back down to the Order corridors seemed smaller to Thomas as he walked without caution. The monks had already told him where the library was, and he knew what he had to do.

John Vail's Diary.

His father was dead, but the threat to the north—whether Hastings', the Order's, or the Box's—remained. The trip south still lay ahead and he, Thomas, son of Turly, had to travel it; but first some answers were needed. *Why did his father have to die?* The young boy felt heavier and heavier as he approached the library door. He could feel the weight of his father's burden fall to him, seep in as if it were the burning weight of fatigue after long work. He felt age, too, and knew he would have to follow another's path and take others with him, whether he wanted to or not.

The dark mountain passages of the Order were still and empty. Thomas knew it was very early in the morning, although he could see no sun, and he moved with the awareness of a lack of sleep which made him feel unreal. Groggy when he reached it, the door of the library was a deep polished tan in which he thought he could see himself. Pushing it open carefully, he stepped through and ignored its vivid squeak, for the silence of the tables and chairs inside seemed to suck him in and cover him with a liquid isolation.

The files, he thought. Where are the files?

Against one wall was a shelf of trays. Thomas went to it and saw that each tray had a letter printed on top. Pulling out the V tray, Thomas flipped through it and was glad once again that his father had insisted on his learning to read: Vacant. Vacom. *Vail, Row Three, Shelf Two.*

Thomas found the place and picked up the heavy box sitting there. He tugged at the nail holding down the lid and when it popped out it made a dull tip, tip as it hit the cold stone floor. Thomas forced open the lid like a reluctant jaw. Inside was a one-page note:

117

You have lost someone close to you. And you have lost this *Diary*. Don't lose Imram. Be the man your father was. Or be the man the monk was. There is no other way.

T.B.

When he finally looked up from the note, Thomas thought that he had been standing there for years. The note, small and white, seemed welded to his hand. He knew that none of the deep dreams of his youth had prepared him for something like that. *Mystery.* He thought he knew now why his father had become so bitter. How could a man live with such mystery all his life? He thought he knew, too, why Turly had walked so freely into the flames. To have an end to the questions at last, whatever the price.

It seemed clear to Thomas, standing there alone in the Order library, that someone else had known of the events at the torch and had taken Vail's Diary so that he, Thomas, could not read it. If there *had* been a Diary, thought Thomas suddenly. What if the monk Dermot had made it all up and had himself left the note as a last joke on the son of an old enemy? He knew there was no way to find that out now. Death held its secrets too well.

As he put the note back into the small box, Thomas wondered vaguely who T.B. was. But the question posed by the author, whoever he was, was a real one. Who *was* he to be like now: his father, an open searcher; or the monk Dermot, a closed and conniving ruler?

There was really no choice, mused Thomas as he closed the heavy library door behind him. He would head south that day with the demanding weight of his father upon him.

Chapter 13

The short man bounded up the three stone steps in an almost comic gesture of grace, his arms flailing like a bird's. At the top he leaned against a wooden doorjamb while pulling open the heavy door. He puffed several times then skipped into the building. Walking rapidly and rising off his toes with each step, he came to a hesitant stop at the front of a large red door and knocked on it softly.

"Come," said a deep bass voice.

The little man pushed open the door and stuck his head in.

"Yes?" said the voice inside.

"Sir, there is news from the north."

"Well, come in and tell me."

"Yes, sir," said the man while scratching a scalp almost bereft of its sandy-colored hair. He tiptoed in, shut the door behind him, and took a chair near one corner of the man's desk.

"Well?"

"Sir, there have been reports that a group from the north has come out of the Lower Mountains and approaches Straiten."

"Who are they?"

"Griff—he is the man who saw them, a good man— says they look like Circlemen."

"Who else lives in the north, you idiot? What I want to know is *who* they are. Did Griff send any descriptions? I want some descriptions; that's what I want. It doesn't help me to know they are Circlemen. I could have *guessed* that."

"Uh, yes sir, there are some descriptions. Some. One of them is young and has milky looking hair. Can you imagine? White hair!"

"Shut up, Norris. No comment, just description."

"And a man who looked like a Danae, and about thirty men who rode as Circle fighters do. Each has a different emblem on his tunic, though."

"An older man with reddish hair was not with them?"

"Not according to Griff. He said nothing about that, but then he did not have time to memorize them all. He thought the young boy would interest you because that was odd. I thought you would be interested, too, and that's why I missed breakfast to come tell you."

The big man behind the desk was silent for a time. His arched ears with big lobes were covered with deep red hair that fell in front and back of his head, although the top was almost bald. He had a full maroon mustache that curled up at the ends like a smile. His arms were large and rested on a stomach that was a vast expanse of flesh. While tapping his fingers on the desk, the man seemed to ponder what to say, and his lips puckered impishly under his bushy mustache. "It is good that you did come, Norris," said the man at last.

"Thank you, sir," said Norris, relieved.

"Quite all right. Now . . ."

Another tap on the door interrupted him. "Come," he said.

"Lord Hastings?" said a skinny man in a white shirt with a gold chain around his neck.

"Yes?"

"John Caine is here."

"Good, good, let him in. I'm just finishing here."

The man, who had stuck his neck inside the room, nodded and left. The sound of his footsteps echoed down the hall.

"Go get some breakfast now, Norris," said Hastings. "Thank Griff that the news got here before winter had gone."

"Yes sir," said Norris as he rose and backed out of the room, letting the door close gently behind him. On the

120

way to the kitchen he saw the man Caine come in and he shivered. Tall, and with wavy hair the color of rusty iron, the man moved with insolence, his thick belt holding a number of weapons Norris didn't know the names of. He was dressed head to foot in dark blue with a single strap of black leather angling his chest from neck to waist. He looked impressive, with a flat stomach and long legs made for running. When the two men passed, Caine nodded to Norris as if the smaller man were a puppy. Norris saw long scars on Caine's cheek—it was the face of a man who took no prisoners—and when he reached the outside of the building he broke into a run for the kitchen.

Hastings met Caine at the entrance to his office. Caine was tall, lean and rugged but Hastings towered over him, and his bulk took on the dimensions of a third man in the room.

"Caine," said Hastings, clasping the man's hand, "it has been a long time since you've come here. It is good to see you again."

"You may not be so sure of that, Lord Hastings, when you hear the news," said Caine, no emotion showing on his face.

"I've just heard the news," said Hastings. "A few Circlefolk coming south. What does that matter? My soldiers can stop them at any point before they get to Straiten."

"I hope so," said Caine laconically, "but that is not the news I bring."

"Oh?"

"The news I bring is about the raids for the Order of Zeno you wanted my men to make on the North Circle."

"And . . . ?" Hastings turned and walked to his desk to sit down.

Caine stood still and watched until Hastings had made himself comfortable. "The best of my Danae went up there, and they got what you wanted for the monk Dermot. But the Circle responded this time and came for them. Most of my men got away, but at least one man was captured alive."

"Get to the point, Caine," said Hastings, one thick hand resting on his chin.

"The man—Barry—is a talker. He will surely tell the Circlemen why we were up there stealing symbols and who was paying us to do it."

"Good," said Hastings.

"What?"

"I said, it was good that you got him back before he could do that."

"We tried. We are paid to do something or die. But . . ."

"Go on," said Hastings, his huge fist coming down hard on the wooden desk.

Caine shifted position but showed no other sign of concern. He was not like Norris, not a secretary. Before answering, he pulled a high-backed chair from the wall and, turning it around, straddled it facing Hastings.

"We went back disguised as one of your green Rider patrols, but we could not get into the Inniscloe Circle. The man Turly has trained his men well."

"Has he?" said Hastings sarcastically.

"Several of the Circlemen died, and so did some of my men. But Barry is still alive, I suppose, and is probably coming south with the Circle group. But since you know of it now, I guess it doesn't matter.'"

Hastings glared at a gray blotter on his desk. He looked up at Caine and shook his head. "You Danae are good at many things, but knowing when something matters is not one of them."

"What?"

"I didn't want the symbols just to decorate my museum. It was to get them down here without knowing why."

"The captured man knows only that you paid for the raid, and that the symbols were to go to the Order."

Hastings sat back after a moment with both hands resting palm down on the desk. "I see," he said. "And what do you think happens now?"

"We must assume that the North Circle knows you are alive and well and that you had us get the Circle symbols for the Order. They may have found out about Dermot at the Lower Mountains, but they cannot know the full reason for it all, not all of it."

"True," said Hastings, looking at Caine's face carefully.

"So they are coming down here to find out why. But with the men they have, coming down is about all they can do. Even my men could take them whenever you wish. We can capture the one man you told us about."

"Who?"

"The North Center. Vail."

"He is not with them," said Hastings.

122

Caine leaned forward. "Why not? You said he always led his men."

"Right. But my man who just left tells me that no man who matches his description was seen *leaving* the Lower Mountains."

"But my men tell me a white-haired man is with the group," said Caine, irritated.

"Vail is red-haired now."

"What? I had heard that it was white."

"It *was*. It is not any longer."

Caine mused about that for a moment. "I see. And so what would you have me do?"

"Let the Circlefolk come on into Straiten, if they can. I want to know now what the *son* of Vail will do. He knows some of what his father does, I think, but not all. But he will be after the same answers his father was."

"And those are . . . ?"

Hastings waved one large hand in the air. "Why I want the symbols. Why I had them sent to Dermot. And, if I guess rightly, why I have returned to power."

"Yes," said Caine.

"The boy may even lead us to the Blessing Papers themselves," said Hastings.

A cunning look settled on Caine's face at the mention of the Blessing Papers, and he thought of the legendary powers they were supposed to possess. "Yes, well, he might," he said. "But then the original question still stands. What do you want me to do now?"

"Watch the Circlefolk and what they do, but let them alone for now. There may be a time soon when I will need you again."

"Of course," said Caine as he rose with a half-smile on his face, which was like a piece of wood. "I'll report back in a few days."

"I'll be here," said Hastings.

After Caine had left, Hastings heaved himself out of his massive chair and walked to the window behind it. He studied the landscape outside with its winter trees and bushes lining the wire enclosure of his compound. He could just see the tall figure of Caine move out of the front gate and disappear down the dusty road toward Straiten to the northeast. Hastings placed his large hands behind his back and rocked up and down on his toes. His face was a mask of solemnity, touched with joy.

Chapter 14

"I'll miss Henley," said Thomas. "He had knowledge."

"Why did he stay?" asked Barry.

"To make the proper connection between the North Circle and the Order. They are old enemies, and peace will have to be made gently. Henley is the one to do it."

"I see," said Barry.

The two had been talking for some time, riding easily in their saddles. Thomas had taken his father's horse, Deep Thought, as his own, and he had let Barry have Burnt Out. Moving comfortably on Turly's powerful stallion, Thomas felt closer to his father than he ever had before. The rippling motion of the horse's muscles seemed to validate his new claim to his father's role.

"You seem to do well as a Center," said Barry after a while.

Thomas looked over at the Danae. The tousled brown hair, blowing in the wind of his motion, tossed itself from side to side and in and out of his eyes, making Barry look almost like a child. But Thomas knew it wasn't so.

"I didn't ask for all this to be placed down in front of

me, Barry," he said with as much authority as he could muster.

"Nor did I," said Barry.

"Indeed. Then that makes us uneasy brothers, doesn't it?"

"I suppose," said Barry. "But think of this. What if I am leading you to your death?"

"Perhaps," said Thomas. "But as long as I have the ability to either kill *you* or lead you to better times, I have your loyalty."

"True," laughed Barry. "As long as you stay in those boundaries." The laugh seemed to be without hidden depths and Thomas felt reassured about his decision to trust the Danae. He knew, however, that he would have to be continually on guard against everything the closer to Straiten he came. That would have to include Barry.

"And consider this," said Barry, while patting Burnt Out on the neck. "By now Hastings knows I have been captured, and that you and yours are heading south. Caine will have told him and we are probably being watched this very moment."

Thomas laughed this time. "Barry, you are a Danae and I think I like you in spite of that, but you don't know me. I may be young, but I am not stupid. I *know* he is waiting. But he will not find us."

"Why not?" blustered Barry, put off balance by Thomas's crisp assertion.

Thomas answered by kicking Deep Thought in the ribs and pulling away from Barry. He could hear the Danae's voice fade as he drew into the wind, and he felt momentarily free and alone. His mind was working well now, after the shock of Turly's death had passed, and he knew it was working for the North Circle and for himself. He would live up to the memory of his father in the south. Like his father before him, he would enter Straiten, challenge it, and beat it. It was a good thought and Thomas rode his nut-brown stallion with an increasing grace.

That night the Circle group pitched camp in a ravine some fifteen kilometers from the caves of the Order. The night sky was brilliant with color but still as an ice crystal. Thomas made sure that defenses were set up. Then food was cooked and some whiskey allowed to pass from hand to hand. Small clumps of men gathered and chatted in the soft glow of the campfires. Thomas ate his bowl of molon soup, its yellow hue clear in the dusk, and sat in his tent alone. He wanted to be alone. The thoughts of the events in the mountains had left him on a new level and he wanted to brood on those thoughts without company. Finally he fell asleep. Later, as if from a deep pit, Thomas heard the men outside begin to mutter among themselves. Their vague chatter rose to a shout.

"Thomas!" yelled Clare from outside the tent.

"One minute," replied Thomas sleepily as he began to get up and put his pants on. He stumbled to the flap of the tent and stuck out his head. "What is it, Clare?"

"Thomas, there is something out there," said Clare, pointing into the dark toward the south. "The men are frightened. They want to know what to do."

"Something out where?" said Thomas, who listened with one cocked ear. He did hear something that was not of the normal night. It was low and multiple like the sound of a thousand giant crickets on the move far off, chirping in an irregular harmony.

"It may or may not be coming this way," said Thomas. "If necessary, I'll go out and find out what it is."

Thomas and Clare walked silently through the camping area where only portions of things could be seen; the dying campfires of the night gave a partially shiny surface to whatever they touched. The two men moved toward the collection of shadows surrounding the bigger fire in the middle of camp. The men there were agitated, Thomas could see that. The ground beyond the firelight seemed like a black hole opening up to engulf whoever was foolish enough to leave the security of the fire.

"Listen to me," shouted Thomas above the excited talk. "My father is dead. He would have known what to do here, but he cannot tell us now. I am his son and therefore the new Center until the North Council meets to elect one. I will go and learn what is making the noise that scares you like children. It is only a mountain full of insects."

The Circlemen looked at each other and nudged elbows into each others' sides. They calmed somewhat, knowing they would not have to go out, and bent to warm their hands at the fire. Thomas pulled Clare to one side.

"Will you come with me, Clare?"

"Of course, Thomas," said Clare without a trace of hesitation.

Thomas scanned Clare's stolid face as best he could in

126

the dark. *He means it,* he thought. *It is good to have un-thinking men like that, although I would not want to be one.*

"Good," said Thomas. "Get some things together and let's go as quickly as we can."

"I'll be at your tent as soon as I am ready," said Clare.

As the two prepared to set off to the source of the strange noise, the sky in the east turned from a velvet darkness to a light oyster-gray laced with pink. The semi-light was unreal at that hour and both Clare and Thomas felt they were in a dream of action, an extension of night thoughts without real substance. They moved out of the camp toward the west and were soon out of sight. The man left behind huddled together with glittering fear in their eyes.

Thomas led as Clare followed. Thomas could almost feel the rigid attention Clare had assumed; the man was a good fighter and an old friend and Thomas was glad to have him with him. Both Clare and Thomas puffed smoke in the cool morning air.

"Thomas, what do you think it is?" asked Clare at last. The sound had remained constant in intensity, although it was becoming louder as they went toward the southwest.

"I remember my father once telling me of something that sounded like this. He called it a Bonesucker. But he never saw it personally and never had the chance to find out exactly what it was. It never came north, and my father did not want to go south again to find it."

"Where did it come from?"

"Father didn't know for sure about that either. He did tell me something about the west of Imram and some strange mountains of purple that made new things out of old ones. But he wasn't clear about it. I was too little to ask, and then later I didn't care to know."

"I'm sorry about you and your father, Thomas."

"So am I, Clare. But that is over now," said Thomas as he walked on, thinking of the pleasant days when he and Clare had played together in the marshes around Inniscloe Lake. Clare had been one of the few children in the Circle who had wanted to play with the odd young son of the Center, the boy with the large white head. This kind of deformity, not jolting but something that would cause a second look from strangers, did not bother Clare who had had his own problems. But the hurt of it had nevertheless stuck to Thomas, and led later to much of

127

his seeming indifference to Circle matters. The Circlefolk knew that Thomas could not be dismissed as a product of the fabulous Shee, and was not therefore simply an idiot. But he had been let alone by his father, and by most of the Circlefolk and their children. Except Clare and Meriwether.

The chirping sound grew almost unbearable as the two approached an outcropping of stone. They crept to the rocks and leaned out over them. Below, in a shallow valley, they could see only chalky rocks glowing faintly in the early light. Clare looked across at Thomas and whispered to him.

"Is that what is making the noise?"

Thomas stared at the chalky stumps and then sat down with his back to the rocks. "It seems so," he said.

"Why?"

"Clare, you always were good at asking me questions I couldn't answer until much later."

"We haven't got until much later," said Clare with a level certainty in his voice. Thomas thought again that Clare had the dogged determination of a turtle which had simply allowed that it was going to move and keep moving no matter how long it took to get where it was going.

"That's true, Clare," said Thomas. "Do you have any suggestions?"

"Let's go to it."

"What?"

"Let's go to it," repeated Clare.

"To what?"

"The noise."

Thomas thought about that for a while. He could see the straightforward frame of mind that resulted in that kind of thinking. He didn't really approve of it. If what he had heard his father say was true, the Bonesucker was more than dangerous. Thomas knew he could not afford to lose any men unnecessarily. On the other hand, he could not stay there and wait to see what would happen. The thing, whatever it was, lay in the direct path to Straiten. To detour might take the group too far out of the way, if they could get out of the way. Thomas had to do something.

"You're right, Clare," he said.

"We will go to it?"

"No. I will go to it."

"We'll both go to it," said Clare.

"Clare, who is Center?"

"You are," said Clare with an instant loyalty.

"Then I go and you stay."

Clare seemed to struggle with the opposing thoughts. He would go too, but the Center told him not to go, and the Center was to be obeyed. Clare put down his sword solemnly, then as solemnly picked it up again. "I will wait here," he said simply.

"Good. Now you watch what happens. Should anything happen to me, should this really be the Bonesucker, return quickly to the camp and take the men back to the Circle. Tell them to pick a new Center, and then decide what to do. Do you understand that?"

Clare nodded his head slowly. His hair, the color of decaying straw, was almost all Thomas could see in the still dim light. The chill air seemed to freeze Clare into a monument.

Thomas stood up and looked down the slope at the chalk mounds. They lay still and composed, the trilling sound rising as if it were a wavering stream of heat vanishing into the mountain coolness. Thomas studied the valley, which seemed to be a curious place of excitement and fear, and which seemed to be reaching out itself to find out what Thomas was.

After leaping up on the rocky ledge behind which he and Clare had crouched, Thomas stepped carefully down the forty-five degree slope toward the trilling mystery. Small pebbles slipped under his feet and kept him off balance. He looked around once and saw Clare's eyes peeping over the ledge.

The trilling quietened for a moment and Thomas stopped. The stones had not moved, nor had anything shown itself. Thomas wondered if it were only the wind playing its tricks like the time at the Inniscloe Lake fishing with his father when they had heard an odd moaning from a nearby cave. It had been the wind then. Both Turly and Thomas had laughed and taken their fish back to the Circle.

A white light rose from the stones like a fog and hovered above the suddenly darkened rocks. Thomas knew then that it was not the wind making the sound. He felt his sword handle slip in his fist as sweat formed in his palm. He tried to feel the light and know how it worked, his mind trying to slip quickly into it, and he thought for a moment that he had found something. He tried hard not to run back up the hill, and he watched as the fog-light churned and then began to undulate slowly toward him, the trill increasing its rate. Thomas felt frozen to the spot. He did not know what to do. The fire in his arms tensed, burned, and made his stomach turn cold. There would be nothing to pierce in that fog, nothing to cut or hit with basu training. The fog thickened like goat's milk and Thomas could see patterns of flow within it. It was about fifteen meters away and rising. Thomas screamed.

There was a rush behind him on the hill and then Thomas felt Clare push him aside and clump on down to meet the hoary thickness. Thomas watched with a cry frozen on his lips. He saw his friend come down solid on each leg alone and complete the motion before allowing the other to rise and fall. Nevertheless, there was great speed involved and soon Clare was in it.

At first there was no change in the thing. Clare was lost to sight momentarily, although his feet could be seen as they continued for a time to clump down the slope. He thought he could hear Clare yelling and cursing, but he was not sure it wasn't a variation of the trilling. Thomas got back to his feet and stood watching, uncertain whether to help or run. *Help do what?* he thought with the clarity of surprise.

The fog thinned out and Thomas could see Clare entirely, his sword thrusting, swirling, his face, when he turned back toward him, contorted into a strange rage.

"Clare!" shouted Thomas in anger and regret.

Clare seemed not to hear. A layer of white foam spread itself over his body, outlining him, giving a strange definition to his features in the growing light of the mountain morning. Soon Thomas could see nothing of his friend but the whiteness which seemed to be condensing on him out of the fog. Thomas thought it was an exact statue of Clare that he saw, a thing of white stone moving in a similitude of life. Thomas remained frozen in his place as he saw the stone-like figure move haltingly downward, stop with its sword raised, then stand rigid, the spell that had made it move having halted. Thomas wanted to scream again when he saw a glow of yellowish white, like an egg yolk partially hidden by a film of heated egg white, move to the front of Clare's face and vibrate while floating there. It pulsated as if trying to talk.

Thomas stared at the thing. Clare did not seem to move or react in any way, but Thomas could see that he was beginning to divide into two things. One was a misty stone-like outline of the skeleton of Clare which moved with the same gait as Clare but as bone only. The other part was a sloughing bag of flesh, its color changing from white back to the original and identifiable flesh of Clare. This part shook as if it were sour milk, and fell away from the skelton; it settled to the ground where it did not move again. The incandescent skeleton continued its walk downhill. But Thomas, in horror, could see that it was dissolving in the fog's light. It grew thinner and insubstantial. At last it disappeared like the light in the eyes after staring at a candle's flame. It was gone into the bulk of the fog.

The whiteness then stopped its movement and held with an odd thickness off the ground on the slope. Thomas woke as if from sleep. He grasped his fallen sword and ran, furious with the loss of Clare, into the very heart of the fog.

In the center of the thing, Thomas could hear nothing from outside it. The trilling was no more and the contours of the mountain were lost to sight. It seemed as if he were covered in a chill mound of white wool. He did as Clare had done and swung his sword wildly, blindly, and felt the fog-like dew fall upon his body, until fatigue caused him to fall to his knees. He sobbed as he tried to think of his father's last moments. He wondered if *his* death would be remembered by anyone at all.

Thomas thought briefly, in his fear and resignation, that the island was truly lost now, and that his foolishness had ended his chance of finding out the things which had always teased and fascinated him. Thinking this, he looked up and saw floating toward him the same yellowish spot which had confronted Clare. Thomas dropped his useless sword and stood up. He would at least honor his father by dying on his feet.

The thing stopped and hovered thirty centimeters from his resigned but horrified face.

A blow struck Thomas between the eyes enough so as to cause them to water. He felt a fullness in the front of his head like a bad winter cold making him feel turgid and heavy. Then the feeling broke and he was astonished to hear words in his head.

"You can hear me?"

From somewhere in Thomas came the answer.

"Yes."

131

"You can truly hear me?"

"Yes."

"You may be the first."

"*What* are you?"

"I am a thing with little memory."

"With little memory? But you speak of a lack of memory. That is memory."

"I remember only myself when I am out of the rock. Behind that is nothing. In front is nothing. That is not true memory. Is it?"

"You are of Imram?"

"Imram? I find myself here."

"And your name?"

"I have no name. Names need memory. I am a thing with little memory."

"You are a thing with no memories and no reason for them. I have a few memories, and no reason for them. I am like you in part," said Thomas, speaking as if cut off from all concern for himself.

"Yes."

"Why did you kill my friend?"

"I did not try to *stop* him. I tried to *speak* with him."

"He is dead. He can never speak again."

"He could not speak with me as you can do. When I come out of the stones, I try to speak with things I meet and always it is the same. When they do not speak with me, I am increased by their bones. I do not wish it, but it happens."

"I am the first to speak?"

"You are the first. Why is this so?"

"I do not know."

"But I am glad. You can tell me why I am here and what I must do."

"I can do neither."

"You cannot tell me why I am here?"

"No."

"Then we will talk of many things. You will stay and we will talk always. Together we will speak it out. We will learn together. It must have been a long time since I began to question like this."

"No. There are other things I must do first. But I will try to learn of these things."

"You cannot stay with me?"

"No. There are questions *I* have. When I can answer them, perhaps I can answer yours."

132

"Yes."

"You must ask questions of nothing else. It will stop them."

"I do not mean to stop them. I only want to speak with them."

"I may be able one day to come back and tell you what I know. You will stay here?"

"I will stay in the rocks of this place."

"Let me go. I will come back if I can."

"Yes."

Thomas made a step backward and when he did so the soft shell of fog separated from him and dissolved back within the cloud. He looked down at his skin and it was reddened but whole. He had his body still and it was not jelly. He watched as the wavering smoke drifted back down the slope to the valley floor. His eyes followed in wonder as the thing condensed into the solidity of rock. The trilling stopped and left Thomas alone. He shook his head several times and rubbed one side of his short nose with a damp hand.

As he turned back to the ridge above him, Thomas saw Clare's body lying like a pool, its eyes staring upward as if from underwater, quivering and changing as a light breeze flowed over it. Thomas bent and retched with uncontrollable sobs. The understanding of the reason for Clare's death did not stop the hurt of that death. The two things seemed to merge in one point of time and Thomas felt responsible for both things, the understanding and the death.

After a while Thomas wiped his clammy brow and straightened up. He looked down at the rocks and waved as if the thing were watching, but he did not look at Clare again.

Chapter 15

The men asked where Clare was, but Thomas did not tell them the truth. He told them the sounds had been made by a small party of Farks. He and Clare had fought them and Clare had given his life to save Thomas's. The men accepted that in fear and allowed Thomas to lead them in a short Circle ritual for Clare. After the service Thomas ordered the camp to be broken.

The group rode on toward Straiten, past the rocks of the Bonesucker, without incident. The sky was clouded over and occasionally they found themselves in a rolling gray mist that covered their skins like cool sweat. As they rode they saw signs of old dwellings to the east of them. They remembered the fearful legends of their youth, however, and had no interest in looking at them closely. They knew, from the legends, that there were more ruins even farther east. They kept their eyes to the south. Thomas rode Deep Thought without once looking back to see if his men were following him, his head held rigid like the stuffed head of a hawk.

At dusk Thomas broke his reverie and called an end

to the day's trip. The Circlemen set up camp in a grove of thick trees like great sponges. Thomas called Barry into his tent after supper had been eaten.

"Yes?" said Barry after folding the tent flap back into place and turning to Thomas.

"Barry, you remember I told you I knew a way to get past Hastings' watch?"

"I remember," he said, "and I remember laughing to myself about it."

"You were right to laugh," said Thomas.

"I thought so. What will you do?"

"Well, I need some information about Straiten itself. I have never been there. My father used to tell me about the ordered streets and the painted houses. About the good sections and the bad. But that doesn't serve me now."

"What do you need?"

"Tell me, Barry, are the streets kept as clean as the houses?"

Barry rubbed his jaw, his dark brown eyes to the floor. "Yes, I think so. Periodically. Stuff builds up but is then washed away out of sight. There are cleaning crews that help. They love cleanliness down there, as far as I can tell."

"Good," said Thomas. "We are a cleaning crew."

"What?"

"A cleaning crew."

Barry stared at Thomas. "A cleaning crew? But you will have to get *into* Straiten to do that. And you'll never do that."

"We have to. You said Lord Hastings waits."

"That's true. He waits. He is the one who wanted the Circle symbols, although I don't know why he asked us to deliver them to Dermot of the Order of Zeno when it is clear that the Order wants nothing further to do with political events in the island. Hastings would have known about that."

"Yes, he would. And that is of concern to us. Why should he order that? There must be other reasons. He will have to be reached."

"Oh, but he is well protected, Thomas. I have been to Hastings Hall with Caine and I have seen it."

"Caine?"

"I told you. He is my old boss. The man who leads the Danae forces on this island. He is the one who set up the

135

attack on the Circle before we left, the one who wanted me. He tells anyone who works for him that capture means either rescue or death. In my case, I knew it meant death. He is dangerous."

"Well, whoever will be watching for us, we will have to fool them."

"How?"

"Barry, my father told me that people see only what they want to see. They don't see anything else much. It is all in the mind, what they see. The image they look for must match the image they expect or they do not see it."

"So?"

"So the troops of Hastings and the spies of Caine will be looking for a collection of Circlemen. They will not see them."

"Disguises? They will be looking for disguises," said Barry with certitude.

"Why should they?" asked Thomas quickly.

"Caine taught us the arts of disguise. It is part of Danae mercenary training. We do not always look like Danae. Therefore all Danae mercenaries are suspicious of things as they seem. Your plan will not work."

Thomas spread out his hands onto the top of the table, stretching the fingers as wide apart as he could. "What, then, do you suggest?"

"You mean, what do I suggest we do since I am a Danae and my life is forfeit should Caine have me in his hands again?"

"Something like that."

"I would go in through the sewer."

"The what?"

"You throw your garbage into holes, or make ditches behind the Circle walls. Right?"

"Right."

"All that stuff that collects in the streets of Straiten, the stuff I was telling you about, all that gets washed away at night. Where does it go?"

"I don't have the slightest idea," said Thomas impatiently.

"Straiten evidently has a network of ditches *under* the streets. It carries all junk out into the countryside to rot."

"Why didn't my father know this?" asked Thomas, suspicious.

"He probably didn't need to know. Nobody goes down there. The cleaning crew just opens holes and lets stuff in.

136

Nobody ever cleans the tubes. Nobody really seems to know what's down there. The people of Straiten know only that the thing works. It has never failed."

"Then how can we get in?" asked Thomas with distaste. He had wanted to do the same thing his father had done and walk right in through the front gates of Straiten.

"I happen to know where one of the ducts opens out into the countryside," said Barry. "It is in a lonely place and it smells and so nobody goes there, or should go there. I was looking for a good place to bed down with a turnip of a girl I had found."

Thomas stood up. "You expect me, Thomas, son of Turly Vail, Center of the North Circle, to enter Straiten through a tube of dung?"

Barry looked uninterested. He was thinking of the girl and picking his teeth as Thomas glowered at him. "You can do what you want. You asked me what I would suggest and I told you," he said.

"This is so," said Thomas, who sat back down tiredly and raised his arms above his head, which tilted to one side as if its weight had finally overcome his neck's strength. "Then I have to think about it a while, till morning anyway. But tell me, Danae . . ."

"Barry."

"Barry. Tell me. How will we know when we are at a certain place in the city?"

"We guess?"

"Careful, Barry. I'm not sure I still need you. Answer me with truth on your face."

"I can't. That is, I don't know if the street markers extend *down* into the tubes. We will have to find out once you decide to go in that way."

"I see," said Thomas.

"Are you through with me now?" asked Barry. "Your friends outside are passing around something that smokes good. They said something about 'framing reality' with it. Odd."

"You offend the Circle with your opinions, Danae, do you know that?" said Thomas, feeling irritated at his new friend's presumption in Mythic matters.

"But . . ."

"*I* have been a Framer. I do not always like the emotions raised, but the images and words made by the beaca smoke are good for the Circlefolk. It helps them keep on hunting and fishing, digging in the earth to plant

137

food, weaving cloth from animal's backs, and giving birth to more who will live on this wretched island and do whatever it is they have to do."

"But your father . . ."

"Outlawed it for fear of its tendency to merge the members into one group. And because of the ambitious excesses of one man he knew in the west where I was born."

"I see," said Barry with a hesitant respect, his rough fingers wandering through his thick brown hair.

"He changed his mind when he finally saw that it helped us more than it hurt," continued Thomas. "I think he also knew all along that it helped the Circlefolk to read his own New Doctrine better, and write his new slogans on sheepskin. The beaca words helped the learning of *his* words. I think finally that was what he was after: simply reading and writing."

"Why?"

"I just don't know. He taught me much better than he did the others. But everyone was supposed to be able to read and write."

"We never did," said Barry.

"What?"

"Read."

Thomas stared at Barry for a minute and then shook his head slowly. "It is a short life we have, Barry, and a dangerous one. My father used to say that my great-grandfather Ellman thought life on Imram was 'nasty, brutish, and short.' "

"A good saying," nodded Barry.

"My father believed it, too. He thought man had had a hard time of it before we were born. That there had been great troubles in Imram and elsewhere. That man had come to grief. That he had 'fallen.' And that we were survivors and alone."

"Danae legend tells of the Falling," said Barry.

"And of the Fires?"

"Yes."

"Well, we may well be survivors and alone. But Father thought we had to help ourselves without outside aid."

"You told me he feared something."

"He did, and it was not necessarily the nastiness, the brutishness, or the shortness of life he feared. He feared the Plan of the Others."

"Danae legend tells of this too, in a way."

138

"Indeed," said Thomas, shaking his head. "Father said he did not want to be robbed."

"Robbed?"

"He was afraid that the Plan would rob each man of his own worth, of the little dignity each man had left. He did not want that to be robbed."

"But all your father did was to maintain the Circles in the north in much the same form they had always had, didn't he?" said Barry with some interest. "How was he going to help anything that way? That would be keeping things the same as they had always been and therefore a design itself."

"Not exactly," said Thomas. "He made a framework for change. The North Circle was given a new set of doctrines—which, as I've just told you, didn't work quite right—and a new emphasis on the uniqueness of each member. You've seen the Circle uniforms, each with a different design on the front?"

"Yes," said Barry.

"And he set up the program I also mentioned: reading and writing Imramian. He never said *why* exactly, but it was to help each man in the same way as the different design on his clothes."

"To make each a separate stone?" said Barry.

"That's what *he* often said, Barry. A separate stone," exclaimed Thomas. "Where did *you* hear it?"

"It just occurred to me," said Barry, shrugging.

"He banished the beaca weed for the same reason, because he thought it also robbed man of his dignity, of each man's responsibility to choose for himself what he called the individual 'rocks of the mosaic.' "

"Mosaic? Was that part of the Plan?"

Thomas was silent for a time. He looked up at Barry and he did not know if he believed what he said but he thought he did. "As far as I know, the Blessing Plan and the mosaic were merely delusions in my father's mind. I only know what he told me of them. The stones were not part of that, at least not a *bad* part of it." On saying this Thomas thought again of his wretched youth. What *good* had the use of written words done *him?* What good had any mosaic done to keep him warm on those cold nights when Turly had stayed out drinking, or discussing politics?

"Then your father . . ."

"What?" said Thomas, caught in a bad dream.

"The fear of your father . . ."

"He was haunted by the past and fearful of the future. He tried to hold things together in the present, hoping for something better, and was increasingly bitter about doing it. I could see him dying in front of my eyes."

"And in the mountain?"

"Dying literally in front of me there," said Thomas quietly.

"So you really don't know if the Blessing Plan exists?"

"No," said Thomas slowly. "No, I don't know if it is *real*."

"You think your father told you only legend?"

"He . . ." began Thomas and then stopped. Once again he wondered if Barry was really what he seemed. He might be what he said he was; he might not be. He thought about what Barry had said about disguises and decided that it was best to keep some things to himself.

"I was saying that my father was a man of many stories. I think everybody in the Circle had heard the same stories over and over. The same warnings. You say you have heard stories like them. My father said he had found the Blessing Box and it was real. And he also said that it could be dangerous if used wrongly. The right way to handle it was not to use it. That is all he would say. He offered no proof of it other than his own words."

"Then you have no problems other than your own," said Barry.

"What?"

"You should not have to be burdened by the things that burdened your father. If he believed all that, you don't have to. He may simply have grown old and sick and stupid."

"Barry . . ." said Thomas with anger.

"Sorry," said Barry, raising his hands. "There are many Danae your father's age who have gone from us in many ways too hard to detect. It is as if the fabled Shee have stolen them away, and then let them come back with less than they had. Odd in the head thereafter. It would not be unusual for that to have happened to your father."

"Perhaps," said Thomas, remembering all the old stories about the Shee. He did not say that he doubted it. But whatever else his father was, he was not stupid, nor a willful liar.

"In any case you are your own man now," said Barry.

No, I am not, thought Thomas. *And I will never be until this business is unscrolled. It sits too deeply inside of me now. I will never know my mother, and I saw my father die in fire. He leaves me a burden as solid and as real as the chalk rocks in which the Bonesucker lives. Barry is wrong. I carry this cursed island on my back.*

"Whatever else I am," said Thomas at last, "I am truly tired. You go sleep now and we will leave for the sewer in the morning."

Barry walked to the tent flap and looked back over his shoulder right before going through. His eyes were in shadow and Thomas could not tell if he gave a smile or a grimace. The muscles of his mouth would not permit a clear distinction. "Good dreams," he said, and left.

Thomas wrapped himself in his white wool blanket and turned on his side. He huddled up for warmth and thought of Straiten. Perhaps his father was right about his needing help in that place. Someone living at streets 65 and 70. It would be another image from the past. Someone who had touched his father once and lived in the same moment with him, knowing him as a youth of real flesh. The past would never leave him alone, Thomas knew that now. It had killed his father, the past, and it might kill him too.

Thomas soon jelled into sleep and did not know himself to be Thomas until the morning sun pierced the brown tent with a thick stifling halo of granular light.

Chapter **16**

The man looked up groggily at a ceiling which was grainy and the color of an eggshell. His head seemed to tick time like the slow dripping of water from one ledge to another. A groan forced its way through his lips.

"Be still a little longer," said a deep voice.

The voice did not register and the man lying on the bed raised one hand to his forehead. He noticed as he did so that his hand was singed as if by fire and he remembered.

He screamed, and hands pinned him to the bed.

"I said be still a little longer," said the deep voice which stirred a memory in the screaming man's head, although the memory was very far away and he seemed to look at the memory as if it were a rider coming at him from a distance. Then all things faded into darkness again.

The eggshell ceiling was still there when the man woke up. This time, however, he did not feel like screaming and he knew who he was. It was a resigned feeling that also felt like knowledge worth having.

"Turly?" said a deep voice.

The man turned his head toward the voice and saw the small man he had met years before on the Arid Islands.

"Blessing?" he said.

"Yes."

"I should have known," said Turly after a moment's silence.

"Perhaps," said Blessing, his rugged and deeply grooved features almost unable to reveal emotion. "But you weren't *supposed* to have known, so you didn't."

"No, I didn't," said Turly quietly. "That's right, I didn't. I have never known what was on the other side of fire."

"Do I hear bitterness?" said Blessing.

Turly gazed at the aged face of Thomas Blessing, a man who was more than one hundred and fifty years old. "I am not dead?" he said.

"No," said Blessing, sitting back in his chair. "But you thought you were dead, were going to die, and your mind and body both accepted that as a fact. Which means, I suppose, that you in fact did die and we merely resurrected you."

"Who did?" said Turly.

"The Church of Spirit and Science."

Turly stared at Blessing. "The Church of Spirit and Science? The one you started in . . . ?"

"2019," said Blessing.

"But I thought it died with the Falling," said Turly.

"It is alive and well. I thought I told you so years ago on the Arid Islands. You remember?"

Turly nodded. He lay on the bed which seemed slick with whiteness; his red hair contrasted with it in a way that set him off, the color of his skin seeming to match that of the bed. "I knew that," he said at last. The room was silent and still but for a faint buzz coming from one of the machines taped to Turly's forearm. "But I thought the Others . . ."

Blessing did not laugh. His face barely permitted a smile, so rigid was it with age. He reached out and touched Turly's bunched fist. His eyes seemed young to Turly.

"There are no *Others,*" said Blessing, after a moment in which Turly thought a secret of great importance was about to be given.

Turly struggled to sit up but Blessing restrained him

143

easily. "But you told me on the Arid Islands that there *were* Others, that *they* made the Box."

"I *implied* it," said Blessing, nodding slowly. "And since you were so eager to believe it at the time, you did believe it."

"But . . . ?"

"*We* are the Others, Turly."

"We?"

"The Blessing line, the CSS, and all those who have helped us along the way."

"*You* did all this to Imram?" shouted Turly almost before Blessing was through. "*You* did? The Falling? The Fires?"

Blessing sat back in his chair and peaked his finger tips into a temple shape. Pursing his lips, he furrowed his brow into even deeper ridges. The lines and circles on his face seemed clearly drawn in the light of the small room.

"Let me show you something," he said at last.

"All you have to show me is Imram!" shouted Turly suddenly. "Imram! and every cursed thing on it!"

"Turly . . ."

"Show me the whole of this place, Blessing!" screamed Turly. "Show it! Show!"

Blessing touched something to his arm and Turly felt his anger and outrage fade gradually into a faint glow like the last rosy tint on a piece of charcoal. He followed the color into darkness.

"You will see it all soon, Turly," said Blessing softly.

Chapter 17

The bushes were thick and green but tinged with brown at the edges of their tiny leaves. Thomas leaned down and looked up into the pipe. It was made of circular brick walls and seemed to be covered on the dark red inside with the smell of charcoal which sheep had urinated on. Thomas turned back with disgust to the morning air.

"We go into this?" asked Thomas.

Barry shrugged.

"Garrett, what do you think?" asked Thomas.

"Is there no other way you can think of to get into Straiten now?" asked Garrett. He clearly did not like the idea of entering Straiten through the pipe either. He scratched his blunt nose and looked around the area as if he wanted nothing to do with it.

"Garrett, that didn't help much," said Thomas. "I know you and my father did things differently years ago, but times have changed. They weren't expecting you last time. There will be people all over Straiten looking for us. In fact, they are probably watching us now. Isn't this so, Barry?"

Barry cast his eyes back over the landscape and nodded.

"If we want to get in, this is probably the only way," said Thomas. "They may know we've entered the city this way, but they can't know where we will come up. This is it."

"Not exactly," said Garrett, who was polishing the top of his balding head with one hand.

"What?" said Thomas and Barry together.

"Some of us can get in through that sewer and wander around Straiten, and others can go in alone at other points. I remember the way Straiten is laid out. It would be impossible for Hastings or anybody else to cover *everywhere*. There is a swamp to the south, for example, where some could easily slip in."

"Well," said Thomas, rubbing his chin. "You may be right. In that case why can't we *all* do that?"

Garrett spat into the earth. "Well, it would be better if we entered singly into Hastings' lair."

"He is saying that some of us will crawl through garbage and others will tramp through swamps and then some of us may get to the bottom of things," said Barry.

Thomas glanced over to the clump of Circlemen muttering to themselves. Touching Garrett on the shoulder, Thomas walked over to them and raised one hand.

"Some of you will stay with me," said Thomas, "and others will go with Garrett around to the south side of Straiten. He will be in charge of those of you who go with him. Remember, we are after the man who plots against the North Circle. If we continue to let him plot, he will destroy it."

The men nodded and clutched their swords in a certain kind of Circle resolve. Thomas knew from his short experience as a Framer that they all loved the Circle and the outlawed Mythic Sequence for the peace and final security it seemed to offer after all the strife of life was done. They were not all solid fighters like Clare had been, or as cunning as Garrett was, but they were all trained in basu skills and could hold their own.

Thomas pulled Garrett off to one side. "Garrett, you pick the fifteen best men of the lot. Be sure they understand they are to look and listen at first. Three days from now we will all try to meet at . . . streets 50 and 49 in the heart of Straiten. All right? If we're not there, come

146

back to this place and then go back to the north. Tell them what you know."

"All right," said Garrett. "But, Thomas, you should know as your father did that not everyone will return to Inniscloe."

"I know that, Garrett."

"It will not be your fault though."

"I know that, too, Garrett."

The older man looked at Thomas strangely, his deceptively skeletal face trying to probe the meaning in Thomas's words.

"Garrett, this island is real and we are on it. It is all we know. Am I right? And if it is sick, we will try to cure it. We hope the whole island will live, but we are prepared for some death, aren't we?"

Garrett replied slowly. "You have not always been so concerned, my young friend. Did your father speak to you about this?"

"Yes," said Thomas. "But it seems only yesterday I was fixing the Circle pumps and not caring a molon about the island or our place on it."

"This is true."

"And now I do care."

"This seems equally true," said Garrett.

Thomas put one hand on Garrett's shoulder. "Then let's be about Turly's business."

"Yes," said Garrett, shaking his head regularly as if he were listening to music. Thomas stared after Garrett's group as it moved off.

Thomas turned away to point Barry and the others to the front of the sewer pipe. He waited while his men bunched around the pipe and listened to Barry explain something to them.

". . . and they lead to the main pipes of which this is one."

Scanlon, a Circleman two years older than Thomas and of full growth, held his nose and said something no one could understand. Thomas laughed and held his own nose. Barry laughed too and went over to a weed patch and pulled up several sprigs of small green leaves. He went to Thomas and, breaking off a few of the leaves, pushed them toward Thomas's nose. Thomas pulled back in surprise but smelled a pungent odor that was stinging yet sweet. He knew what Barry was doing.

147

"You have found a way to blunt the terrors of our passage, Barry?" he asked, smiling ruefully.

"Yes. The smell of these leaves is strong in the nose but not as bad, I think, as the smell in there," he said, pointing to the sewer.

"I will have to agree," said Thomas, eager to try whatever would work.

Scanlon bent down and tried to sniff up into the two-meter wide pipe. He turned around and crammed some mint up into his nose, too. The others followed suit, each sticking the prickly leaves, with their dusty green coating, gently into place. Some eyes watered but soon they were all ready. Thomas beckoned them to follow and stepped gingerly into the thick wetness settled at the base of the pipe. When he had disappeared into its gloom, his shoulders bent and his hands extended in front of him, Barry stepped into the same muck and the others followed in a line.

Thomas took the first candle from his pack and waited as Barry joined him. The two wicks caught from Thomas's flint and the light grew into a hesitant glow. The light did not seem to want to reach any farther into the pipe's interior than it had to. The rest of the Circlemen lit up.

"Barry, you lead," said Thomas with a nasal twang. The sweet-smelling leaves were working, but the imagination of each man made the odor of the pipe pervasive. Each thought he was in a tube of offal.

"Very well," said Barry. "This way please."

Barry stepped off into the pipe's length, the surrounding walls arching up and over the men. They looked like a glowworm trapped in a bowl of thick mush.

The corridor of the drainage pipe, as best Thomas could make out, was ribbed about every four meters with an extra brace of bricks. There were marks on the wall to indicate that the level of material in the pipe varied. There were signs that the level had once been as high as their necks. Thomas hoped they would not have to learn what that meant. His thighs were growing weary of lifting his feet high up and out of the heavy putrid matter that tied to suck his boots off. Soon he called the first halt and his men, not wanting to sit down, leaned back against the wall and tried to shift the weight of their belongings to the wall.

"Barry, where will we find the first branch pipe?" said Thomas, wiping his damp forehead. There seemed to be a small breeze in the pipe but it did not help to keep him cool.

"Branch pipe? Listen, Thomas, I told you I personally never came down here. I just knew about it, that's all."

"All right," said Thomas, rolling his eyes to the darkness above his head. He wondered what his father would have thought.

After ten minutes' rest Thomas shouted to the men to get up in line and keep going. They walked without talking for about an hour more. Thomas was very tired and he knew the others must be, too. But there were no other pipes as yet, and he wanted to go on until he knew if there would be markers coming down from the streets. He called another halt anyway and patted his bag to determine the number of candles he had left. Four. They would last another hour or so. He knew he should have taken along enough torches to get them through, and he was angry at himself for not having done so. But then he reflected that he hadn't known what *through* was.

Something on the ceiling of the pipe caught his eye. He lifted his thick white candle and looked closer.

"Barry, look at this!" he whispered.

Barry clumped over to where Thomas was standing. He squinted his eyes and moved his face from side to side like a cobra.

"What does it mean?" he asked.

"It is the sign drawn on my father's chest," said Thomas, forgetting for a moment that Turly was dead.

"What?"

"Once in the west of Imram, in his younger days, he had been leader of a tribe of people there, the Ennis. At the Settling rite of a new camp of theirs, he carved that sign on his bare chest. I saw it often. And the sign was on a map he drew."

"The next question," said Barry, "is, what is it doing up *there?* Am I right?"

"Right."

"Well?"

"He said that it was the sign of the builders of the Blessing Box."

"Who said that?"

"Turly did," said Thomas.

"The *builders* of the Blessing Box? But, as you said, there is much legend involved in all that. What if the Box *does* exist?"

149

"It is what my father said, Barry. And you see the sign up there. There it is. It is real. Somebody, or something, put it there."

"Then *they* made this pipe?" asked Barry, with some hesitation in his voice.

"Might have," replied Thomas uncertainly.

"But who are the builders?"

"Father told me once that someone called the *Others* had built odd things all over the island. And they were the ones who had done the things that caused the Falling of many years ago. He said they had kept people in fear of each other until he had found the Blessing Box, and fixed things."

"What did he fix?" asked Barry, his voice still hushed as he gazed up at the sign of the Others.

"Listen, Barry," whispered Thomas. "Every Circleman knows the story. You said you knew a lot about Imram. Why don't you know *this* story?"

"I can't know everything," shrugged Barry. "I had other stories told to me as well."

"You'll have to tell me sometime," said Thomas.

"Yes, well, tell me now what it was your father fixed."

"He said he was able to make the Box stop causing Imramers to hate anybody who was different or not a part of the immediate area. The Circles of the north were then able to combine into one big Circle. It also made it easier for us to travel in the countryside. We grew richer than we had been. There are many more crops now and . . ."

"I don't care about crops," said Barry. "What I want to know is, if any of this is true."

Thomas thought for a moment. "I thought it was something he had made up; but then I wasn't there, and I *was* born in the west of Imram. That much is true."

"A good story."

"My father told me that stories can do anything they want. Nothing wrong with that. It is like Framing."

"Maybe," allowed Barry.

"Anyway, my father did some strange things as he grew older. That was none of my business, once I was able to move out. But he was convinced it was all true. I myself will have to put my eyes to it first."

"Me too," said Barry.

"Certainly the legend of the Blessing Papers, whatever they are, is one of Imram's best stories."

The two men then looked at each other in silence.

"Thomas?"

"Yes?"

"Why is it the 'Blessing Papers' once, and then the 'Blessing Box' next?"

"I don't know. Same thing probably. Box the papers are in. Papers in the box. That kind of thing."

"I see. Do you think we will see any of the 'Others' down here?"

Thomas looked around. "If we do, they are worse off than we are. Why anybody would want to be down here is beyond me."

"I'll keep my eyes open anyway," said Barry.

Thomas backed away from under the sign of the Others and motioned to the men, who had not seen the sign, to join them. Barry and Thomas then started off again, their heads bowed in thought.

The small band seemed to walk for hours, days. There was no sound save the solid splash of their walking and the grunting; the tepid glow from their candles still weakly outlined the stained brick walls. There was no sign of anything else in the pipe with them. It curved gently from time to time but in no great degree. Thomas wondered if they had already passed completely under Straiten and were to wind up in the sea.

"Thomas!" hollered Barry from up ahead.

Thomas snatched his thoughts back to the pipe. The sound of a human voice was a shock.

"Barry?" said Thomas, trying to catch up with the Danae, wondering if blood were to be drawn at last.

"Look," shouted Barry excitedly. "A marker!"

Thomas saw a gray shaft depending about twenty centimeters from the ceiling of the pipe. It bore the numbers 1 and 50. About five meters ahead of them a similar tube, but not as large, ran at a right angle to them.

"We are in Straiten," said Thomas.

"We are *under* Straiten," corrected Barry.

"Yes," said Thomas. "But this means we can find our way to any of the streets, get out, and then get back in to escape."

"Where is the exit hole?" said Barry, who was standing with black muck up to his ankles and one fist resting on his hip. He had a wry look on his face like a man with plenty of candles but no flint.

Thomas glanced around quickly, raising his candle, burned almost to the nub, to search the rounded top of the pipe at that point. There seemed to be no way up and out. He scratched his head and thought for a moment that they might spend the rest of their lives beneath Straiten looking for a way out.

"Thomas," said Scanlon.

"Yes?"

"Yes?" repeated Thomas, looking squarely at the younger man with the peaked head and short-cropped hair.

"Could this be an outlet?"

"Where?"

"Here, against the wall. See, there where the brick breaks from the wall and becomes the ribbing. There seems to be a wider break than is necessary. I just checked at the last ribbing and it was not that way at all."

Handing his candle to Scanlon, Thomas pushed his fingers to the rib bricks and ran them down the lines like nerves. He could feel the separation. Reaching high up and on his toes, he ran his fingers until he met another line branching off. He felt the hinges as if they were printed on the wall. They could have passed right beside the exit had they not been looking for it.

"Barry, see if you can get your Danae nails into the lower edge of this thing. No, see there just above the slush line. Yes, now push your nails in. Ah . . ." Thomas had hold of the top lines and the lines gave.

A slim opening appeared in the semi-darkness. Thomas peered inside and looked up into a light dimness that seemed to float in space.

"It may be a way up into the streets," he said. "But we don't want to get out on street 1. We ought to go to 51 at least. We have more walking to do."

"True," said Barry wearily.

Thomas stepped back from the concave door in the wall and wiped his hands on his pants. He then pushed the door closed and took his candle back from Scanlon. The men were standing around him in a ragged semicircle. Thomas saw their haggard faces like ravished half-moons, lit by the sparseness of the candlelight and surrounded by shadows. There were various degrees of distrust and fear in the faces. Thomas wondered how many of them he would grow old with. This thought was not something he could entertain for long, and he moved away into the narrowness of the sewer pipe, the lighted space in front of him reaching weakly into the dark.

Chapter 18

The upper door opened into a side alley. Thomas stuck his head around the surprisingly thin brick doorway and glanced about. There were a few people walking randomly on the street just off the alley, which was like a small cubbyhole. The air seemed mild and sweet, the sky a cobalt blue in the early afternoon sun.

"See anything?" asked Scanlon behind him. The younger man was eager to put his face out into the freshness, too. The smell of the pipe behind them seemed to reach up and wrap itself around them like a fist to prevent their escape.

"Nothing," said Thomas, pulling back inside. "But you and the others stay here for a while. Barry?" whispered Thomas. "Come up here."

"I am here," said Barry, who had already pulled the mint leaves out of his nose and was shifting from foot to foot eagerly.

"Barry, you and I are going out to look around for a minute. You say you know the place. If nothing seems wrong, we'll come back and get the others. Scanlon, keep them all in here out of sight."

"All right," said Scanlon with some regret.

"Should we not be back in, say, fifteen or twenty minutes, go back the way you came and wait at the entrance to the pipe for Garrett to return. If *he* doesn't return in three or four days, go back to the North Circle. Elect a new Center as soon as possible."

"Twenty minutes and then go back," said Scanlon.

"Yes," said Thomas, and motioned to Barry to follow him outside. The two men stepped through the alley near the corner of 50 and 51. Thomas went to the edge of the alley opening and leaned forward to look out. There seemed nothing unusual there, but then Thomas knew he did not know what was usual in Straiten. The rows of triple-decked huts were impressive and clearly of better construction than anything in the north. Their fronts were painted with a variety of colors, some of shades Thomas had never seen before. It was like a shattered rainbow, chopped into pieces and laid out in random order.

The streets to the east were wide and clean; the ones to the south were thinner but equally clean. Thomas thought the people he saw—dressed in roughly the same kind of clothing Circlefolk wore—looked well-fed and contented.

Barry said something and stepped out into 50 street. Thomas reached out to grab him back but could not quite reach him. Barry moved with a smooth step, and he was soon gone around the corner into 51 street. Thomas stepped out of the alley after him and let the afternoon sun wash over him, which made him blink as if light dust had been thrown in his eyes. Thomas guessed that they had been in the underground pipe for almost three hours. He looked down at his boots and winced when he saw the still wet, green-and-brown stains on them, and on his lower pants legs. He stopped and tried to scrape the boots clean. His mouth puckered and his brow lowered over his eyes in disgust.

"Thomas, what are you doing?" whispered Barry, who had slipped back from around the corner.

"Cleaning myself off," said Thomas. "If anybody sees this stuff, he may wonder about where we came from."

"Listen, that man over there is going to wonder why a common worker is so worried about the way he looks. Now quit."

"All right," said Thomas reluctantly. He knew he had to trust Barry in some things.

154

"Good. Now we should look around this block at least once," continued Barry. "Then we can get the others up here and start looking for the best way to get to Hastings."

"You're right," said Thomas.

The two started off again down the narrow strip of inlaid rock running in front of the houses. When they turned right onto 51 and headed west, their eyes were in the sun. In front of them about fifteen meters away was a group of beggars in tattered tunics that seemed to have been torn by dogs. The beggars' faces at that distance looked like pieces of charred wood. One was legless and was riding on a flat board with tiny wheels on it, rolling with a bumpy ease down the sidewalk.

"Tinkers," said Barry under his breath.

"Tinkers?"

"Country people from the south coast. They would sell their own children for coin."

"Are they dangerous?"

"Sometimes yes, sometimes no," said Barry with disgust. "They are one of the worst features of this part of Imram. Not like the north."

Thomas wondered why Barry seemed to hate country people so much. He wondered if that hatred extended to *any* country people.

As they drew close to the tinkers, Thomas and Barry saw that they would have to step off the sidewalk into the dusty street as the tinkers showed no inclination to do so. Thomas wanted no trouble that soon and so tapped Barry and motioned to the street. Right before they met the group of beggars, he touched his hand to his forehead and stepped off into the dust.

A fist caught him on the forearm, just missing the throat. He leaped instinctively from the direction of the fist and doubled over, feeling the rough surface of the Straiten street scar his flesh. His basu training made him stop fighting for breath and roll to a point where he could stand and face his opponent. Before he could quite maneuver, a stick came down hard on his nose and a blossom of pain grew on his face. Nevertheless, he kept rolling. With an effort smooth as a lack of thought can make it, Thomas came to his feet and saw the group of six tinkers divided—half coming for him, and half already on Barry. The tinker on the board was rolling off fast to the western part of the town.

155

Thomas gave himself to his training. He threw the palm of his hand into the face of the first man to his right and it hit with the sound of a stick hitting wet ground, the man's eyes snapping shut as red pumped from his nose. The same instant his hand did this, Thomas's left leg shot up in a tight arc into the crotch of the man on his left, who did not have the opportunity to see either the hand or the leg move. Both of the tinkers seemed to collapse at the same time. Before their cries could be heard, Thomas had leaped into the air and smashed the third tinker's chest with both feet. Then, coming back up quick off the street, he checked the three and popped each in the side of the neck where the blue artery carried blood to the brain. All three stopped their moans.

Thomas glanced up and saw that Barry was not having the same luck. One tinker was on the ground with Barry's blut blade sticking in his right armpit, the red creeping down his shirt. But the two others had Barry held against the wall of one house, hitting him in the face and crotch.

Leaping again, Thomas broke the back of one of the men. Before this man had arched backward, or Thomas could begin his fall to the sidewalk, the young man from the north flicked out his arm and grazed the head of the last tinker with his fist. The man released Barry's throat and stepped back, stunned, allowing Barry to slump to the ground. Thomas was up and facing the tinker now and the man's face was twitching with fear and sweat. His eyes were bulging like that of a cornered animal. Thomas leaned forward in the basu defense while quickly glancing at Barry who seemed unconscious.

"Why did you do this?" hissed Thomas, his voice coming through clenched teeth.

The man stared at Thomas's arms which were held in front of him like two crossed swords. There was blood on both of the fists. Thomas popped one fist to the man's shoulder. The man jerked, clutching the shoulder bone with his left hand.

"Why did you do this?" repeated Thomas.

"You are from the north?"

Thomas did not answer. His broken nose was beginning to throb with the beat of his blood.

"You are rich?" said the tinker.

Thomas continued to watch the man closely. He did not answer.

"We need your coin," said the tinker with a rasp to his

voice. "We wanted to take it and drink good all night together and then go back to Clanholly."

"Clanholly?"

"Where we are living for now," said the man.

"You are just tinkers?"

"Yes. You hate tinkers too?"

"I have never met a tinker before," said Thomas. "I think I hate tinkers now."

"This man hated tinkers," said the tinker, pointing to Barry with his chin. "He hated us. We could tell. It would have been easy and good to take his money."

"That is why you tried to kill us?"

"One way to get your money," said the tinker, shrugging.

"Get back to Clanholly," said Thomas. "Now."

"What of my friends?"

Thomas looked around at them. "They are of no use to you now," he said. "Leave while you can."

The tinker stared at Thomas, his eyes seeming to widen at the vision of the boy's head and hair. He nodded slowly and began to back off down the street. Thomas turned quickly to Barry and felt his neck. But he was not so absorbed by his friend's wounds to miss the sound of whistling air. He ducked his head to one side and heard the sound continue past his ear. Arching his back and balancing on his hands, Thomas sent his legs flying up and back. He heard a gurgle as the heel of one foot caught the last tinker by the throat and crushed the cartilage there. Thomas looked back once to see the man fall to the ground and lie still, his eyes open and staring into the sun. He then turned back to Barry.

"Barry?" he said. "Barry!"

Barry groaned but did nothing else. Thomas stood up and looked around. He could see no one else alive on 51 street except far up toward the east. He remembered that the seventh tinker had rolled off to the west and that he and Barry would have to get back to the sewer fast. Bending down, Thomas grabbed Barry's arms and pulled him up and over his shoulders, resting him there with his head hanging toward the street on one side. He then staggered back to 50 and 51, breathing heavily; Barry was like a sack of dirt.

Thomas grew cautious as he drew near the corner. Someone now knew they were in Straiten, and he would have to improvise even more than he had thought. It was about past the twenty-minute meeting time he had told Scanlon about. He hoped the boy would have more sense, perhaps less loyalty or heroics than Clare, and return to the outside as he had been told to do. If he did follow orders, he and the men would soon be on their way back down the sewer pipe and then eventually back to Inniscloe Circle. He and Barry could catch up to them somewhere.

Thomas laid Barry down at the corner and looked up and down the street. Up toward the north he saw what he had feared. Red uniforms. The red guard of Hastings.

"Ah, bats at night," muttered Thomas with the knowledge that he could not now carry Barry around the corner and into the alley without the red soldiers seeing them. They could not now rejoin the others. Thinking as he acted, Thomas bent to pick up Barry and hurried back the way he had come. Reaching 48, he turned south down to 53 running east and west. He found the alley for the entrance to the sewer pipe at that corner and put Barry down while he tried to find the opening. He found the seams, but the door would not come open. Thomas cursed again and again. He and Barry seemed stranded.

"Thomas?" said Barry groggily.

Thomas rushed to Barry, who had slipped over onto the street. Propping him back up in the alley, Thomas opened Barry's tunic and checked his wounds.

"What happened?" said Barry, looking around, his eyes puffing closed.

"The tinkers," said Thomas.

"Where . . . ?"

"One got away," said Thomas. "I think he may tell someone important that we are here. We need shelter."

"They were with Caine," said Barry after a moment. "I should have known."

"Caine?"

"My old employer. I told you."

"Not Hastings?"

"No. They had to be with Caine."

"Well, can you walk?" said Turly.

"I think so. Let me try." Barry stood up shakily with Thomas's help. He thought the earth was slipping beneath his feet and so fell back against the alley wall.

"Barry?"

"I can do it. But where can we go? I don't know anybody here that wouldn't sell us in a moment."

"The red soldiers are down where we were by now. No way back there," said Thomas, thinking fast. "We'll go to the address my father gave me."

Leading the half-blind Barry, Thomas moved out of the alley and walked carefully down 48 until they reached 65. Turning to the east on 65, Thomas pulled Barry to hurry him on. When they got to the corner of 70 going north and south, Thomas drew Barry into an alley there.

"Listen, Barry," said Thomas. "I don't know who is in this house. But my father said I might be able to find help here should I need it. I think he saw this danger."

"It is everywhere, Thomas," coughed Barry. Some blood had come up and lay on his lips like drops of red rain. Thomas tore off a piece of Barry's tunic and patted off the blood. Handing the cloth to Barry, Thomas looked out into the street like a cornered animal.

Like an animal, thought Thomas. *I am hunted.*

But Thomas could see no red shirts in the streets and so walked up the steps of the house on the northwest corner. It was freshly painted a light pink like the earliest light of sunrise. The green shutters were all drawn, however, and Thomas wondered why he was there. If the people who lived there were not the old friends of his father, more Straitens would know where he was. He knocked on the polished front door carved with the likeness of a huge branched tree, its whorls intricate and fine.

After a moment the door opened and Thomas looked into the shocked eyes of a woman about the age of Meriwether.

"Turly?" said the woman with incomprehension.

Chapter 19

Barry was in the first-floor bedroom asleep. The ragged mounds of flesh on his arms and face had been washed and dressed by Derva, who closed the door of the bedroom gently as he began to snore.

"If he is lucky, he will sleep for a long time and wake up feeling bad," she said. Her hair was pinned up in a brown, gray-streaked bundle on top of her finely shaped head. Thomas admired the way her eyes, riding high above her cheekbones, could look sad and beautiful at the same time. He let his hands hang helplessly at his side as he listened to her tell him what was wrong with Barry.

"But he may lose one eye," she said. Her small ears, rounded and held close to the head, had a circle of gold in each lobe.

"One eye?" asked Thomas at last.

"Yes," replied Derva softly, looking up at his nose. She placed a hand out and wiggled it gently. Thomas winced.

"Can you breathe?" she asked. He said no, and her red tunic swished to one side as she went quickly to an upstairs closet. She came back with a bundle of clean rags, a bowl of water, and a jar of jelly ointment. She motioned for Thomas to sit down and then proceeded to pack one of the rags into his mouth.

"Bite down on this," she said. "This will hurt. Hold your arms down and grab the sofa."

Thomas screamed deep in his throat as Derva twisted his nose with a jerk. Tears stung his eyes and he squeezed them shut. He could hear Derva, very far away, telling him that she thought it would heal all right now and that he could breathe again.

Thomas opened his mouth and spit out the bloody rag; he swallowed a few times to get moisture back on his tongue and then gently flared his nostrils. The pain was duller. He could breathe better, although he still felt as if his face were nothing but a nose. He lay back on the sofa and waited until he thought he could safely open his eyes. When he did, Derva was not there. He heard her in the rear of the house washing something. Thomas shut his eyes and thought again about why he was there.

Because of the Circle.

His father.

Himself.

Thomas thought about all three for a while. He could not readily distinguish them. Where did one begin and the other leave off? He, Thomas, was what he was because he was the particular son of a particular man living in a particular place and time. He could be no other than what he was, he thought. *Except for the dreams.*

"You are better?" asked Derva, coming back into the room.

"I am. Thank you," said Thomas. "Thanks for Barry too."

"He is a Danae, isn't he?"

"Yes."

"How did you two come to fight on the same side?"

Thomas told her, briefly.

"I believe that," she said. "The Danae are in and out of Straiten now. Have been for almost three years, ever since Hastings came back."

"He *is* back then?"

Derva nodded her head. "Oh, yes, he's back."

"Tell me about him," said Thomas with a sudden lunge forward on the sofa. It pained his nose as blood seemed to wash forward and fill the front of his face.

161

"Later," said Derva. "I want to know about your father. What happened to him after he left my house years ago? I know that he helped pull down Hastings in the rebellion and that he got to Boulder Gap where Sean died. After that I could find out nothing."

"Sean?" asked Thomas. So many names. So many people.

"Your father didn't tell you about Sean?" asked Derva, surprise peaking her eyebrows. "I would have thought he had told you all about Sean. A good man," she added, a veil of memory falling over her. Thomas watched her eyes fade in and out of the present, seeing what was in front of her then, and in front of her years before.

"My father and I didn't get along well after I grew to a certain age," said Thomas. "We only talked about a few things after that."

Derva seemed surprised again. "Turly? He didn't seem that way when I met him. He seemed kind and full of curiosity about many things. Too intense, I thought, but still a man who would love a son."

"He was, once, I understand," said Thomas, who found himself apologizing for Turly.

Derva looked into the present and saw Thomas's pain. "I am sorry, Thomas. You look so much like your father in certain ways. I thought it was him, you know, at the door. But I can see that you are also quite different. Your mother's influence, I'm sure. That would be Meriwether, I think I recall."

"Meriwether? No, it wasn't Meriwether. It was Jeneen, an Ennis who lived in the west. My father met her after he left Clonnoise Abbey."

"What was at Clonnoise Abbey?"

Thomas stopped himself. He seemed too willing to give away the secret of the location of the Blessing Papers. Turly had warned him about that. He had not believed its value until that night at the Lower Mountain when Turly had come to him and then walked into the flames. His father—almost in a final wish—had been certain that the secret had to be kept by Thomas and that it might be needed one day for some reason. Thomas had almost come to believe him about that, too.

Thomas had known Derva only a few hours. She was lovely in her age and Thomas wanted to trust her completely. But he held back and told her he did not know

162

why Turly had been at Clonnoise Abbey, but that he had gone farther up the coast and so found Jeneen.

"And where is she now?" asked Derva, while touching her slim fingers to her gray-brown hair.

"She is dead," said Thomas.

"In the north?"

"No. I never knew her. She died in the west after I was born. My father took me back to the north after she died. I grew up there."

"I see," said Derva, who looked down at her fingers spread wide in her lap. Thomas felt a strange emotion, but he said nothing and simply watched her.

After a time Derva looked up and caught Thomas staring at her that way. She smiled and cocked her head. A slight flush spread across the top of her chest, revealed by a flap in the tunic open at her neck. "You are your father's son," she said.

"I'm sorry?" said Thomas, who had not been listening.

"You and my daughter would be about the same age," she said quietly.

"Daughter?" said Thomas, looking around the room. "You have a daughter? Where is she?"

"Dead."

"Dead?"

"The hunger that came after Hastings fell killed many people here in Straiten. She was one of them. I could not feed her."

"I'm sorry," said Thomas. "How old . . ."

"Almost four when she died. Sean saw her only once."

"Sean was her father?"

"Yes. Events in this island do not always please the heart, do they?"

Thomas thought she meant something deep and he looked at her carefully. She seemed only a mother in an old bereavement. Her eyes were glistening lightly and Thomas thought he might see himself in them if he were close enough to them. He did not move. The past in the room was palpable.

Derva looked up with brave sorrow, sorrow that could accept whatever came and make the best of it. It was the look of experience. Her chin was held up high as she spoke, her wet lips throwing off light. "And where is Turly now?"

Thomas coughed and leaned back in the sofa.

"Everybody is dead, it seems."

"What?"

"My father, not a week ago, walked into fire and is gone."

"Turly did that?"

"Yes."

Derva breathed in deeply and held it. She let it out and shook her head. "I suppose I knew that someday he would do that. He seemed fascinated by fire, light. But I thought it was just a need to show that he wasn't afraid of it."

"I guess he wasn't," said Thomas.

"What? Oh, yes, I see you might be right. There must have been something there for him."

"Yes. I hope he found it."

"Well, enough of this," said Derva after a pause. "You wanted to know about Hastings. Let's get on with it."

Thomas sat forward and concentrated on her words so as to forget the flat hard sore of his nose.

"He is now at Hastings Hall," said Derva. "About three years ago he came back to Straiten with a large force of his red soldiers. No one knew where he had been. He quickly took back what he had lost to the rebels years before. They had grown fat and lazy anyway. They would fight among themselves, and they could not manage to choose anyone to lead them. And the people of Straiten, those who were left, were tired of the chronic hunger and the brutality in the streets. The rebels had come to accept everything as their due, had taken *anything* openly, without regard for . . ."

Derva trailed off and Thomas could only imagine what she meant. He himself had never seen anything else other than Circle order at work and its concern for the individual and others in the middle of life. The immensity of Straiten, the free-floating strangers, the lack of food in one's own backyard, must have caused great fear.

"That is when your daughter died?" said Thomas.

"She died a year after Hastings had been driven out. Her stomach was always so large and round but beautiful in its way. Her eyes seemed never to blink. She came to smell like dry straw and died one night without a sound. I buried her myself in the Heron Swamp to the south of Straiten. I was very nearly dead myself. I could live on roots or berries, you see, but a child could not. I was bone and skin."

Thomas could not see her as bone and skin. He did not

want to see her as that. It was hard for him to picture the kind of trouble that would lead her to such a condition.

"Hastings built back his empire of the south," continued Derva. "Within less than six months crops were in, pigs and goats were back from somewhere, and people were again buying and selling what they needed. Hastings was then openly welcomed back. There was dancing in the street. We all forgot why it was we had ever wanted to be rid of him. Good times were back and we all wanted to keep them. I grieved that my daughter Neece had not been able to live until good times had returned, but it was no great regret after the first grieving."

"And now . . . ?"

"Now Hastings seems to be moving. The southwest has been taken; the south and the island's center have always been his. But now we hear that he is ready to move north and take it, add it to his empire." Derva was speaking as if she were reciting a list of things needed from the market. Thomas nodded his head, hearing what he knew he might hear. He was even more afraid of Hastings now, and afraid for the North Circle. He knew he would have to do what he could do to meet Hastings and stop him if possible. He thought briefly of the Blessing Papers but shook the thought off. The room was very still and filled with soft light; dust motes drifted in the rays that slanted down from the one window in the room.

"Derva, you know I have to see Hastings," said Thomas at last.

"I suppose. Turly did too."

"Yes," said Thomas. "But I cannot do it like Turly did. I am not Turly. I am his son Thomas. We did not think alike, he and I. We did not do things alike."

Derva asked Thomas how old he was. Thomas answered and she made a face, her eyebrows up again. "It will be hard," she said.

"It *should* be hard," said Thomas, who was not sure what that meant, but it sounded good and seemed to lessen the tension about any upcoming struggle. He stood up and stretched. Mentioning to Derva that he had not eaten all day, he followed her into her kitchen, watching her from behind.

Thomas was surprised to see all the kitchen tools in a Straiten kitchen. The floor was a polished square of dark wooden tiles. There were cabinets on the walls filled with dishes, some with bright country scenes painted on them.

There was a door to one side that led out into the rear of the house.

The Circlefolk he grew up with seemed very far away from Thomas now. He remembered clearly how he had dreamed often that there were other ways of doing things than the Circle allowed for. He remembered how the dreams of these differences had seemed vivid and real, with the texture of true knowledge. Perhaps Straiten had been his dream. Looking around closer, however, he didn't think so.

Derva fed Thomas cheese and slices from a tube of meat. There was black bread and golden mustard and cups of Straiten tea. Thomas stuffed it all into his mouth as if he were a thief. The bread loaf sitting on top of the white tablecloth looked like a mountain with a knife stuck in it. Thomas chuckled several times as he thought of it. He felt good again and wondered if he could stay with Derva and go no farther.

After the meal, Thomas wiped the golden stains off his lips and followed Derva back to the front room. She started to arrange some flowers in a vase while Thomas stretched out his legs and folded his arms contentedly on his full stomach. It was growing dark outside and he looked out the window and watched small points of light blink into the night sky.

Thomas looked back at Derva, still arranging the red and white flowers, and thought again that she was beautiful. The years had been kind to her, in spite of her troubles. Her lips, moist as she licked them, seemed to move slowly as if in some kind of invitation. He remembered Meriwether and he remembered certain girls at the Inniscloe Circle whom he had never touched. Derva seemed better than any of them. Her body moved with the experience of more than years and, as the shadows in the room grew, he began to feel something that he had rarely felt. Thinking this, he began to rub his hand along the inside of his thigh.

Derva straightened her pale tunic and watched the young boy rub his leg. She thought he was of uncommon good looks, although his head was larger, his eyes more piercing than she could account for. She felt comfortable with Thomas, thinking she was able to talk freely and without guile. More than twice his age, she felt little difference otherwise. She had never held the years tightly

166

before, content to let time do what it did. But the slipping of youth had recently seeded urgency in her and it was growing, would grow. And there were some things she did not wish to give up.

Standing, Derva looked down at Thomas who was half hidden in shadows. She ran her hands over the top of her legs, matching Thomas's motion. His large head, covered with its luminous hair, slanted questioningly up at her. She stepped to the boy from the north and touched the palm of his hand, which seemed to shiver lightly, his fingers turning up and touching her.

The two rose and went upstairs to the room where Derva slept. It was dark there and Thomas did not mind as Derva began to remove her tunic.

Thomas thought he was tasting the sweetest fruit as he sucked Derva's lips, which were moving on his mouth with a slow haste. He could feel her hands brush the cusp of his legs lightly. In that cusp was a deep, spreading heat, and it quivered up into the air. Thomas proceeded to dream in a way he had rarely done before, and then only when he was alone and moving himself with the rapid flicker of his wrists which then drew from him the anguished moan of fulfillment.

The air in the room was like moist heat and Thomas lay curled over Derva, his tongue now tasting her body, the skin and the weight beneath it smooth and rolling. He stretched his tongue, as if it were a finger, and rubbed lightly over it.

Derva moaned and flexed her legs as if waking from sleep. Her hands were clasped around Thomas's neck as he bent over her, touching her fiercely as if she were a hidden surprise which might be taken from him. He was holding back, not wanting to end it all, feeling no fatigue. He thought he could go on forever.

Suddenly Derva rose and tossed her head like the unexpected flip of a mare's neck and Thomas rolled to his back. The liquid capturing of her mouth made him suck in breath and hold it. She bit him softly and squeezed with her lips. Running his fingers roughly through her hair, Thomas stared up into the dark and did not know if his eyes were open or closed.

Much time seemed to pass in sweat and heat, the voices of the two blending in various ways, pain and joy, the explosive sounds of great exertion. Derva alternated with Thomas as mover and Thomas acquiesced, knowing the feel of innumerable bodies that had touched hers before he had. Derva was full of flesh and its knowledge and she used it, bringing Thomas to the pitch of release and then holding him back; plunging him again and again to that pitch, herself seeming to reach an end and still going on, her motion like a sickness of fever.

Then she was lying on him the full length, gliding forward and back, he not moving by her request. He felt himself rigid in her, surrounded by the heat which he could no longer tell as separate from his. Derva moved with a slow rock, but the breath of the two labored. She seemed to be telling Thomas something in a delicately harsh way. A long conversation. And then, as if by an inverse law of their feeling and the weight of their need, her body slowed and slowed. Thomas knew he was on the very edge of life, and he held all the breath he could.

Derva drew in breath of her own, becoming one with Thomas's held breath, and jerked herself once, twice, tightening the aperture of her legs. Thomas felt himself abruptly flow into the very heart of her, the force of his release seeming to hit high inside. He cried out and could not tell his voice from hers.

Thomas dropped to sleep. When he woke, he felt that Derva wasn't there. He fumbled to find light and lit a candle which was on a table next to the bed. Derva's bedroom had a bed and a three-tiered shelf across the room stacked with various kinds of clothing. Thomas noted that her clothes were mostly of a dark pink. On one end of the bottom row of shelves was a selection of bottles. Thomas uncorked each one and sniffed the aroma. Each was sweet and fine. He stumbled over several pairs of high-heeled silver sandals with skin like a lizard's. On the wall over the narrow bed were two paintings. One was of a small child; the other was of someone Thomas did not know but guessed was Sean, the girl's father. He dressed and turned to move out of the bedroom, but heard the kitchen door below open and close.

The stairs down seemed longer and more dangerous. Thomas gripped his blut and breathed shallowly as he circled down to the first floor of Derva's house. At the entrance to the kitchen he stopped and listened. He thought he heard a slithering sound, the sound of iron rustling against leather. He pressed back against the wall and leaned his head backward. Beads of sweat stood out above his lips. Through the muffled enclosure of the night

Thomas could hear several dogs barking far away. The kitchen door was pushed open. Thomas waited for the figure to come through and then he went for its neck, his arms swiftly circling the person's head and drawing it to his knife. But before his mind registered a face, his nose knew the sweet aroma of one of the bottles upstairs.

"Derva! Where have you been?" he said, agitated, his good memories erased by a sense of danger.

The beautiful Straiten woman seemed to show no dislocation at being attacked in her own house, and patted her tunic down.

"I had business out, Thomas. My business. At the same time I had to check with some friends about whether Hastings is actually at the Hall now. He is."

Thomas believed her. He could not disbelieve her. He could feel the belief well within him, pouring out into relief and shame. After a while he allowed that he had thought she had gone for Hastings. She repeated that in a way she had. They sat down at the kitchen table after Derva had lit a candle. She got out two heavy glasses, marked with clever lines that wound about the stems like ivy. She poured red wine into each glass.

"This is not what I hear called Circle brew," she said, "but it is good. It is made from grapes, not potatoes."

Thomas sniffed the glass and took a sip. He approved and downed it with one gulp. Derva filled the glass again and sat down to sip hers.

"How is Barry?" said Thomas.

"He is all right, in his sleep at least. I checked him before I left."

Derva stared at Thomas's hair for a moment. "You thought I was going to tell Hastings you were here? I mean, you felt it as a certainty?"

"No, I didn't feel it as that. That is why I did not run at once. I thought you would be back. But I did not know who would be behind you," lied Thomas.

"You're lying," laughed Derva. "And I can't blame you. Straiten is tricky if you're not used to the weaving lines that are not represented by the straight streets."

"What?" said Thomas.

"Thomas, I have the impression that you know things, but that you cannot truly understand *why* you do. Is that right?"

"I think so."

"Has it always been like that?"

169

"As far back as I can remember. I've always been good with tools too."

"Why is that?"

"If you can tell me, I will be happy," said Thomas. "Sometimes I think it is a gift, other times a curse. My father seemed to fear what he knew of it. I learned to hide it. But even though he did not trust me, he wanted me to do certain things."

"Such as?" Derva's violet eyes seemed to pierce the dim light.

Again Thomas felt doubts creep into his mind. Derva kept asking about the instructions of his father. What did this mean?

"He wanted me to become Center of the North Circle one day," he said. "Even though he thought me part of the Blessing Plan for Imram."

"The Blessing Plan?"

"Yes. Turly thought it was a plan to force all Imram into a particular mold."

"Why did he fear it, Thomas? Imram needs *something,* I think." Derva seemed genuinely interested in his father's story, but Thomas still wanted to hold back as much as he could. If Derva was a friend, he would not want her to suffer for her knowledge. If not, he wanted her to know as little as possible. He told her only the stories of Turly's trip to the west that he thought safe. Except for his mother's role, he suggested that much of the story may have been made up. Derva did not comment on that.

". . . and so he grew to hate the manipulation of any one Imramer," finished Thomas. "If any child should have to die for the Blessing Plan, Turly wanted nothing to do with it. He wanted men to be like grains of sand, responsible alone for *their* fate, and to *choose* their part in a larger mosaic."

"I see," said Derva. "And do you agree?"

"I never saw Blessing or the Box, or knew its Plan. I never asked for any of this," answered Thomas truthfully. "And besides, nobody in the north ever knew how much of Turly's story to believe. He was respected and so he was given *some* credence. . . . Do you believe it?"

Derva smiled and showed her perfect teeth. She seemed a woman of comely youth yet, and Thomas was drawn to her even more. He was about to reach his hand to her when the back bedroom door flew open and

170

Barry staggered out. There were new stains of blood on his neck; Thomas was up to him instantly, holding him.

"Barry? Barry, what is it?" he said.

"The light in the dark," he gasped. "The light . . ." The Danae slumped in Thomas's arms, his hands quivering and jumping like two fish out of water. They leaped as Thomas held him, and played about his chest and shoulders in random agony.

"Derva, here, help me get him back into bed," said Thomas with nervous fear. The two struggled with the jerking Barry and finally got him prone. Derva wet a cloth and wiped his forehead and neck. Thomas then looked rapidly around the room but could see nothing unusual. There were no candles in the room; the shelves held only small figures of animals carved in wood. But the window was partially open, and it had not been before.

"What could he mean by 'light in the dark'?" asked Thomas, closing the window, his stomach growing cold.

Derva shrugged. "He may be delirious in his fever," she said, wiping Barry's chest and then pulling the bed covers up over him.

That might be true, thought Thomas. He had seen the fever of wounds in battle. Sometimes men would die of it, sometimes not. He looked closely at Barry's face, which was still the color of a crushed plum. He thought some of the wounds were fresher than others, but he wasn't sure. There was a bright glazed look in Barry's eyes when he suddenly opened them and rolled them around the room. They lit on Thomas and would not move, even though his head did, as if it were an old man's, shaking lightly.

"Don't . . . go to the Abbey, Thomas," he said in a hushed tone that made Thomas bend down to listen. "Caine . . . knows . . ."

"What? Knows what? I'm not going to the . . ."

"If you value your father," whispered Barry urgently.

"What? My father? What of my father, Barry?" Thomas had to hold back from shaking the badly injured man, who looked now as if he had stuck his head in the roar of a burning wind, the hair blown back, the eyes surprised with the blast.

"Don't, Thomas . . . *don't,*" he breathed as his head rolled away to one side and stopped as if locked in place.

171

"Barry!" shouted Thomas, this time with great anger. No death was what he wanted, and no more mystery.

"He is dead, Thomas," said Derva after a time.

Thomas slumped on the bed, feeling drained. He was not sure how to feel about the Danae he had come to like as a friend. "What did he *mean?*" he said.

"I don't know what he meant," said Derva. "Strange things can happen in the mind."

Stranger than you can know, thought Thomas.

The room was as still and quiet as a sunset. Thomas fidgeted for a while, lost in his own thoughts. "I have to go, Derva," he said after a time. "Will you be all right here with his body?"

Derva was surprised. "Well, yes, of course. There are carts to carry away the dead. But I thought you would stay here awhile. Where will you go?"

"I've got to meet some of my men at the north entrance to Straiten," he lied, this time sounding convincing.

"Yes," she said, glancing at the still form of Barry and then at Thomas. "Will you come back?"

Thomas hesitated. "You told me nothing was certain in this place. Is that right?"

"If you come back, I will be glad to see you," she said, holding her head slanted to one side.

"Then I have to go now," said Thomas, who felt alone again, as if he had been told that his was a world full of actors and that he had to continually guess who all of them really were. But if *that* were so, he thought, he was after the identity of only one of them at the moment: Lord Hastings.

"Goodbye, Derva," he said quietly.

Derva let Thomas out the back door. For a moment she held on to the edge of the door as if it were a human being, her eyes wandering over Thomas's face. He thought for a minute that he would have to confess to her his real plans, but he did not, could not. Waving back to her once at the exit point to the street, he began to run. Headlong as if wild beasts were after him, he did not stop until he reached 93, then paused to lean back against a wall. There were lamps on the street at every other corner and they looked like fireflies frozen into place. As he again hurried beneath them, his shadow would catch up to him and then be sucked swiftly away to the next lamp. His skin was prickly and damp.

Thomas turned west on 93 and slowed to a walk. He

was more careful after the first full flush of his escape and he kept to the shadows. Soon to the south he heard the distinct croak of frogs and the liquid quiet of a large body of water. The swamp. Garrett had said there was a swamp to the south of Straiten. The Heron Swamp, he had said. Thomas turned south on 50 and moved stealthily down to 99, the last street in the city. He stood on its edge and tried to look out into the swamp. He could smell it, but he could not see it. The starlight allowed only the vague dark bulk of immense trees, covered with what must have been great vines, splayed out on the horizon like hunched-over giants, waiting.

Walking west on street 99, Thomas thought of his past and his future. He was in a web from which he did not think he could escape. This seemed to weigh on him like truth and he brooded as he strolled with his hands clasped behind his back, his head to the ground, his feet kicking at small stones on the hard surface of the street. Given the web, he knew he would have to go see Hastings, make an attempt to prevent the loss of the north. It would be the only thing he could do. Hastings had known Turly. Thomas felt more and more the other half of whatever his father had been.

There was a scuffling of feet and Thomas could not unclasp his hands in time to avoid the blow on his head. He crumpled while thinking about his father, his scowling face accusing him of stupidity.

"Thomas? Thomas," said a voice floating just outside pain. Thomas first felt a wetness brushing his neck and he raised a hand to touch it. "Ah, Thomas, good," said the floating voice. Thomas remembered that he had eyes and he opened them.

"Thomas?" said a man squatting beside Thomas.

"Garrett?"

"Yes. I am sorry. I didn't dream it was you. I thought it was one of the men from the Green Moon Room, one I could question further about something I had heard there tonight."

Thomas searched his head with his fingers. There was some blood. Now it was the back of his head as well as his nose that hurt. He felt awful.

"I am sorry, Thomas," repeated Garrett.

"All right. I'm all right," said Thomas, irritated that he had been caught by one of his own men. He looked closely at Garrett. "But you did get into the city then?"

173

"Easily. We came through the swamp near here and scattered out. I've arranged to meet the others later. Where are the men who were with you?"

Thomas told him and Garrett nodded in understanding. He had been to Straiten before and knew what could happen. Because of that, Thomas felt somehow safer with Garrett there. The man's balding head seemed to flash in the dim starlight.

"I've got to go on to Hastings Hall, Garrett. We have to know what Hastings is going to do. But I'm not sure which is the best way to get there."

"I think I've found a good way. A way that might get us in the front door."

"Get *us* in the front door?" said Thomas.

"Yes, whatever you think is best," allowed Garrett. "But that's why I hit you. I wanted to get more details about it."

"Yes?"

"Tomorrow morning early, what time I don't know, a wagon from the Green Moon Room leaves for the Hall. It will deliver the week's supply of beer for the troops there. There will be one driver. The wagon is big and will be filled with barrels of beer, and covered with a large wooden top. It should be easy to get inside it, just outside the city, and so ride in it to the Hall. I understand that there is little security at the gates nowadays. There is little fear of rebels or of anything else. Life is very easy here now, it seems."

"So I hear," muttered Thomas, still holding his head. He rolled his shoulders and rubbed the back of his neck. Looking up, he thought he could see the first faint streaks of pink begin in the east. Another hour and dawn would bloom. "Try to meet Scanlon if he hasn't already left. Gather them all and come to the northeast corner of Hastings' estate. Wait for me there. Give me four days. No more. Then go back to the Circle."

"But I'm going with you," said Garrett in exasperation. "I know the inside of the compound."

"You can tell me about that while we go to that road leading to the Hall. You can help get me on that wagon, but then I'm going on by myself. One man can do better than two in this case."

"But . . ."

"Just me," said Thomas with a definitive edge to his voice.

174

"You are a fatalist like your father," sighed Garrett. "Very well. We'll wait for you outside. As many of us as I can find. We'll try to be there at least by tomorrow. You wait. We wait."

"In three or four days, go home," said Thomas. He was anxious to be going and so did not wait for Garrett's reply. He felt his legs move shakily at first and then gradually regain their strength. Garrett padded up beside him. The pair from the north went like disobeying children through the dawn streets of Straiten.

Chapter 20

Garrett swayed drunkenly in the middle of the road, his face and upper body smeared brown with mud. His arms were waving as if he were trying to fly.

"Here, move away," yelled the driver of the wagon.

Garrett held up his hands and collapsed in the road. The driver swore, reined in his horses, and climbed down out of the wagon. Walking to Garrett with a tired rolling gait, his huge belly lumbering in front of him, the man looked around and then bent ponderously and went through Garrett's pockets. He found nothing, cursed again, and rolled Garrett off the road, giving him a parting blow in the side with his foot. He strolled back to his wagon with majestic gravity, hauled himself back to the front seat, took a long swig from a black jug, grabbed the reins, flicked them, and was off.

Thomas settled in between two large barrels near the front of the wagon, directly behind the partition that separated the load from the driver. He had checked it while the man had been preoccupied with Garrett. The spot could not be seen from the rear opening of the wagon unless all the barrels were crawled over. Thomas hoped guards would not want to do that. He moved slowly, carefully, so as to avoid splinters.

The trip to the Hall took about an hour on the dusty road. Then Thomas could hear the driver begin to mutter to himself and bustle around to hide something that sounded like a jug. A few minutes later a voice told the man to stop. The driver and the other man chatted about the weather. The driver got down and rustled some papers which he passed to the guard. There was a grunt of approval and the two walked around to the rear of the wagon. Thomas listened tensely as the man asked where the beer had come from. The Green Moon Room, said the driver. Good, said the other. Good. Go on through, he said.

The wagon creaked on for another ten minutes and then stopped. Thomas heard the driver get down and shuffle off to the front. Thomas waited until he was sure the driver was out of sight, and slowly and quietly crawled up and out of his hiding place. He looked carefully around the sides of the wagon and, seeing nothing, jumped down lightly and ran for the nearest clump of bushes. Just as he reached them, a door opened in the large gray building the wagon had been parked in front of. Two men came out. They were talking animatedly about something Thomas could not hear. One of them was checking the papers of the other while pointing to the back of the wagon.

Thomas lay hidden and watched the men check the wagon and then drive it into the building through the door in its side. When the door was closed behind it, Thomas glanced around to place himself in the reality of the image Garrett had given him of the Hastings Hall area. He knew that he had to find the L-shaped building that held Hastings' personal office. Looking around once more, Thomas moved at a stooped run from the bushes to the spot where the building was supposed to be. It was there.

Several figures in red were walking in and out of one end of the main building. There were lots of bare trees and shrubs near it; Thomas thought there would be enough shelter to hide there and so ran in a zigzag until he was near the door opposite the most heavily trafficked one. It was still very early in the morning and Thomas thought the working day there had not yet fully begun;

he was feeling good about finding Hastings, although he still did not know exactly what he was going to do if he did find him.

The inside of the large L building was cool and dark. Thomas quickly and easily found a highly polished door with a raised H on it. Garrett's memory was good, thought Thomas.

There were sounds coming from down the corridor and Thomas put his ear to the large door, heard nothing, and pushed it open. The room was well-lit, with a huge desk in the center and behind it a window which framed part of the large front lawn of the Hastings compound. On the left wall was a board which held a map of Imram.

Thomas made sure the room was completely empty, and then he moved to the map. It was not like any map of Imram he had ever seen. There were pins in the north and west in places he was not familiar with.

He knew the Inniscloe Lake. And Bellsloe. The Lower Mountains. But there was a large round emblem by the mountains that was not on the map his father had had him learn. It was the sign of the Others. This bothered Thomas as his finger traced the pins from the northeast down to the south of Imram, to the Clonnoise Abbey, and around and up to the north again. He could not make out what the pins signified other than a location. The pins in the north were orange and in the south green. Some odd pins to the west were white. Near the Lower Mountains, beside the sign of the Others, was a large pin with a red head the size of a small wart.

Thomas continued around Hastings' room, being careful to disturb nothing and to keep one ear cocked to the corridor outside.

On Hastings' desk were only a few papers. Thomas could see that they were routine orders for food and drink. Pulling out the top middle drawer, he found a cube like an odd yellow rock. Thinking nothing of it at first, Thomas gripped it as he used his fingers to move lightly around the various other objects inside the drawer.

Presently a warmth spread through Thomas's hand, the one holding the cube, and he looked at it in astonishment. He felt strange, as he had many times before when faced with tools he did not know the use of.

Listening to his head speak, Thomas held up the cube and placed one eye to its side. He drew back as he thought he saw tiny figures moving inside. Overcoming his

IMRAM

North Circle

Bellsloe Circle

Harven Circle

Inniscloe Lake

Inniscloe Circle

Purple Mt.

Forham Dam

Lower Mts.

Arid Island

Straiten

Heron Swamp

Gort

Ennis Camp

Leeve Desert

Hastings Hall

Tombs

New Ennis Camp

Boulder Gap

Clonnoise Abbey

fear, the young boy from the north put the cube to his eye again. There *were* figures inside, like moving paintings. Aghast, Thomas watched a young child follow its mother through a garden and join a man who lifted the child over his head and then looked out at the viewer. The action promptly began all over again.

Thomas watched the motion for four or five repetitions. Not sure what to think about the marvel of the cube, Thomas placed it down on Hastings' desk and looked out the window at the deep brown of the grass. His father had been right. There had been many things in Imram which he, Thomas, had only dreamed of. But now it all seemed dreams turned into truth. It was the truth of dreams. What else was there, he thought, dazed. He looked startled a moment as he tried to envision the Blessing Papers. They lay there, in Clonnoise Abbey, with a solidity they had never had before. They *had* to be real. And he knew he would have to go there to find out. His dreams demanded it.

Thomas was pulled from his revery by a noise coming from one wall. He whirled and listened. It was the sound of two pairs of feet and low conversation. It seemed to be coming through the wall on which the map was hung. Glancing around quickly, Thomas noticed that two large wooden shelves, each with drawers climbing up one above another, were jammed close together on the opposite wall. Between them was a narrow space which might hold his body hidden in the shadows. Stepping to them, Thomas turned sideways and wiggled in and back against the wall. His vision of the room was now limited to a small section of the room, and the map, which seemed to swing open with the wall as he settled back and held his breath.

". . . will be here soon. The reports are that he is erratic but moving as we would like. My men have been told what to expect. There should be no trouble, although there may be obstacles."

"He can do it," said a voice that sounded strangely familiar to Thomas. "I taught him."

"Yes, you taught him," said the other voice, "but the ability and the fever does not always stay where you want it to."

"I know."

"Here, let me show you his route so far," said the deep voice Thomas had never heard before.

A small hand entered the slot of light Thomas had. He

180

squinted his eyes and watched tiny fingers point to the map.

"He has to be about here now. Very near. He will try to come to the Hall next, and then we can see him, too."

"Are you certain?"

The small hand fell away from the map. "We are not able to know everything absolutely. That would destroy what we are after in the first place."

"What are you after?"

"Soon, you will know soon," said the deep voice quietly. "The Plan will work as it works."

Thomas shivered. He thought he was hearing legend discussed as fact, and his eyes were straining to see the other man in the room. The beat of his heart was speeding up and he was afraid its sound would be heard by the two men.

"I will do what I can," said the more familiar voice, "when he comes."

"That will be enough." Having said this, the owner of the deep voice moved through Thomas's field of vision and he was surprised to see a withered gnome.

"We can only wait?"

"Yes," said the gnome. "But we will see the one who works for me first. Everything is almost ready."

The other man passed through the narrow shaft of light then and Thomas almost screamed, his eyes turning dark, his head fighting dizziness.

Turly! It is Turly! No!

"I see," said the man whom Thomas now knew.

"Imram and the world are ready to bloom again," said the gnome almost happily. "I'm glad it has come down to this."

"Are you?" said Turly.

"You will see," said the gnome.

"I am still held somewhat by what I was, Blessing," said Turly.

Blessing?

"Ah, yes, you are."

"It is hard for me yet to see your world as mine, old man, and I won't be sure until . . ."

"Yes," said Blessing. "Your father was the same way. I suspect your son is, too. You were strong enough to defy what you could not understand."

"Thomas has that and more, I'm afraid," said Turly in

181

such a way as to make the listening Thomas feel strange to himself.

"That of course leaves all in doubt until the very end," said Blessing. "But when we have a chance to talk with him as well, I think he will believe us as will you."

Thomas could not fully retain what was being said. He had many thoughts spinning in his mind. Should he go out and announce his presence, and hug his dead father? Or should he remain hidden? What was the meaning of his father working with the very man he had always said was his greatest enemy?

"Are you ready?" said Blessing.

"Yes," said Turly.

Thomas heard the two men move back to the wall from which they had come. He started forward after them but stopped, suddenly feeling he could do nothing but remain where he was. The years behind him had made him too independent a thinker to give in so easily to another's plans. He also thought that perhaps his father might not be himself at all, that he might really be dead but animated in some fashion by the magic of the south to fool him. Turly would be a false father then, and his old father had warned him of such tricks. He would wait, even though his heart yearned to rush out before it was too late.

"It is time," said Blessing. "This way please."

There was a whirr and a click and all was silent again. Thomas waited for several minutes until he was sure the room was again empty. He slowly moved out of his hiding place and looked around. Nothing. He shuffled out and over to the wall they had come through. Putting his hands and his ears to it, he listened. Hearing and feeling nothing there as well, Thomas took one last look around the room and at the map and then went to the door leading to the corridor. His eyes still seemed to be glazed from what he had heard and seen, and his head was filled with disconnected thoughts about himself and his place in Imram life. There were tears in his eyes for his father Turly, whom Thomas did not know how to consider now. He had recognized the love he had had for him when he had witnessed his death by fire. But he was dead, and now alive. What did it mean? And an old foe of his father, Thomas Blessing, was with him and he had seemed to accept him without being restrained in any way. A brooding old man, and an oddly renewed younger one.

Thomas was confused, but his own past prompted him to action. Looking out the door carefully, glancing up and down the hall, he knew what he would do. And it would not be what either Thomas Blessing or his own father wanted him to do. He, Thomas, thought he had to do what *he* had to do.

The back lawn was almost empty. Three red soldiers were standing and talking beneath a large elm tree, its many branches massed into a large shade which covered them like a liquid. Thomas fidgeted as they stood and laughed while pointing in different directions. He looked back down the corridor where it stretched straight to the L bend. The shadows inside were as wintry as the shade outside. Thomas hunched down beside the door as he twisted to see out. One of the soldiers had left and the two others were flipping a coin about something. One of them slapped his thigh and put out one hand. The third soldier reached into his pocket and drew out something, putting it in the other's hand. They walked off together.

Thomas breathed easier. He stayed where he was for a few more minutes, then pushed open the door and stepped out. The huge grounds in the rear of the building were beautiful and well-kept. Thomas faded into the bushes near the building and worked his way to the end of the wall, looked around the edge and saw that the front gate was well-guarded. No escape there. He looked back over the way he had come first and saw that it, too, was guarded. The shed where the beer wagon had been put was now surrounded by soldiers.

There seemed only one way to go. Thomas inched back along the wall and waited until he could run to the nearest tree. He reached the tree and squatted to the ground. No sound. He looked up and back at the L building. There were soldiers coming out of the rear door where he had been. Feeling trapped, Thomas looked the other way where, through the thick tangles of underbrush, he could see the beginnings of the Heron Swamp.

"Colin!" shouted a soldier near the building.

"Over here!" answered another soldier coming from the shed.

"Have you seen anyone?"

"Not out here."

"Do you think he's here?"

"I don't know."

"Have you checked the swamp yet?"

"No. I'll send out a group. But few could get here easily through that swamp."

"The rebels did, years ago."

"You were one, right?"

"Watch your tongue, Colin my man," said the other.

Thomas now knew which way he would be going. To the swamp. After the two soldiers had drifted back to the shed area, Thomas breathed deeply several times, then broke for the less dense part of the swamp. He had almost reached it before he heard shouts behind him. They were high and thin, too far away and too distant to his own hopes to bother him. He had entered the swamp.

The water and the cold first brought Thomas back to himself. He was running and splashing with knees pumping up almost to his chest, his arms flailing away at the branches and vines that tried to hold him back. The sunlight was coming down through the trees, hunched over and above him, like blind spots. He had no clear sense of where he was going except forward and away from Hastings Hall. He knew the Heron Swamp was on the east side of the compound and that was all right with him, even if it was in the opposite direction from the Abbey.

Thomas turned once, in a looping spiral, to see if he were being followed. He saw no one as yet but believed that he had in fact been seen and so could not stop. He plunged on, bearing to what he thought was the line toward the northeast. He would find Garrett and the others and go back north. With his father Turly somehow in league with Blessing, he wondered how the North Circle could ever combat what they had in mind. But that could wait.

The water in the swamp grew deeper, and Thomas found it even more difficult to move in than the sewer pipe. His muscles were soon burning with fatigue and he began to look for a place to rest for a moment and hide. He could see nothing but water and huge trees with thick vines that swung down like the engorged webs of spiders. Thomas kept on, desperate now. The sun was high but could not be seen, the dim glow inside the swamp like sundown.

At last Thomas, thinking he could go no farther, saw a large hollow in one of the giant trees. Moss hung down over part of it and Thomas thought it a good refuge. Splashing clumsily to it, he collapsed inside its dank interior, the bottom slick and cool. He wiped his brow and pulled his legs up to his chest.

After a few moments Thomas thought his eyes were filling with water. The inside of the tree hollow was fading and running apart as if dripping into the ground. He tried to get to his feet but could not, as his trauma and flight had drained him, and he watched helplessly as the small space folded in on him, over him, enveloping him in the smell of his own sweat. He seemed paralyzed but felt the hollow shiver slightly and then begin to pull back and off him. He looked up **and** through the opening in front, his eyes widening in disbelief.

"Hello, Thomas," said a creature that looked exactly like the demon emblazoned on every Mythic Sequence Ritual Cloth.

Chapter 21

The corridor beneath the earth was straight and narrow
and shiny with the same inhuman molding that Turly remembered about the tunnels beneath Clonnoise Abbey.

"Is it far?" asked Turly.

"No," said Blessing. "He is waiting for us."

"Who?" said Turly.

"You will see, you will see," said Blessing, hobbling
with an unnatural quickness, his high boots making almost no sound on the floor.

After a moment's silence Turly repeated an earlier
question. "Why aren't *you* in control of all these things?
You started them."

Blessing looked back and up over his shoulder. "True,"
he said. "But one man can't do everything, and when
your father died I had to have help. There are many
things that need to be done from day to day."

"Probably," said Turly, walking slowly to keep even
with Blessing. His mind tried to visualize the man who
could so cleverly have access to the rooms of the hated
Lord Hastings of the south, the one man who might dis-

rupt the Blessing Plan. But Turly wasn't yet sure which side he was on. The conversations he had had with Blessing since he had passed through the fire of the torch on the mountain had been limited. He had first to spend time recovering both physically and mentally from the ordeal. It had been hard. And Blessing had told him several times that they were to go south to meet the man who was in control of the CSS operations in Imram. Blessing had promised him a full explanation of the Falling at that time. Turly had reluctantly agreed, the journey through the flames seeming to have at last calmed his life-long insistence on having his questions immediately answered. He felt purged in that respect. But there were still some things that gnawed at him and he looked forward, as he followed Blessing beneath the ground, to meeting the man in charge.

The corridor opened up into a room that reminded Turly very much of the room in which the Blessing Papers lay. There were black and white tiles on the floor, glossy silver walls, and a high roof which held lights that dangled at different lengths like grapes on a vine. There were two doors into the room beside the one by which they had entered. Blessing did not stop but hobbled toward one of the doors at the far end of the room.

"The CSS built this room?" said Turly, almost whispering.

"What?"

"Did the CSS . . . ?"

"Oh, yes, we did," said Blessing without stopping. "We did a lot of things," he mused.

"Yes," said Turly.

Blessing glanced at Turly but did not reply. He hurried to a strip of colored ribbons posted near the door. Reaching the strip, Blessing touched it in a certain rhythm. The door swung open into darkness. Blessing looked at Turly and motioned into the darkness.

"The Church Head waits," he said.

Turly hesitated. He wondered again why he was with the old man who, by all accounts, including his own, had caused the Falling of all mankind more than a hundred years before. The implications of that had yet to come to the surface fully. "All right," he said.

The darkness seemed to thicken as Turly walked into it. He heard the tiny Blessing follow, and he instinctively put his hands up in front of him. There were no obstructions and he quickened when he saw a point of light in what he took to be the center of the dark. It grew as they walked to it and became the open crack of a door. Turly stopped in front of it.

"Open it," said Blessing.

Turly opened it.

The room inside was lined with what looked like red ceramic tiles running in regular lines. The floor was a solid block of red and in one corner, placed all alone, was an immense red chair. In it sat the acting Head of the Church of Spirit and Science. Turly's eyes widened in shock and alarm. He turned back to Blessing who nodded and pointed with one arm. Turly turned back to face the man across the room.

"*Hastings!*" he screamed.

Lord Hastings of the south smiled and gripped the arms of the chair. His legs were crossed and his large paunch rested above them. Turly could see even from that distance the balding red hair and the thin fringe of reddish beard like rust. Hastings was silent and then roared back:

"Turly of the North Circle! Welcome!"

Hastings laughed in a deep resonant voice, then rose to his feet, his arms spread wide as if to take in the whole world.

Blessing prodded Turly from behind. "Go to him," he said.

Turly stood frozen to the tile. His head was reeling with new answers and they rolled around like heavy rocks going downhill. He moved forward woodenly as Blessing took one hand and they headed toward Hastings, who was coming toward them now. The meeting seemed to take a long time, Turly walking in a dream of memory.

"Thomas," said Hastings jovially as he reached the two and picked up the aged little man, whirling him in the air like a child.

"Put me down, Hastings," said Blessing, unperturbed, his set face not showing any emotion. "We have questions to answer."

Hastings set Blessing down and seemed to sober. He looked at Turly and nodded his head. "Yes, we do," he said.

"Hastings," said Turly.

Hastings looked down at Blessing. "What have you told him?"

"What I thought he could take," said Blessing.

Turly shifted his eyes from Blessing to Hastings and back again. The world seemed much bigger than he thought it could ever be.

Turly, Hastings and Blessing went to a smaller room, pulled chairs together, and talked of many things. Turly's sense of what was normal and what was not had not yet fully recovered, but a new sense of the way things really were in Imram—and around it—was growing in him.

"So *you* did it all," said Turly.

"Yes," said Blessing. "We started it, as I told you. It seemed a necessary moral decision: Was man in charge of his evolution, or wasn't he? Was his movement and growth in time to be grandeur or servitude or both?"

"And . . .?"

"We still do not know if it was worth it. A lot was lost."

Turly rubbed his chin. "Why did you lie to me on the Arid Islands? Why didn't you tell me all this then?"

Blessing sat back and spread his hands wide. "You weren't ready," he said. "You hadn't *chosen* anything yet, not really. And I didn't actually *lie* to you. A certain point had to be reached in which you—of your own free will—had to choose either the Blessing Plan or one of your own devising. I merely put some thoughts into your head to help you."

"Or confuse me," said Turly. "What you were telling me sounded inhuman. You suggested there were *Others,* aliens perhaps, who had involved themselves with us for some unknown reason. I wanted no part of that."

Blessing glanced at Hastings. "I told you that *we* are the Others," he said. "Do you know of anything more alien?"

"No, but . . ."

"Turly," broke in Hastings, who had been sitting with his large hands folded over his immense belly. *"What* we did is now clear to you, I think. But *why* we did it is not."

"Yes," said Turly.

"Think of what has happened, and is now happening, this way," said Hastings, gesturing with his hands. "Pretend you are standing on top of a cliff looking down at a river which is bending in a semicircle in front of you. The bends to your left and your right curve down and back to wherever they go. The river directly in front of you is the topmost point of this semicircle."

"All right," said Turly.

"You look down and can see a boat on the right curve heading up toward the topmost point. It cannot see anything at all on the other curve."

"That's right," nodded Turly.

"But *you* can see both curves. Should another boat be coming up the other side on a collision course with the first boat, you would know it."

"I suppose."

"Now, you want the first boat to be saved. You know its fate. What would you do?"

Turly sat back and thought. "Yell at it?" he said at last.

"And if it couldn't hear you?" said Blessing.

"Throw rocks? Get its attention somehow?"

"What if it ignored you, Turly?" said Hastings.

Turly felt very tired. "I don't know," he said. "What should I do?"

Hastings and Blessing looked at each other briefly.

"Perhaps do what we did," said Blessing.

"You stopped the boat with the *Falling?*" said Turly, incredulous.

"We did," sighed Blessing, "and have regretted it in part ever since."

"But . . ."

"We threw not stones at the boat, but boulders, and they nearly sank it entirely. It was almost as bad as colliding with the second boat, but not quite."

Turly considered Blessing's posture. He was a man who was obviously used to authority and the use of it, but he seemed genuinely in anguish as he spoke of the Falling. Hastings seemed more possessed, his big hands now resting on his knees.

"It had to be done," said Hastings. "There were at least some survivors of the attempt to stop that boat. There would have been none at all had it continued on to collision."

"But the 'regret' you speak of?" said Turly, not understanding.

"The regret comes from the method used, the necessary deception, and not the actual doing of it. We regret the means, but not the end. There was a good reason for trying to stop that boat. But ever since the Falling, and the unfortunate Fires that followed, the CSS has been guided by a new and rigid tenet," said Hastings.

190

"Of what?"

"That even though we have a design for rebuilding Imram, an active design, there must be *free will* involved in the participants' fulfilling of it, in the acting out of it, otherwise it will all have been for naught. We can only *watch* now, more or less. We want to put the boat back on the river, but this time let it do what it will."

Turly stared at Blessing. "That's what you meant by my *choice* in the west?"

"Yes," said Blessing.

Turly was silent for a moment, the room seeming to vibrate. "You said you would tell me why you wanted to stop the boat in the first place. What was in the second boat?"

Blessing coughed. "I—we—did what we did to try to keep from losing the one thing man had, in evolutionary terms, that had enabled him to survive, and survive meaningfully, throughout his history."

"Which was what?" said Turly, sitting forward, troubled.

"The word. Words. Written and spoken words. What those words could do, could make, could cause to come into being for man's understanding."

"But to make such a Falling . . ."

"Caused much grief to the planners of it. But for various reasons we had to put man back into the same environment that had given him his verbal origin and his brain. Which had, in fact, given him his soul. We had to put man back into an almost machineless state."

"Soul?" said Turly.

Blessing nodded. "The thing that you have inside you that makes you wonder who and what you are and where finally you are going and why and what you are going to do until you get there."

"Words gave that to me?"

"Yes," said Blessing. "In a certain way."

"These words were being lost in the old world?"

"In a way."

"And the soul too?"

"Yes, that too," said Blessing, his rigid face showing little emotion.

"But what of Myth Time in the Circle?" said Turly.

Blessing arched his heavy white eyebrows. "The Mythic Sequence Church was an early attempt by the

191

CSS to begin the restoration of the word. It will continue to be helpful in its way."

Turly then thought of the huge Ennis Stone he had once believed in. "But I also found words to live by in the whirls of the Ennis Stone. You would have known that. It seemed better to me than the Blessing Plan then. Why shouldn't it be so now, if words are the key to mankind's soul?"

"Yes, you found words there, Turly," said Hastings. "But they were your words alone. The whirling loops of that old Stone were random whirls and nothing else. *You* were therefore the only one who could live by those words they inspired. It would not have helped Imram at all for you to have stayed there."

"But you said I could choose," said Turly. "And I chose."

"Yes," said Hastings sadly now. "But then you left the Ennis and went back north."

"Only because Jeneen was killed," said Turly, suddenly rigid. "Did you . . . ?"

"No," said Blessing, "no. We had nothing to do with her death. That was wholly Dermot's doing and he lived to regret it. In the end he did his part in this drama by helping you through the torch. We, for our part, were prepared to live with your choice to stay with the Ennis. We were prepared to lose the final link in the Blessing Plan, what I once told you was the 'final secret' of the Box."

"Yes," said Turly. "I remember."

"We had been prepared to see the Plan ended there in the west," continued Blessing. "But you went back north, your son was alive, and the Plan was again in force as far as we were concerned. You have received premonitions ever since, one way or another."

"Premonitions?"

"Images. You remember the images the Box gave you? And the images in the little cubes in my cave? And the images you saw in your stay in the Leeve Desert?"

"Yes," said Turly, astonished.

"And those images you have seen, or thought you have seen, all your life in fire?"

Turly paused, his head churning. "Yes," he said.

Fire.

"All were images meant to point you in the way you had to go, and to what you had to choose to do."

192

"Have to do, and *choose* to do," said Turly. "They go together in the Blessing Plan?"

"Yes," said Blessing. "It was the old tenet of our faith, if you will. It was necessarily part choice and part fixed design."

"But why didn't my father simply *tell* me these things?"

"We had to use images many times, Turly, and for a particular reason," said Hastings, unfolding his hands and leaning toward Turly. "Your father and I used to argue about it. But he agreed. We wanted to keep certain things on your mind, but we did not want to convince you of them so that you would be truly unable to act as you saw fit. It was a delicate business."

"I remember the images," murmured Turly almost to himself, recalling vividly the licking pictures of flame on cold winter nights.

"They finally brought you to us, through the torch," said Blessing, "and that made it all worth while."

Did it? thought Turly.

"But we used images cautiously," continued Blessing, "because it was the *overuse* of images that had brought on the need for the Falling in the first place."

"What?" said Turly. "How?"

Blessing nodded his head. His eyes seemed large enough to Turly to see anything and everything. "Yes," he said. "We are now at the heart of the matter: Images. Hastings and I both have told you at different times bits of the past. Now let me tell you more of the old days."

Turly sat back, his shoulders slumped, his hands resting in his lap. "Will it be truth this time?" he said.

"It will," said Blessing, smiling as best he could. "There is no longer any need to shade the truth. The time is ripe."

"All right," said Turly after a time. "Tell."

Blessing settled back in his chair, his small hands punctuating the air for emphasis. "Images were rising in importance in the world," he said. "There were images that could show many things, some marvelous, some banal, but none in such a way that could allow the viewer either to savor them or reject them or even change them if he thought it necessary. It was an *emotional* reaction only."

"You mean like the pity and fear in the images of the Box?"

"Exactly," said Blessing. "You *felt* those things, but

193

you could not tell if they were true or not, given the circumstances."

"No," said Turly, remembering the harsh fury of the images, coupled with their smooth flow.

"Such images, a constant barrage of them, were causing a change in the human head," said Blessing slowly. "And it was a change that seemed to be putting man back almost to where he had started in time."

"How?"

"There have always been two sides to the human brain," said Blessing, tapping his forehead. "The right side and the left side, if you wish to put it that way."

Turly nodded.

"Each side has a variety of functions. Too many to go into now and not that important in our story. Except for this: In the beginning of human history, before man was conscious of being man, the two sides evidently did not work closely together, or recognize each other as being two parts of one thing."

"Why not?" said Turly.

"We don't really know," said Blessing. "But we do know that one side—the right one—could learn from experience. The left side could carry on many of the tasks of life without trouble. However, when something new or odd occurred, it needed help to decide what to do. The right side 'told' it what would be good to do, based on its past experience."

"Oh?"

"Evidently. And when man was young this was helpful. It helped him survive in a world of survivors," said Blessing.

Turly thought about that. "But you said the two sides did not recognize each other as being two parts of one thing."

"That's right. It must have been rather like a god talking, or guiding a man, leading him in the right path. A comforting thing in a time of stress. The god always knew what to do, you see."

Turly thought immediately of the butterfly-wing sensations in his head when the Box had been active there. He started to ask about it but Blessing pressed forward.

"But then something extraordinary happened," said Hastings.

"What?" said Turly.

"A breakdown in this one-way conversation began."

"Breakdown?"

"Yes. And it started when men first learned to read and write—primarily to keep farming and business records. The silence of the act of reading words caused the importance of the right side of the brain to lessen. Instead of relying on a voice to direct action, a voice which a man thought was that of a benevolent if jealous god, he began to see that it was *his* own mind making the decisions. Through the act of the word, man gained his consciousness. A stage was set up in his head and he was on it alone; the *me* became an *I*. The breakdown of the old conversation thus led to something new in history, and we are the result."

"God," said Turly.

"Yes," nodded Blessing. "The little gods fled when the word began. This caused confusion, of course; early man felt lost and alone because of it. He felt abandoned. Nevertheless, *man* was made when his brain recognized itself as one thing."

"Man without his Stone," said Turly, thinking of the reliance of the Ennis on the supposed interpretations of its random whirls.

"Something like that," said Blessing, knowing what Turly was trying to say. "Men have always retained a need for certainty. And that is why—even in the imagistic world we had created—the revelation of the old holy man as a machine was so shocking to the world at large."

"Then the holy toy *did* play a large part in the Falling!" said Turly. "You lied about that, too!"

"Another half-truth," admitted Blessing. "But, yes, such an exposé of what you call a 'holy toy' tore at the very heart of a world that still wanted comfort and direction."

Turly brooded for a minute. "Was there a *real* holy man such as that?" he said at last, his words almost a pleading.

Blessing and Hastings glanced at one another. "There seems to have been," said Blessing.

"He was not simply one of the right-brain gods you speak of?"

"Oh, no, he seems to have been at least a man speaking to other men. But then perhaps he was *made* into one of the many substitutes set up by men to replace the old gods in the brain."

"I see," said Turly. "And after man knew he was man —alone? What then?"

"Even with all the uncertainties and terrors of his new estate, man went on to create much that was good in his history," said Blessing. "And much that was bad."

Turly looked at both Blessing and Hastings and wondered where they put themselves in such a scheme of good and bad. Blessing's eyes crinkled as if he knew what Turly was thinking.

"The world of our more recent ancestors, the world of silver needles in the air—one of which I think you saw in Hastings' museum—and of much greater wheels that could spin above the earth and below the moon, was the creation of men who thought for themselves."

"Then what was the problem?" said Turly. "If all that was good, then why was the Falling necessary?"

Blessing was silent for a moment as if collecting his thoughts. "You remember I once told you about 'old ghosts' that had come back to haunt man and cause him to do things that some of us came to see as wrong?"

"Yes," said Turly.

Old Ghosts.

"Well, in part, the old ghosts were a result of the re-emergence of the right side of the brain as a separate decision-making entity."

"What?"

"The problem arose from one of the things man had created for himself."

"Yes?"

"And that was the ability to make images, a plethora of images, which increasingly bypassed the written word. Such images were not only visual, but sensual as well. The growing dominance of these images was causing the abrupt rise of that old linkage we just talked about—a man coupled with his own separate god who could speak to him and guide him through such a jumble of images."

"You mean men grew backwards?"

"Something very like that," said Blessing. "Men increasingly came to act like obedient children who would jump when their voice said jump; they would make love, or fight, to the same voice."

"God," said Turly.

"And what was even worse," added Hastings, "one personal voice could be invested as a small communal

196

god. These small groups could then act as a unit against other groups."

"And cause trouble, Blessing?"

"Precisely. There was every indication to those who became concerned—like me—that the human brain could be changed faster than had been thought possible, although this change was more of a reversion than anything else, the mind trying to adapt, to protect itself against the new surge of images it couldn't make rational sense of."

"Images alone did that?" said Turly.

"The brain did not take millions of years to change, but less than one hundred. The *environment* the brain had put itself in was causing it to change itself into something less than human."

"*That* was the boat on the other side of the curve!" said Turly suddenly.

"Exactly," said Blessing. "It seemed clear to me that either man had to be forcibly returned to the ways without images and try another rise back up the curve of knowledge, or lose everything anyway."

"Why?"

"The new relationship of the two spheres of the brain —in the absence of the written or spoken word—could not for long have maintained what it needed to keep itself in the image state. The split brain would not have the understanding necessary to sustain the level of tool—the things that sent out and received all those images—that had caused the problem in the first place."

"You mean the Falling would have taken place anyway?" said Turly.

"Very likely. It was predicted. And without the small semblance of control the Blessing line has now, man's history would have then perished utterly. There are only a few men left now," he said. "But we may be on the verge of a new growth."

"Through the Blessing Plan?"

"Yes."

Turly shifted position in his chair, which was growing uncomfortable. "So you and the CSS decided to cause the Falling and so keep the fall short?"

"More or less."

"But man cannot live by words alone," said Turly, trying to imagine the huge waste of the Falling.

"No," said Blessing. "But even his ability to *know* that

depends on his words. You could not, for example, have tried to convince me of that thought without the words you just used."

Turly balked. "Man *needs* visions, images to force the words," he insisted, remembering all his Myth Time dreams, and his Ennis verse.

"That is true, Turly," said Blessing softly. "But the words, *words,* must come or they cannot stop the images, hold them for whatever they are worth. Otherwise all dreams are behind you and forgotten almost as soon as you see them."

"But words can lie too, and be forgotten," said Turly, stubbornly trying to hold his own in a world newly born to him.

"Yes," said Blessing. "But if they are written down, or carried on faithfully by mouth, at least man has a chance to tease out the faults in them then. But not so in an image that comes and goes more quickly than the blink of an eye."

"Like those in the Box?"

"Yes. And that is what your father meant when he wrote down certain Order of Zeno paradoxes: 'The Box that is *seen* can never be known.' Remember?"

"Did the images of the Box lie to me wholly?" asked Turly, after reflecting on what Blessing had said.

"No," said Blessing. "They showed you what they were supposed to show you. The *Papers* were the important things in the vault."

"I see," said Turly, his face showing dismay.

"No, your first trip to the Abbey was not in vain, Turly," said Blessing quietly. "You were *not meant* to see the Papers then."

"What?"

"That was to wait until later, and perhaps for another to do."

"Who?" said Turly.

Before Blessing could answer, a knock on the door interrupted them. A thin man with no hair at all came in and went straight to Hastings, who bent his head to listen to what the man was whispering. Hastings nodded, then frowned. Waving the man away with two fingers, he turned to Blessing. "Before you go on, Thomas, I must tell you that we have a problem."

"What is it?" said Blessing with no change of expression.

"Turly's son has been here and is gone already. He was seen going into the swamp to the east."

"Away from the Abbey?"

"Yes."

Both men looked at Turly, who did not understand. "Why is my son so important?" he said.

Hastings got up and started to pace to and fro. "The Box is a connection, Turly, to the last library of words on earth, except that it is not *on* the earth."

"I don't . . ."

"When the Falling seemed inevitable, Thomas and certain other groups had it placed in a high earth orbit that unfortunately puts it over *this* island only once every ten years. We can talk to it then. It contains records of all that man has ever done or thought. And it waits, Turly, it waits."

"It waits for *us,* Turly," said Blessing. "But we must *want* it again. The orbiting Home, as we call it, can do nothing until a permanent connection with us is made. And that connection is the Box itself."

"And until that connection is made in the proper manner," said Hastings with some agitation, "we cannot know if anything has gone wrong up there since the last time we talked to them almost seven years ago, or for them to know if anything has gone wrong down *here.* But we had long ago made plans for a definite date to make this connection, whether or not we were in temporary contact— and we knew we would not be after your father was killed in the vault. His death upset the schedule."

"What?" said Turly.

"The Box is the *only* link with the orbiting Home we will ever have, Turly. Your father knew that, and he wanted it badly. If the link is made at the proper time, we can talk with the Home all the time, and so leave behind at last the swamp we have been in all these years. Man can begin his rise again."

"Rise?"

Hastings leaned toward Turly. "You remember when you were down here the first time I told you that the getting of knowledge of any kind was rather like an S-curve?"

"I think so," said Turly. "There is a limit to knowledge of all things large or small. The stars and the atoms, I think you said."

"Yes. A slow gathering at first, a rapid upward loop,

and then an abrupt leveling off and an ending to the knowledge that is *possible*. Of course this makes for a boxed-in effect. An ultimately closed universe. Your father knew man had to see it as open in order to go on. The CSS in fact had conceived of it as both open *and* closed. Thus the symbolic 'sign of the Others,' as it is known."

"And when is the proper time for the connection to be made?" said Turly.

"Now," said Blessing. "Now."

Turly stood up, his hands clenched. "Then do it," he said. "Have the Home make the final connection."

"No, you don't understand," said Hastings, moving around behind Blessing. "We *down here* have to make the last move. *We* must choose to do it, to want it, or it will not happen."

Blessing leaned forward. "You and your son must go to the Abbey and choose to make the link *now* or Imram will remain forever the way it is, or worse. The prearranged time of choosing will come for us only once."

"And," said Hastings, "matters are further complicated by the fact that one of the Danae I have used for various reasons knows something of the Box. He wants its power without its knowledge. He will try to get to it too, my agents tell me."

Turly thought for a time that seemed very long but was only a second. "But why me and my son? Why can't your CSS agents go and make the link?"

Blessing chuckled. "You are quick, Turly. I can see why your father was proud of you."

"What?"

Blessing raised one hand. "First of all, by its own choice, the CSS will no longer direct the end of this matter. That is the *new*, and final tenet of the CSS. None of our agents will act now, except indirectly, to help you find Thomas, for example. But our job is done," he said, nodding back at Hastings.

"Why me and my son?" repeated Turly.

Blessing lowered his hand and smiled as best as his withered face would permit. "It took some doing to arrange you and your son, you know. That was the last of our direction."

"Arrange?" said Turly with a crack in his voice.

"Yes, to be sure that the line of Blessing would be a good one, with the best chance of choosing well."

"The *Blessing* line?"

"You are not a Vail, Turly," said Blessing softly, almost tenderly.

Turly shifted his position. More and more answers were coming and he did not know if he could absorb them. "Not a Vail?" he said, whispering now.

"You are my great-great-grandson, Turly. You are Turly *Blessing*."

There was silence in the room. "And my son Thomas?" said Turly, the thought staggering him.

"Is Thomas Blessing, and the whole of Imram history, past and future, may now ride on *his* shoulders."

Chapter **22**

"What are you?" asked young Thomas, the sounds barely escaping his mouth.

"I am of the Shee," said the creature, shorter than Thomas, and much fatter.

"You are a legend only," said Thomas immediately, his mind trying to belie his eyes:

The devil folk who steal men and make them mad.

The demon held its full sides and rolled with laughter. Its sardonic grin matched that of the one on the Sequence Cloth.

"I am that I am," said the Shee after it had regained its composure.

"But the Shee are of the mountains and are only stories," insisted Thomas.

The thing glanced at Thomas who was still lying in the hollow of the tree although it was no longer a hollow and no longer a tree.

"We took the name from Imram legend because it seemed to fit," it said. "No other reason."

"Then you are not the Shee," said Thomas.

"We are now," it said.

Thomas took his eyes from the thing and looked around at the room it was standing in. There were heavy chairs and desks ornamented with silver candlesticks and odd round objects perched on three-legged holders. On one wall was a cloth that matched the Sequence cloth. Thomas stared without meaning to, not wanting to. The demon saw the stare.

"You are familiar with our art," it said.

Thomas tore his eyes away and looked at the Shee demon. "It appears in Mythic Sequence art. Why?"

"That is a long story, young man. If you would come with me I will try to explain." Saying this, the creature turned and shambled off toward a door that was too big for the room. Thomas got to his feet and went after the thing. He had, he thought, no other choice.

"This way," said the demon, holding the large metal door open for Thomas to pass through.

The way was narrow and dark. Thomas had to grope with his hands several times to be sure he was with the demon. When he reached out, his hands touched a skin moist and warm. It did not repulse Thomas as he thought it might.

"Now here," it said. Thomas saw a crack of light split open into an even larger room filled with books and glass jars, the full lights overhead reflecting off the jars like single eyes. There were several chairs, all shaped like the half-barrels Thomas was used to playing with at the Circle, placed at various spots around the room. The demon picked two near the fire crackling at the farthest end of the room and motioned Thomas into one. Thomas sat down and watched the demon with amazement.

"This has been a long week," it said, also sitting down.

"What?"

The demon looked at Thomas who was sitting awkwardly in his chair. "I said it has been a long week."

"Why?" said Thomas, wondering if the creature actually knew what a week was.

"You have been able to stay one step ahead of me," it said. "You, like your father, have been helped again."

Thomas ignored the business about *help*. The immediate problem was the demon. "Why have you been one step behind me?"

The demon chuckled. "You have more humor than your father had, and that's good."

"You know my father?"

"We fought, in a manner of speaking, at Clonnoise Abbey years ago."

"You? That was you? But he said he fought with Oliver, the old Head of the Order of Zeno!"

"He fought me as well," said the bulky creature which nevertheless had a certain grace about it. It had two small horns on its forehead, and its rugged eyebrows slanted up and out at their ends. Thomas thought it looked like a depraved toad. "There was little joy in it for me," it said. "Oliver really wasn't alive at all. But I had to do it, for Blessing."

"For Thomas Blessing?"

"Yes."

"Father told me he won," said Thomas, no longer surprised at Blessing's name.

"He did. But winning doesn't last, just as losing doesn't. It is all part of the run."

Thomas did not know what the demon meant. But there was a reason he had been taken, he knew that. "What do you want me for?" he said.

"Kerning. Earl Kerning," said the fat demon.

"What?"

"My name," said Kerning. "I have a name, not just 'demon.' "

"Oh."

"I took you, as you say, for a particular reason."

"And that is?"

"The Shee, my people, want Imram to be as it once was."

"Why should they?" said Thomas, surprised to hear the demon sound like his own father once did.

"Because we have a place in such a world, and *you* have the means to bring it back."

"Me?"

"You."

Thomas frowned. The thoughts circling in the bottom of his head began to surface. His father and Blessing had spoken of the burden of change that he, Thomas, carried. But such thoughts had been held down by him, submerged past consciousness. Now they moved.

"Why me?" he said at last.

"You are the heir, whether you know it or not, to a line of men that made a profound change in this island. It caused the original change that led to *now* and, among

204

other things, to the Shee. But that change soon caused the loss of something that the Shee love: the excitement of joy in the motion of flesh and the mind. The original change froze Imram in a certain position, and now we wish to help resurrect the old Imram. We need you."

"I know of none of this," said Thomas, dazed.

The demon face seemed to smile, one fleshy finger rubbing the lower lip of a heavy jaw. "You were not supposed to know what you know," it said softly, almost dreamily.

Thomas sagged into the chair. He knew that perhaps part of what the creature said was true. He had long imagined things for which he could find no counterpart in his world. Where else could they come from but from something in his head that he could not seem to control, or that was not his?

"I see we understand each other better," said Kerning. "Good."

Thomas tried to assert himself, restore his own confidence. Sitting forward, he pointed one finger at Kerning's face. "Why should I then help you to do something that I cannot otherwise *not* do?"

"A good question. That's why you are here," said Kerning, extending a thick finger of his own toward the floor.

Thomas sat back, and Kerning paused for a minute.

"Some men in this island plan to keep it in a condition more to their liking," said Kerning at last.

"My father?"

"No. I am talking of other men who do not want to do what your grandfather John Vail wanted. They do not want to proceed with the Blessing Plan as it was originally conceived."

"My father loved the Blessing Plan and then hated it, and now seems to love it again," said Thomas abruptly.

"Exactly," said Kerning, leaning forward with a new light in his eyes. "He is now a part of the thing he wrongly hated in life."

This jarred Thomas. "In life? He is not dead, he is . . ."

Kerning waved his big hand. "In a sense he is dead. He is no longer an *active* part of Imramian life. He has passed into . . . the line of men who help Blessing, and that line cannot help us anymore."

"Why not?"

"It is too long to go into."

"Then what did Blessing want that he can no longer help us—you—with?"

"A world where the *run* I told you of can begin again. And a world where the Circles of the north can be changed and allowed to grow even more. A world where the dreams you have always had, dreams of strange shapes and tools, will have a place. A world where discovery and its excitement will again be possible. A world of driving joy where even the Shee will have a role."

Thomas stared at Kerning. "What *proof* do you have?"

"Of what?"

"Of the run. Of what you said."

Rubbing his heavy thighs, Kerning rose and went to a small red box. He picked it up carefully and took it to Thomas who did not raise his hands to take it.

"Here," said Kerning. "Take it, feel it, *know* it. It will show you."

Thomas reluctantly lifted up one palm and received the little box. It felt warm and strange in his hand and objects began to form behind his eyes. Time seemed to stop as Thomas was touched at first tenderly and then with a mounting urgency by solid images in his head.

The curve is dark and steep with light increasing at the top as the eye moves toward it with a sense of wind blowing in the face. The top comes. There are motes of light that then weave random twists in the air. It is like snow on a calm day. The snow packs and grows in a thickness, which turns red, which blackens and seems to rot into a dank richness out of which grows the head of a man.

The man pulls himself up out of the rich darkness, staggers, looks upward at a new curve in front of him. He is tired and tries to sit on the earth. He cannot. Each time his legs jerk him erect and he plods one more step upward. His face twitches, and his arms swing with a weary sway, a curious twist like a half-circle that cannot stop, in a piston movement. The lids close as he walks but the eyes beneath them turn in upon themselves, make frantic gestures as if there were restless insects under the skin.

A slope rises before the man who does not notice. He walks for a long time, the slope only gradual but increasing. Suddenly a smile comes to the man's lips. His arms speed up and his legs receive a bounce they had not had. The slope steepens and the man runs, his naked loins bouncing, and his chest rising and falling with regularity. The eye that sees focuses in on the two nipples on the man's chest. They are light brown and thickly hairy but change as he runs to a soft rigidity that rides above a mound of shivering flesh. His loins no longer flounce but are contained and smooth. The slope in front of the figure is steeper yet and is almost straight up, but it goes faster and faster.

The arms of the running figure reach up and clasp the shaft upon which it is moving. Running, climbing, exploding up in a rhythm of speed, the body reaches its peak and the peak of the slope. With a great heave the body spreads out over the top and lies, flowing, on the top of the curved slope as if fulfilled. There is nowhere else for it to go. No running room. It seems to flow without direction as it reaches the end of the curve.

The mass that was a body glides to and fro like a listless lake. Its fringes lap at nothing as it rests in itself, and the slope seems to rock forward slowly, tilting, allowing the mass to drip languidly to the bottom on the other side. There seems to be no concern as the mass dwindles at the top.

The drops are seen as they gather at the bottom. They catch bits of light and are beautiful as they separate and meet in a sparkle like varicolored bits of glass thrown into the air and falling together slowly in space. There is peace and motion at once. The eye that watches them circles them and seems to touch them with love.

A figure enters from the right. He is small and his face is marred with tangles of skin etched into ridges and valleys. It is a face that is old and concerned. The face moves close up and the eye sees the concern in the face. The eyes of the face look at the drops of the mass and they squint. The man rapidly scoops up the pieces and molds them into a single ball which flickers in random flames as he does so. He trots back to the rich red darkness at the front base of the slope and digs a hole into which he places the burning ball. He stands up and smiles. He looks up at the slope and then down at the spot where he has placed the ball. The face of the man is again shown up close. It grins without guile. The scene shifts downward. A head begins to rise from the muck.

The image closes into a brown warmth that cradles and holds the eye. Features appear, and its dimness clarifies into the head of a demon.

"Well?" said Kerning.

Thomas rubbed his eyes dreamily and arched his eyebrows as if to clear his head. "What does it mean?" he said.

"What do you think it means?"

Thomas thought a moment, trying to remember. "That a man must run upward and that the run is both good and bad. The beginning and the ending of the run seem natural."

"A good meaning," said Kerning.

Thomas blinked. "Who was the small man?"

"Your father has told you of Thomas Blessing?"

"Yes. I have seen him."

"You have?"

"Yes."

Kerning paused. "Did you think the little man was Blessing?"

"I think so," said Thomas slowly. "What was he doing?"

"What did it look like he was doing?" said Kerning.

"Starting the runner over again."

"Good, good," said Kerning. "You saw it well."

"But what does that mean?"

"You mentioned the Blessing Plan."

"My father hated it most of his life."

"Do you think what you saw was the Blessing Plan at work?"

"You mean to start man back on a run up such a slope?" said Thomas, startled for a moment as he remembered the images.

"Yes."

Thomas pondered the images. If the motion upward represented the Blessing idea of what man should do, then he could see why his father had come to hate it; it seemed a hopeless cruelty: the run was forever. But it was also motion and the joy of life; therefore Thomas thought he was beginning to see why his father had turned back to it, if he had done so. It was all there was. Life and motion. And Thomas felt, especially after his night with Derva, that life and its many motions could be good. Although not certain of this, he felt a rush of warmth that seemed to cleanse the coldness of his youth, to right a balance somewhere inside him.

"Well?" said Kerning.

Thomas looked up at the demon-like creature who

seemed kind and concerned. "Why do *you* want this?" he said.

"I have told you."

"Is that the only reason, to have a role in Imram again?"

"Of course."

"Nothing else?"

"What else could there be? We have to live with your kind even if you are not running. It would be better for us if you were running. There would be more joy in it. Don't you feel that to be true?"

Thomas held back. "I . . . think so," he said.

"Do you?" said Kerning, smiling his almost grotesque smile.

Thomas sat silently for a while and then stood up, his fingers moving absently through his white hair. "What am I to do now?"

"What do you think you should do?"

He shrugged as if throwing off an unnecessary weight of some kind. "Go to Clonnoise Abbey as my father said I should, find the Box there, the Papers perhaps, and see what he called the 'final secret' of it."

"Ah," said Kerning. "Let me tell you something."

"Tell me what?"

"If you do that, if you go to the Box, you will find a bulb shaped rather like an eye."

"Yes?"

"If you touch it, first there will be a shock of a certain kind. Then the Box will open."

"And . . . ?"

"Then you will find at last whether your father was right or wrong about the Blessing Papers."

"What do they say?"

"That is for you to find out. But I do know that you are to touch the bulb a second time. If you do, the run can begin again."

"How?"

"I don't know *everything*, Thomas. I am, like a number of others on this island, merely a player."

"Are you playing now?"

Kerning cocked his head. "Not exactly," he said. "But I think Blessing would approve. As I told you, *he* will do nothing further to help you."

Thomas paused a moment and scratched his chin. "What if I *don't* touch the bulb, Kerning?"

"Why, nothing will happen, nothing at all, and that is the point. If you do not touch the bulb, Imram will remain as it has been, a festering swamp of trouble and pain. The inhabitants of this island—north, south, east, and west—will still have their problems to deal with, problems that cannot, it seems, be solved by themselves alone. No one will surrender to another his sense of rightness without a clear case being made for it. No surrender at all."

"Will the run solve that?"

"There will be a better chance for it."

"I see," said Thomas, believing that was so, although he wasn't quite sure why. *Both lies and truth hide in the trees,* he thought.

"Will you do it?" said Kerning, a note of insistence in his voice now.

Thomas had another line of thought. "Are you like the Bonesucker, Kerning?"

"You have met the Bonesucker and lived?"

"I have talked with it."

"Talked with it. You have talked with it? You must be the first."

"Yes. *It* wanted to know why *it* was here in Imram."

Kerning laughed and nodded and then asked Thomas why he thought he, Kerning, was like the Bonesucker.

"I wondered if the Shee came from the same Purple Mountain in the west where my father once told me certain 'changes' were made."

Kerning nodded, one finger rubbing his right eye. "Yes, as far as we know, we came from the Purple Mountain. But our origin is less important than the fact that we are now here. Same for the Bonesucker. Same for the molon and the Fark and Fallow. All are here now and cannot go away."

"They want what you want?"

"If they could think it in the same way, yes," said Kerning.

Thomas brooded on that. He had promised the Bonesucker he might come back one day and give him an answer to his questions about his origin. "Can you all live here?" he said.

"We *are* all living here," replied Kerning. "But we can do so in even better ways if the Blessing Plan is carried out."

Thomas stood up. In a fraction of a second he had

made his decision. "It will be," he said simply, many images of motion and odd tools crowding his mind.

Kerning chuckled. "I'm glad to hear you say that. I have waited a long time to hear a . . . Vail say that. I wish you luck."

"Luck?"

"The men I told you about. Those who oppose the Plan, or do not understand it. Mercenaries. Renegades to their own kind. If they find you before you reach the Abbey, they may kill you. Trust no one."

"Renegades?"

"Yes."

Thomas nodded. "Which is the way to the Abbey from here?" he said at last, brushing dried dirt from his pants.

"To the southwest. Follow the evening sun to the river. Cross it and go straight on to Boulder Gap. After that, slant to the left of the sun. The Abbey is in a deep valley marked by one of the signs of the Others. You will see it."

"Others?" said Thomas. "*Are* there Others?"

Kerning was silent for a moment. "I can't say," he said, shaking his head in a slow rhythm. "Your father may try to find you, however, if he can. Ask him if there are Others. And remember, he *is* your father, Thomas, love him for that if nothing else."

Thomas tilted his head as if listening to something else. *Love?* "The Plan will work, Kerning," he said. "With or without my father. I once thought he was not human. You know that? But he always was. And now so am I, I think."

The bulky demon patted Thomas on the shoulder with his thick hand. "Good, Thomas, good. Now come with me."

The two walked back to the room in which Thomas had first appeared. Motioning the boy to an odd looking chair in one corner, Kerning walked to a panel against one wall and pushed a brown strip. He waved as Thomas's eyes grew watery and the room faded and dripped. Kerning smiled to himself as the boy disappeared, then scratched his big chin and began to laugh with something like joy.

Thomas erupted from the hollow of the tree in a headlong plunge through the swampy water.

211

Chapter 23

Turly, tired from his quick journey, looked back down at the valley in front of the Boulder Gap. The scene was calm and still, sluggish clouds rose in slow tremors over the winter hills.

Turly turned to one of the CSS agents Hastings had sent with him. "Colin, have you got the Finder working yet?"

"If we are in the right," said Colin, whose hands were fumbling with something in a heavy beige bag.

"How much longer?"

Colin checked the bag. "Maybe tomorrow. If he is within range of the Finder, and is actually going to the Abbey, we'll know by then."

"Does that toy really work?" said Turly, now unimpressed by Hastings' machinery, which used to seem like magic to him but was now only the paraphernalia of the Blessing line. *It will all come down to hands,* he thought, *in the end.*

"Most of the time," said Colin casually. He looked up at Turly. "If you believe in it, it helps."

Turly wondered if Hastings' men weren't laughing at

him for his ignorance, while still knowing that he was heir to all that they gave their allegiance to. "Then let's keep on," he said at last. "If I remember rightly, we have about that long to get to the Abbey."

"How long?" said the other man.

"You said one day to find him if he's here?" said Turly impatiently.

"If your son is coming this way, yes," said Colin.

"Then we might make it," said Turly.

One day, thought Turly. One more day and then Imram would be either left the same or changed forever. He reached down and touched one of the cold rocks he had been leaning against. The events of years before stirred the blood in him, and he momentarily felt that he was again a youth fleeing from Oliver and that he was again in pursuit of his father.

In a way he was, he thought. This time he had to be sure of the touching of the milky bulb he remembered being on the Box, and this time to get the papers *inside* the Box. This time he was to save more than himself or his father. He had to save Imram with the help of the boy of white hair.

The boy from the north with the white hair who threatened all Imram by finding the Blessing Papers.

Turly chuckled in spite of himself. How legend roils, he thought. How it twists and turns and finds its own course. He had thought that *he* was the boy of the legend. But it was his *son* who was the legend. Thinking of this, he knew it did not disturb him. He thought that he had long since lost the ability to be greatly astonished at anything. Too many times burned, he thought. Too many flames passed through. They had put a hard crust on him.

"Turly?" said Colin.

"Yes?"

"We should leave now."

Turly nodded and the three men moved off toward the southwest. Turly looked back down once to the spot where Sean had immolated himself to save Turly's little group years before from an attack by Oliver. Turly knew now what Sean was, an agent of the Blessing line, one among many, one who was supposed to do what he had done. The specter of Sean's aged face, worn out by the forces he had used, rose in Turly's memory.

"Is that what Ghosts are like?" said Turly aloud.

"What?" said Gravely, the other agent.

"Nothing," said Turly.

That afternoon they saw from a great distance a line of Fallow weaving up a far hill. Their bright yellow vest suits were like a bed of small flowers waving in the wind. Turly motioned his two helpers to remain still while the Fallow were in sight. He knew that they had enough trouble without asking for an encounter with one of the changed groups of the island. He remembered the one Fallow in the west who had died while struggling to get away from the sign of the Others he had shown him; and the entire fighting troop of Fallow who had fled in wild abandon from the carved sign on his chest at the Ennis camp the day Jeneen had died. He had had no opportunity to ask Blessing about the Fallow.

Turly wondered briefly if the Fallow knew that the sign of the Others was of human origin. Perhaps that would make no difference, he thought. The Fallow, if they were once human, were human no longer. Men were as foreign to them now as anything that could come from beyond the earth.

The Fallow passed and the men moved cautiously down the hill and across the valley toward the next hill. By the end of the day they were all weary. Colin and Gravely went to look for wood, and Turly helped prepare supper, making biscuits to go with the molon they had caught.

Turly lifted the yellow lizard creature from the bag where it waited. Swiftly slicing off its head with his blut blade, Turly skinned the hide, stripping it off its six legs. Gripping the stump of the neck in his teeth, Turly then balanced the molon from the rear, pushing it upward toward his face, making its belly bloat and shiver slightly. Turly guided the tip of his blade to the white mound of the belly. Quickly puncturing it in just the right spot, Turly moved quickly away from the ocherous fumes which gushed out of the mound. As he did so, he remembered the many times he and his grandfather Ellman had practiced the molon rite.

Ellman.

Was Ellman of the Blessing line? He had forgotten to ask Blessing about Ellman, too. His eyes watering, partly from the molon fumes and partly from memory. Turly touched the place on his forehead where a red mole used to be, where an apparition of Ellman had seemed to touch it years before and made it disappear.

Colin and Gravely came back, built a fire and boiled

water. Turly shook his head to clear it, and dropped the prepared molon into the rolling water, his face expressionless. Sensing Turly's absorption in something they could not fathom, the two agents were silent as the red-haired Blessing watched the fire burn without ever wanting to touch it.

The next day the Finder indicated that Thomas was indeed on his way to Clonnoise Abbey ahead of them. Turly sent Colin and Gravely back to Hastings Hall to report, and he set out alone to meet his son.

A new day was coming, he thought.

Chapter **24**

The morning was as clear and beautiful as Thomas had
ever remembered one being. The thick blue of the sky was
punctuated by clouds white and delicate like dandelions.

Putting his hands on his hips, Thomas stopped for a
moment to admire the view. His hair was tousled and
there were bruises on his face due to the troubles of his
trip south, but he didn't care. He felt near the end of a
long journey. He felt possessed by a new duty, and
everything else seemed only incidental. Moving off to the
river that flowed quietly in the early morning calm,
Thomas was reflective. His mind put each piece of the
Imram puzzle together so that the end result seemed to
stand out almost as clean in his thoughts as the trees by
the river. It would be good to see the Blessing Box at
last, he thought, to find that what he had believed was
only a story was the truth.

Thomas swam the green river easily. The cool undercurrents played around his booted ankles as he kicked,
but caused no great problem. He used his arms, scooping
water out in front of him as if he were clearing chickens
out of a Circle yard. The sun warmed his face somewhat
as he sucked in air.

On the far bank Thomas rested. He let his clothes dry for a while and then he got up to continue to Boulder Gap. The map of Imram that he held in his memory was clear. The way to the Gap was to the southwest; it lay between the river there and the Abbey at Clonnoise. Looking up at the sun, Thomas reckoned that he would reach the Gap by that afternoon. He did not think he would have any trouble finding food or shelter. Circle teaching insisted on the ability of each member to survive by himself. Those were additions to Circle doctrine made by his father, and Thomas smiled that it should be so. He felt warmer than he had in a long time.

Thomas was very tired by the time evening came. After crossing the Gap, he saw a promising valley, packed with trees, from a distant hill and he trudged toward it. Along the way he found tiny blackberries full of sweet juice, and he ate two handfuls of them. There were several large snails which he picked up and stuffed into his pocket. They would be good even without salt, he thought. He wished he could find a molon, but they were quick and cautious and it usually took two men to catch one. No matter. Thomas's thoughts were not really on food. *Curves and motion.*

The valley was narrow and the sides steep. Thomas had to lean backward as he walked down the northeast side toward a small creek he had seen through the trees. His toes were chafing in his wet boots, and he thought he would be glad to sleep that night. The sky overhead, before it was obscured by the heavy vegetation, was fading from blue into a light purple.

The water in the creek was cool and good. Thomas lay flat on his stomach and scooped up handfuls to splash in his face. As the water ran and dripped back into the creek, Thomas could see his reflected eyes and nose quivering, drawing in and out like a bowstring in the reflections of the water. He smoothed back his hair and wiped his mouth. Rolling over into the grass and weeds, the young boy closed his eyes and tried to recapture the images Earl Kerning had shown him. He dozed off for a moment, the scarlet curve he had seen haunting his dreams.

A faint sound of music wakened Thomas in a soft darkness. He sat up and stretched, his lower back slightly sore. The music seemed to be coming from deeper in the valley, and so Thomas crept toward it cautiously. He had forgotten about the snails, and his stomach was empty and growling. But the music played on and drew Thomas with its wild swirling melody like an underground stream bubbling and boiling in a whisper.

There were lights fading in and out of the darkened trees. Thomas thought they were torches being whipped about and he became more careful. If it was the mercenaries at play, he would have to skirt them and find another place to sleep. But he caught sight of something that eased that thought and also made him wonder. A stout figure in a red and white frock danced into the full glare of one of the larger lights and it was Kerning.

No. Not Kerning, but one like Kerning. *The Shee*, thought Thomas, *it is the Shee*. But he was still suspicious and stayed near the outer fringe of the area where the Shee were dancing and whirling in what seemed to be a celebration of some sort. Thomas could see now that there were about thirty of them in all, the men all looking like Earl Kerning, but the women slimmer and less ugly in the face. There were even a few that looked human. Thomas strained his eyes to see these few and was soon caught up in the spirit of the place, lightly clapping his hands and bouncing his head.

The fluid and hot globe of lights seemed to drift to Thomas. He did not move, except to nod and clap his hands, as the motion grew in him and eventually surrounded him, enfolding him in the Shee revels. Thomas soon had to crane his neck to each side to watch the awkward grace of the Shee dancers, their leathery feet stamping and pointing in the air, their full bodies swaying and whirling in constant delight. Thomas thought theirs was a gaiety of ecstatic animals, their faces stretched in joy of themselves at play. His own hands continued to clap, harder and harder.

One of the Shee—Thomas did not know whether or not it was Kerning—separated from the group and came in a heavy swoop to Thomas. His hands and eyes invited Thomas to join them, to rise and dance as they were. Thomas moved easily to his feet and began to rotate his hips and jerk his legs, a huge grin spreading his face into enjoyment of the moment only. His youthful coldness continued to crack and break like winter ice in spring. In his dark eyes shone lights of green and yellow.

Sweat gleamed on Thomas's body. A ring was formed with all hands clasped, Thomas not feeling the rough skin of the Shee, not caring. The music came from a small group of Shee dressed in light pink trousers. One plucked a V-shaped stringed instrument, his long thick fingers strumming it with abandon. Another blew into a long reed with holes running down the front. The third player held a round drum between his knees and beat on it with short quick flips of his wrists, the staccato rhythm booming out in soft explosions. They all had a curious glaze in their eyes, their expression one of both distance from themselves and an immediate involvement, as if something else was joining them in the dance and was actively moving their limbs in a bubbling joy.

The night was one blue dew. All about him Thomas caught glimpses of desire made flesh, couples breaking off from the ring and disappearing into the woods and returning later with an even greater look of ecstasy etched on their faces. Thomas leaped and pivoted with his own beating heart, desire welling up in him as his blood grew in heat and fire and the night.

A cup of brew was passed and each member took the cup and drank from it. When it came to Thomas, he stopped and stepped back from the ring, the cup in his hands. Lifting it, Thomas saw his face momentarily before he let the Shee drink flow down his throat. It was good, like a thin honey. He felt it in his throat and stomach, twitching and pulsing. Gleeful, Thomas drank more until one of the Shee near him took the cup and passed it on. Thomas laughed and rejoined the ring, his eyes shut, head thrown back, neck tossing like that of a young horse running in a field.

Thomas felt hands touch him from behind. He turned with desire and saw a girl who looked like a Circle woman dancing lightly in front of him, her coal-black hair blowing freely. A part of Thomas's mind recognized that she could not be there, and he tried to make her presence fit in place. But it did not fit and that part gave up in the assault of the frenzied Shee dance. He did not care that the girl was not in the Inniscloe Circle where she should have been. She was there, with him, and he felt a need for her that he had never had before for any Circle girl. Reaching out to her, Thomas moved in a new way, and it was a way that burned and rose and spilled out from a deep part of him, a part that had been frozen to that point.

The girl, smiling, backed away from Thomas, leading him by slow degrees to a grove of saplings shining with the light of the Shee torches. More in obedience to himself than to her, Thomas gradually ceased dancing and began to circle the beautiful girl of the north who had unbuttoned the top of her pale green tunic. As they reached the grove, she turned and ran into it, hidden from Thomas for a moment by the shadows of the trees. Thomas ran too.

The branches and leaves of the trees were thick and broad and were brushed with a dim light that was dusty and fresh. Thomas forgot that it was winter as he whirled through the grove with the girl one step in front of him. Almost beyond the sound of the music Thomas caught her and pulled her down and down. Her clothes rose like a bed sheet blowing in the wind, slowly, and filling with billowing hoops. Thomas fell among them as if pushing against a heavy wagon, his muscles seeming to strain at a slower pace, his face flushed.

Two hands pulled at Thomas's cheeks and one loosened the belt of his pants. This oddity did not register with Thomas as his head was full of smoke. He felt at the very heart of things, and he was committed to go to the end, whatever that was. He and the girl would unweave the night.

Something pulled gently at his legs, lifted them, and moved under them. In a moment Thomas was in her and she was around him.

There seemed to be talk, loose and inside his head, but tinged with a primal urgency.

Time to go soon. Something that needs doing.

Yes.

I will give you Imram.

Yes.

And to Man.

Yes.

Yes, I do.

Yes.

Yes, and more.

Yes.

In the morning Thomas woke alone on the cold hillside, but he felt that one important part of himself had come fully awake and that he would not let it sleep again ever. He rose and moved on quickly toward Clonnoise Abbey and the curve that was waiting there for him.

Chapter 25

The valley was shaped like a bowl pushed together in the middle. Thomas stood behind a tree on the top of one of the sides that had been pushed in and looked down into the valley where the Abbey lay, broken and ruined. Beside him squatted a large brown rock which had stamped upon it the mysterious sign of the Others.

Thomas hesitated. The words of the Shee, and the acts of the night before, were in his head but so were those of his father. Turly had told him to go to the Abbey if necessary. The Shee had told him it was necessary to go there and find the Box. They had agreed with his father who had evidently returned with love to the art of the Blessing Plan. And they had shown him a vital secret of the nature of mankind, and a part of himself that he had kept buried for too long. They wanted to extend their way of life, and now so did he. Why did he pause?

The Abbey looked sunk in shadows in the seemingly peaceful depths of its valley, and Thomas thought it a good sign. He glanced around at the other sides of the valley and saw nothing. Gripping his blut blade, he moved down the hill slowly, weaving his way among the trees. Near the bottom he stopped and craned his neck to see into the graveyard behind the Abbey. There were a number of headstones. Crosses with circles on them; stones that tapered near the top; a figure with wings that seemed forever trapped on the earth, its solid weight hanging it at graveside. Thomas almost unconsciously ran through the songs about the Abbey his father had taught him. They were keys to the vault of the Box, he knew that. But he would have to get closer to unravel the puzzle. Rubbing one leg that had a large bruise on it, Thomas continued his way down as a light rain began to fall.

In the distance a movement at the front door of the Abbey caught his eye. Stooping beside a bush, Thomas watched. There was no other movement for several minutes. Then a patch of blue appeared. Thomas squatted lower as a tall man dressed in blue moved out onto the front steps and looked up at the sky. The man seemed satisfied and turned back to the door. Another man, wearing red, joined him and the two talked for a time, motioning up to the northeast. A group of ten men came out and moved off up the hill in that direction. The two men in red and blue walked back into the Abbey. Thomas tried to think what to do. With the men there, whatever their purpose, he would have a difficult time getting to the Blessing Box. He would simply have to wait to see what the men would do. He had the time, he thought.

Evening came softly in the valley. Thomas saw no other sign of the two men, and he relaxed to wait them out. He ate berries and divided his time between watching the Abbey and the sky.

Almost as the last light was fading, Thomas heard a man running down the northeast slope. He sat up and watched through the branches of a small tree. There was only the light sound of falling feet at first, and then Thomas saw his father Turly break out into the open near a large cedar whose limbs were arched upward. Thomas wondered if he were with the men who were already in the Abbey. *Turly.*

He found out quickly. As Turly approached the front door, Thomas saw the patch of blue again. Turly stopped. The man in red moved languidly around the other and stepped slowly to where Turly was standing. Both of the strangers had long swords with them, and they were drawn and ready.

222

Turly stepped back from the first man and drew his own sword; the man in blue joined his companion and the two moved in a semicircle in front of Turly.

Turly was obviously not a part of the group. Thomas knew that his father was very good with his sword, but not against two men. It would be an unfair fight and Thomas wondered why there was to be a fight at all.

The man in blue was talking to Turly and Turly was arguing back. All three swords were cocked up, pointing at each other.

The fight started when Turly seemed to shake his head as if to say no. The man in red stepped in and thrust at Turly.

Turly parried the thrust and spun away while the man in blue stood watching. The red man went after Turly but was not as agile as he was and, before he could stop his rush, Turly flicked his long blade and pricked him on the shoulder. Thomas could hear the man yell, and saw him grasp his shoulder. Turly reached out and hit the man's weapon, which then fell to the ground. At that point the blue man arched his sword and began to stalk Turly.

Thomas watched with rapid breath as his father crouched and waited. It seemed like hours before the two were face to face, and Thomas felt a growing tension. He did not know who the man in blue was, but he felt that the tall man was more than capable with his sword, a man who could kill easily and without care. Thomas had seen his father die once, and he did not want to see it again. Rising to his feet with resolution, he started toward the Abbey, his own sword drawn.

Turly thrust and missed, the other man sidestepping and lunging in as he did so. As Turly rushed by him, the taller man brought the sword down on Turly's shoulder blade and made him lurch forward even further. Spinning, Turly was again face to face with him, grim but determined. The Center of the North Circle swung his blade in the air and then brought it down quickly, the stroke almost smashing the other man's sword. But the man in blue whipped it away and then slashed it across Turly's chest. Thomas, who was running now, could not see the damage, but he was growing afraid for his father.

The injury seemed to make Turly come to life. Tossing the sword grip from hand to hand, he grinned at the man. With the swift touch of a lizard's tongue, his sword licked out and hit one of the man's hands. The man swore loudly and for the first time seemed worried. Thomas cheered for Turly. His father had been good in basu practice, Thomas knew that, and he was glad to see that some of that remained.

The man in red, who had been squatting to one side of the fight watching, shouted something as Thomas entered the Abbey grounds. Holding his wounded arm, he pointed to the youth. The man in blue separated from Turly warily and looked back at Thomas.

"Thomas!" yelled Turly. "Stop!"

Thomas said nothing at first but advanced on the three men, not knowing what he would do.

"Let my father go," he said, looking from face to face.

The man in blue, his face scarred and weathered, gave Turly a cautious look and stepped toward Thomas. "I am Caine," he said with pride. "Head of the Danae mercenaries."

"You knew Barry," said Thomas.

"Oh, yes," said Caine. "Pity."

"Pity?"

"He knew too much."

"*You* killed him?" guessed Thomas.

Caine ignored him. "Why are you here?" he asked, raising his sword point.

"He is my father," said Thomas, pointing at Turly.

"Is he?" said Caine with a bare twitch of a smile. "Then you must be Thomas."

"Yes," said Thomas.

"Then neither of you will do anything but show us the way to the Blessing Box."

Thomas stared at Caine for a moment and then looked over at Turly.

"Hello, my son," said Turly.

"Father, I saw you die in the Lower Mountains," said Thomas softly, as if there were no one else present.

"It was not true flame you saw," said Turly. "I went through it into another part of the mountain." When the young man nodded, Turly wondered why he could so easily accept the unbelievable. *Well, so could he.*

"The Order is then with Blessing?" said Thomas.

"In a way, yes. They want only to be left alone now that they have done their part."

"And their part . . . ?"

Turly smiled. "To get me here, to this moment."

"You hated the Blessing Plan once," said Thomas. "I saw you with Blessing in the room at Hastings Hall."

"You were there?" said Turly.

"I was there."

"Quiet!" shouted Caine, agitated. "The Box. Show us the Box!"

"I know of the Plan now, Father," said Thomas without pause. "And I am for it."

Turly smiled and said nothing. But he seemed relieved.

"For my own reasons I will go to the Box and . . ."

"Do what, Thomas?" said Turly.

"I have to go to the vault first," said Thomas.

"What vault?" said Caine quickly. "Where?"

"I want to press the bulb on the Box," said Thomas. "And open it."

Caine and the man in red looked at each other. "Where?" they said together.

"Thomas . . . don't," said Turly.

Caine seemed to become enraged at Turly's interruption, and suddenly, before Thomas could react, he leaped at Turly, who had lowered his sword while talking with Thomas. Surprising him, Caine drove home the point of his sword and Turly fell to the ground.

Thomas yelled in rage and instantly slapped one fist into the nearby red man's throat, then ran and leaped, with his legs bunched, toward Caine's chest. Caine turned with a startled look on his face, but he could not move in time. He went down with a rush of air bursting from his lungs. Rolling on the ground, he still had the nerve of purpose and groped for his sword. Thomas moved to him and crushed his nose with one heel. Caine jerked and lay still. Then, hesitating only briefly, remembering Barry and his father, Thomas kneeled and plunged his blade deep into Caine's heart. *Nasty, brutish and short.*

Behind Thomas, the red man cursed and tried to get up; Thomas stepped back to him and chopped his neck sharply on one side. Some birds overhead wheeled and cried out as the man fell.

It was over.

Thomas heard Turly moan and the boy fell to his knees beside him, cradling his head in his lap.

"Turly? Father?" said Thomas.

Turly's eyes seemed sunken deep in his face, which was drained and whiter almost than Thomas's hair. "I . . ." he said, his voice faint.

"Father, don't talk," said Thomas, rubbing his face gently.

Turly's hands moved slowly as if they were just learning how to work. They pulled from his pocket three coins which Thomas instantly saw had on them the face of the demon. He dropped them on the ground, his jaw falling open to expose what seemed a great darkness to Thomas, who bent his ear to his mouth to listen.

"I love you, Thomas," said Turly, his voice scratchy and almost breathless with pain.

Thomas held Turly and cried. All of his youth seemed distilled in that moment: all the love lost, all the rejection and suspicion, all the pain—forgiven.

"I love *you*, Father," said Thomas. And it was a new world.

Turly stirred slightly and seemed to smile although his face was contorted and his eyes glazed. Thomas put his ear to his father's chest and heard a faint heart beat. Quickly checking the wounds, he knew they were serious but not, he hoped, fatal. Ripping lengths of cloth from his own tunic, Thomas carefully bound up the torn skin and covered the punctures as best he could. When he was through, he brushed back his father's red hair and saw that he was trying to speak again. He placed his ear next to Turly's mouth.

"Thomas . . . for you . . . the lock is here . . . the keys . . ."

"Yes, Father."

"The coins . . . too . . ."

"Yes," said Thomas, stuffing the coins into his pocket.

"The bulb . . . Thomas . . . the bulb . . ."

"I know," said Thomas slowly and clearly. "I . . . know of the bulb and the curving run."

Turly seemed to pause and smile again at his son in what Thomas took to be pride. Then his face achieved a strange look, his eyes fluttering and slanting toward the Abbey walls. "The vault . . . Thomas . . . Blessing . . . songs . . . coins . . . soon . . . by nightfall . . . Thomas . . ."

"What?" said Thomas, wondering why his father had mentioned Blessing. And why the urgency? He had to hold himself from shaking him.

"Soon . . . soon . . ." said Turly and fell silent, his eyes closing. Thomas thought he had a peaceful look on his face but wasn't sure, nor was he sure how long he would be unconscious. But, looking up and around the bowl of the valley, he thought he had to get to the vault as quickly as he could. He had sensed a need for speed in his father's voice, and more of Caine's men might be coming back.

Carrying Turly carefully to a secluded corner of the Abbey, and covering him with one of the heavy tapestries pulled from the wall, Thomas felt that he would live, and that soon they could both return north and live out their lives with Smith, Meriwether and the rest of the Circlefolk, whatever else happened. This pleased Thomas, and he left Turly and went out the rear of the Abbey.

The cemetery was silent. Thomas stood for a time at the rear door and glanced around at the various stones. Turly had taught him as a boy that there was a puzzle there to which he had the appropriate keys.

Keys.
Songs.
Riddles.

> Where life and love are justly through,
> Where all is loose and light and free,
> The stars are burning brightly still,
> And sit upon a blackened hill.
> *Fol de rol de rolly o*

Thomas trudged through the tall weeds among the dead. *Where life and love are justly through,* he thought.

> Make your eye to rise in time
> And it will see its rightful due;
> For frozen in its ancient day,
> The old can never have its way,
> *Fol de rol de rolly o*

In front of Thomas was a huge stone figure, a creature with wings like the ones he once had liked to draw on Circle demon pictures. It stood tall and impassive, streaked with gray and green. He ignored it and continued his journey in memory among the external images of that memory.

> High above the scene is set:
> All remains and all is changed.
> What have you to do with this, O,

227

Who live and love and die below?
Fol de rol de rolly o

What indeed do I have to do with this? thought
Thomas, smiling softly, the smile serving as a recognition
to himself that he was now indeed an actor in his father's
drama. *All remains and all is changed.* He could not imagine himself as he had been just a few short weeks before,
sulking and scheming against his father in the far north
of home. Changes. The same body, a different mind. The
same world, a different landscape.

The young boy reached the far end of the burial ground
and turned to face the Abbey, lying in its gray rubble.
He saw several birds wheel above the ruins and then dart
beyond the hill down which he had come earlier.

*Where is it? Where is the vault of the fabled Blessing
Papers? Where do they lie?*

Thomas finished the song from his youth. As he did so
his eye fell upon the rear exit of the Abbey. The words of
the song seemed to move his feet. He knew he was where
he ought to be.

So seek from near the corner door,
Where age goes through but once, no more,
Where bones of men are set in stone.
Then you will have what few have known.
Fol de rol de rolly o

Thomas's feet stopped at the stone angel he had passed
earlier. He looked carefully around the rest of the graveyard and saw only the one figure with wings. Walking
around it, and placing his hands carefully on the base of
the marker, Thomas could slowly feel, like a sleeping
hand refilling with painful blood, the sensation of gears
and wheels inside the stone. Stepping back, he began to
sing "Turly's Song":

"Upon A Knee
A Nothing Sings
And When It Does
It Gives Us Wings."

At the final vowel, the stone wings of the angel began
to fall slowly and the cover of the grave in front of it
shifted to one side, creaking, grating with a hollow sound.

Thomas walked to the gaping hole and looked down into it. There were steps leading deep into the ground. Having no candles with him, and not knowing where to look for any, Thomas stepped quickly down into the earth, his father's urgent words seeming to whisper in his ear. Ten, twelve, twenty steps and the cover closed over him. He was alone and in a stale dark that seemed like rough silk.

The rock tunnel was smooth to the touch and Thomas traveled through it as fast as he could, his hands serving as his eyes. His booted feet seemed to make a thin layer of dust scatter as he shuffled across it. After a time, his own eyes seemed to flicker with internal lights of their own, deluding him several times into thinking that he had seen movement ahead in the tunnel.

Thomas thought over the alternatives he still had. Should he actually find the legendary Box at the end of the tunnel, he knew he could do one of two things: touch the bulb he had been told about, or not touch it. If he did touch it, he wasn't sure what would happen. *Would* man make another rise up that long swift curve he had seen in the cube of the Shee? Would there be no damage if he did *not* touch the bulb, or would Imram remain the preying ground for men like Caine?

There seemed no answer to that last one. And he now felt committed to touching the bulb; he could only go by what he had been told, that it was necessary to touch the bulb for man to be man again.

Thomas stopped in the dark of the musty tunnel and thought about that. He had learned of the bulb in two strange ways. Once in overhearing Blessing and his father while they were talking in Hastings' office where he was hidden. The other time was from the Shee, Earl Kerning, who had seemed concerned for the human race. Or was he? Thomas's sense of self bothered him. What was the *truth* of things?

The question bothered Thomas as he shifted uneasily from foot to foot in the earth beneath the Abbey. His father had just mentioned the bulb, but was he telling him to touch it, or not touch it? What *was* he going to do when the Box was found?

If it was found.

Thomas decided to puzzle out the answer when he actually had the Box, and he stepped off into the dark again, trying to move even faster, the problem of his final choice lending a hotter edge to his feelings.

Then Thomas's sensitive hands found metal. Racing over the surface of it, his fingers knew it was a sealed door of some kind. He felt along the opposite side of the tunnel wall and realized he was stopped. But further study discovered a vertical slot in the center of the door, and his fingers fondled it to discover its use.

Riddles.

Keys.

Coins.

Thomas seemed to hear his father's voice as he fumbled in his pocket for the coins. *The lock would find you.* The young man slipped the coins into the slot one at a time, stopping and waiting after each drop. When the third coin had gurgled down into the dark, Thomas felt a slight rush of air as the door seemed to slip upward and out of his way. He extended his hands and passed through the now open space.

The blind journey continued. Almost hitting his head at one low point in the tunnel, during which he bent and half-crawled until he could stand again, Thomas began to fantasize about the end of his search. He imagined many things. Stranger creatures than he had yet known; wild pursuits with even wilder weapons; reconciliations beyond his finest dreams; tools that seemed to form and dissolve in his hands. It was both good and terrifying. All of Thomas's world was in his sensitive fingers on the rock wall, and in his wheeling mind.

After an interminable length of time, Thomas fantasized that a stark red light had snapped on a long way in front. It was some time before he knew it to be real, and his breath grew more rapid as he stared at it. The light pained his eyes as he drew near. Then, one hand shielding his face from the glare, Thomas reached a giant door which lay open to a room floored with huge black-and-white squares.

The room was awesome. The walls were shiny and metallic, one of them holding several rows of silver lights that seemed to dance in a silent rhythm. Thomas stepped inside hesitantly. He forgot for a moment the urgency with which he had entered the underground tunnel. The overhead lights, making the room shine as bright as day, were like white grapes hanging on a vine. Thomas craned his neck to look up at them and then around at the room itself. There was no sign of a Box of any kind. There was a layer of dust on the floor and Thomas thought he saw old tracks on it. He shook his head, and went quickly to the far wall of silver strips. Putting his hands to them, he could feel nothing but an odd humming as if something were sitting and waiting impatiently. He turned and glanced about him with squinting eyes.

The Blessing Vault, he thought.

On the floor there was one white square which seemed to have been wiped almost clean of dust. There were dark stains to either side of it, and Thomas walked to it carefully. Squatting beside it, he placed his finger tips along its edges and felt melody. Knowing the tune, Thomas began to sing the long song of his father. *High above.*

It worked. *The song and the riddles worked,* thought Thomas, as he stood up and watched the square draw back and a tripod whisper up from beneath it. A luminous black box, the color of a moonless night, rose on it. The numbers 2020 were etched on one side, and a small black bubble was on the other.

The Blessing Box, thought Thomas, his eyes misting. *The bulb!*

The Box lay silently on top of the tripod. Thomas stared at it and then remembered what he was there for. To open the Box. To touch the bulb. Flexing one hand, he reached for the bulb. He touched it lightly and was thrown backward, stunned, and stark images came to him without speech, as they had to his father years before:

The darkness is lush and full of silence. The stone floor is gritty and there is a vague and distant sense of light that cannot penetrate the darkness but is trying to. The dark floats in wait. It moves by the eye as the eye remains open to see into the liquid black.

A bare length of whiteness, horizontal in the form of a cocoon. It stands out in the gloom when looked at closely. It cannot be seen in its entirety at that distance, however, and the eye backs up as if to take in the imagined whole, the dun-colored wrapper widening and swelling in its roundness. The eye goes back, back until it is at maximum visual range to see it when it explodes in light, a slow-motion sparkle outward into intensely blue-white dots massing and unmassing like moths in an erratic frenzy.

The eye does not blink, and the cocoon shape rises to a sitting position as the glow from within it fades and shrinks to the steady pace of a candle's light. The thing within rustles and moves. A clipping falls to the gritty floor and one edge of the dun wrapper unfolds like a leaf, curls back and exposes an arm that is of the purest brown. A hand reaches out and it is a hand that is also curled like a leaf, but it straightens and reveals holes crusted with dark circles.

The entire thing is out of the confining cloth now and it stands by the slab of flat rock upon which it had lain. It looks at the wrapper and smiles.

The eye that is watching this tracks to the discarded binding. It hovers above the unrolled light and sees with no astonishment the beautifully clear lines there, the lines of a man perfectly revealed as if in a mirror after a bath, or in the process of memory waking after a night of troubled sleep, returning to the true textures of day.

It is an exact picture: The light coming up through the cloth pushing up again through each pore and hair and onto the receiving cloth. This is repeated several times to engrave the image of it happening.

The eye watches it still as it notices from one corner of its vision the thing from the wrapping moving slowly away to the wall of rock and beyond. The eye seems willing to know what it will do, that it is about to enter history, and it does not care.

The room is large but crammed with people of various colors and sizes. They press upon one another, push for position, move their heads from side to side to see, to hear. The eye pauses briefly to take in the variety of shapes it sees. It moves to the front of the room where an impressively polished table sits solidly upon a floor clear of any imperfection. The eye could see itself in it if it looked. It does not. There are tiny flags upon the table, and glasses partly filled with liquid which are periodically lifted to the faces of men and women sitting at the table.

The eye tracks close to each of these faces. One is large with fatty tissue like a doll, pink and white and lined with eternal contentment. Another is haggard and worn, thin with clusters of moles on the cheeks like constellations; the forehead is creased and vaguely worried as if something were biting its leg under the table. Another face is glancing from side to side, to the face of contentment and the face of care. It cannot seem to decide which role it wants to assume.

There are documents on the table and the eye rotates

232

to see them. There are the large letters CSS on the top sheets. The eye looks up and out at the small sea of faces that perch in the crowded air like birds, waiting. They seem uncomfortable as they nestle close to one another.

The eye tracks to the rear of the room, the way it had come, turning back to look at the now small table at the front. The figures at the table are still sitting. They are looking at a door to their right. The eye does not move as the door opens. All heads and faces swivel to the door.

The man from the cave walks in and smiles kindly. He raises his arms as if reaching for something.

The people in the room begin to file out. The eye catches their backs as they leave. It cannot see their expressions. The people at the table watch as the man with no clothes on waves to them. They get up and leave too, a look of profound disgust on their faces, their lips turned down. The man leaves through the door he had entered, and the eye is left in an empty room, the tiny flags on the table quivering only slightly from an unseen wind. The room darkens slowly as the sun outside sets.

A large circle of red and white pebbles. They form the mosaic of a single rose, surrounded by the clarity of limpid space, untainted. It is a rounded piece of work, labored upon over many years of patient toil. It lies serene, finished.

Dark feet kick at this work of rock. The eye watches only the feet as they thrust and poke with heel and toe. The outer rim of white-gray pebbles shatters into disarranged clumps like trampled insects. The rose lies contained at the center. It is reached by the sandaled feet and it seems to pull away from them. It cannot. Each of its measured petals fall away into mere rock and loneliness. The chiseled red beauty of its outline, massed and held by the unfelt pull of the earth, dissolves, under the prodding of the feet, into ragged color.

The eye tracks upward to the brooding face of the man from the cave and the large room. He looks down at his sandals and bends to brush off the dust. When he is through, he turns to the ragged pile and picks at it. He frowns and concentrates as he seems to try to rearrange the pebbles. He bends forward to reach one and, as he does so, he topples and falls onto the pile of senseless rock. He falls slowly and seems to hit with great force. His arms are up to break his fall and his elbows scrape sharply against the individual pebbles. The eye sees this and retains its position. It sees flesh tear away from an elbow and catches the barest glimmer of metal as a fading sun it never really focuses on flashes once.

The thing stands and shrugs. It is sad now in its face and it looks at the barren pile of pebbles, shakes its head and walks away.

A long darkness and a knowledge of that darkness as it passes. Then the rising of light as on a stage, slowly and inexorably; there are glimmers and flashes, random and startling to the eye.

The pebbles reappear, lying still and unconcerned with only a hint of their former pattern as if a cloud had loosened itself from a familiar form and had frozen itself in an uncertainty of recognition. An arm reaches down toward the bits of rock and dust. It picks up one of the white pebbles and places it apart. The arm hesitates for a moment and then goes back to the pile for another pebble. It places that pebble beside the first one. Another pebble, then another. Soon a curve is formed.

The arm and its fingers take a long while to work and arrange a few pebbles. It does not touch the red pebbles at all, leaves them in disarray in the center of the pile. The fingers twitch and pause. Another arm joins the first. The eye sees the arm as it moves in the half-light. When it rotates it sees the long purple scar spiraling down the arm from the outside of the elbow to the inside of the wrist. It is like an artery on top of the skin, a thick line on a map, a curve that points to something.

Another arm joins the task and the three work at the pile. A fourth, with eager fingers, joins, and another and another. They continue to reach and touch, push and align. A pattern begins to emerge but it seems meaningless to the impersonal gaze of the eye. It is a circle within a circle within a circle crossed partially by a rising curve.

The eye seems to blink several times, and closes.

Light bursts onto the horizon with no flare. There is an arc of pale yellow dividing sharply with the blackness around it and above it. The eye floats in front of a bed of stones, its image of circles and a curve almost complete. But there is no rose there, nor anything else. It is the merest pile of pebbles, gray and white like decaying teeth.

A tall figure dressed in white is walking toward the mound from a great distance. The man walks for a long time, and the eye seems to grow weary waiting for him. He treads heavily as he walks. When he does arrive at the mound he slows even more; he smiles at the eye and then down at the pattern on the mound. The eye follows him as he circles the mound once and then seems to reach out one foot as if to disrupt that pattern as well as the one with the rose. As his foot wavers, he begins to fall toward the pebbles and he throws out his elbows to catch his fall. The skin tears with a wrenching sound.

The eye holds on the tearing skin, up close, and there is metal and wire beneath it. The man stands back up and dusts himself off. Bending forward over the pebbles, he begins to arrange them and the eye cannot see the action.

The man stands erect after a while and walks to the other side of the mound. Before the eye can track down to the pile, the man falls again. His skin is already hanging in rags at his elbows, the metal within shiny and bright. As he falls the eye follows him as if to help. He falls slowly as if on rusty wires. When he does hit the ground, the metal elbows absorb the blow. The metal makes a sound like the grinding of teeth and breaks as had the skin.

The eye closes in. Beneath the metal and wire there is flesh, pliant and pink. The eye seems to stare without comprehension. The man rises again and proceeds around the mound of stone. The eye still does not look at the pattern there. It stays on the man as he bends and seems to make figures or words with the pebbles. When he is through, the face looks up at the eye and smiles. It is no longer the face of the man from the cave, but an old face, withered and age-worn, with well-furrowed grooves and whorls in it. The old man's eyes seem to glitter as he points down to the mound. The eye follows the motion. There are words in the mound now and they say:

You have chosen.

The eye closes and there is darkness.

When Thomas awoke the Box was open. Lying on his side, he stared at the deep rich black of the Box, its color seeming to be continuous with the pictures he had just seen. Sitting up, he wondered if his father had seen the same things: The strange toy that had risen from the dead; the confusion of its appearance in a meeting; the scattered mosaic; the line of men who seemed determined to piece it back together; the man who was a machine who was a man.

You have chosen.

The images had been intense and persistent. Thomas thought there had been both regret and apology in them. But the final pictures seemed to have been clear: only the line of man could restore what had been lost. Human arms and hands reaching to replace displaced stone, stone displaced by man himself, by the Blessing line. Thomas felt guilt as he rose to his knees. He remembered what his father had called him, and he had recognized the face of the old man in the last pictures: Thomas Blessing. The thought that he himself might be a descendant of Thomas Blessing disturbed Thomas only briefly; he knew it made no difference one way or the other. He was there in that room for a particular reason, and that reason was solidifying like a piece of ice.

Shaking his head to clear it, Thomas crawled forward to the Box to look inside. There was a massive quiet in the giant room and it seemed to focus on the Box, the inside of which Thomas saw to be orange and shiny like the color of an Order robe and looped and whorled in bulging ridges. At the bottom was a sheaf of papers. Thomas froze as the full impact of that fact sank in.

The Blessing Papers.

After so many years he, Thomas, would see them, read them, would know what his father had called the "final secret" of the long drama of Imram. He reached inside and gingerly lifted out the thin packet of papers. He put them on his lap and dropped his hands to his side. Lifting his face for a moment to the huge lights overhead, Thomas took one deep breath. He lowered his eyes to the small paper on top of the stack and began to read. It said:

IF YOU ARE HERE AND CAN READ THIS, YOU ARE OF THE BLESSING LINE AND ARE ABLE TO SAVE IMRAM AND THE WORLD OF MAN.

OVER YOUR HEAD IS THE LAST STOREHOUSE OF HUMAN KNOWLEDGE. ONLY YOU CAN NOW MAKE THE LINK THAT

WILL RELEASE THIS KNOWLEDGE BACK TO MAN. WITH IT MAN CAN ONCE AGAIN BEGIN HIS RISE TO WHAT HE CAN BE.

YOU CAN READ AND SO YOU ARE FREE OF THE CURSE THAT TOOK THIS KNOWLEDGE FROM MAN. YOU CAN REFLECT ON WHAT YOU SEE AND SO ARE IN CONTROL OF WHAT YOU DO.

CONSIDER THE IMAGES YOU HAVE JUST SEEN. NOW CONSIDER THAT THE IMAGES WERE MADE BY MEN. THEY WERE MADE TO TELL THE STORY THAT THEY SHOW. THE IMAGES ARE NOT NECESSARILY TRUE; BUT YOUR SEEING OF THEM MAKE THEM SO. THEY ARE HARD TO DENY AS THEY ARE GIVEN.

ENCLOSED WITH THIS NOTE ARE COPIES OF THE TRUE STORY OF THE MEN WHO MADE THE FALLING.

READ THEM. IF YOU ARE NOT CONVINCED OF THE VALUE OF WHAT THEY HAVE DONE AND WHY, DO NOT TOUCH THE BULB AGAIN.

IF YOU ARE CONVINCED, PRESS THE BULB.

SHOULD THE BULB NOT BE TOUCHED AGAIN, THE LINK TO THIS KNOWLEDGE WILL BE LOST FOREVER. MAN WILL ALWAYS BE SOMETHING OTHER THAN HE ONCE WAS. BUT PRESS IT AND THE LINK WILL BE MADE. MAN CAN BEGIN HIS RISE.

IT IS IN YOUR HANDS NOW, BLESSING. DO WHAT YOU WILL.

—John Blessing, 2105

Thomas lowered the papers slowly. *The word.*

If you are here and can read this, you are of the Blessing line. . . .

Was he? thought Thomas. *Was he?* If so, and his father was right, he and he alone was to decide whether or not the human curve of growth would be worth the return. His mind was rushing with the images of a lost past and the promise of a resurrection. Uncertain about his true identity, but thinking again that at that point it did not really matter, Thomas began leafing through the papers and reading slowly the evidence that seemed to him to confirm what the first paper had said. Memoirs. Notes. Time-tables. And the *Diary* of John Vail—Blessing. He knew he would have to study them more, but man seemed to have had a past unlike anything he had guessed at; and it had all been scattered by man himself, *deliberately*, by the line of his father and his father's father and on back to the original Thomas Blessing.

To destroy man to save him. Was that it?

Thomas could not fathom the why of it, but he understood that the past could be returned with the spread of man and his tools. Man could make his run up the curve of knowledge once again. The Sigma curve that his father had told him would begin slowly but then speed almost straight up until the last possible piece of knowledge was gained. And then . . .

And then *what*? thought Thomas in perplexity. Again a Falling? Again the Fires? How big was the next curve to be? How big *could* it be? And how often would man have to run the curve? Forever? Was his father and the mysterious Shee right in wanting man to make that energetic and violent run? And were the images he saw correct in projecting a successful remolding of the broken pieces of the past if he *did* touch the bulb?

Thomas gripped the Blessing Papers. Both the images that Kerning had shown him, and the evidence of the Papers themselves, suggested that man `could not be man` without such a curve of growth. *He had to do it, to hurry, to run upward to whatever was there.*

Strong emotions ripped through Thomas. He wanted to avoid the troubles that had robbed his father of his youth; but he also wanted the dreams of his own youth, the dreams of strange events, dreams that the Papers promised him if the bulb was touched a second time.

Thomas leaned toward the now grayish bulb. The Box itself seemed to hum in anticipation and the bulb blended to pink. The young Thomas could feel the portentous nature of the next few minutes. If he did not touch the bulb, life in Imram would remain the same. *A swamp*, Kerning called it. If he did touch the bulb, seeming to stare at him now like the eye of a savage beast, what would open to him and to Imram? His left hand flicked out and hovered near the bulb, the index finger trembling. His legs also trembled, as if they wished to move.

Pulling himself closer to the Box, Thomas reached a point directly over the bulb. The seconds passed slowly in the great room, the figure of the boy dwarfed by the immensity of it. As he watched, the bulb began to glow in its pinkness, flipping from weak to strong, the light almost frantic in its enclosed space. Thomas stared at it, numbed. Then, steeling himself, he squeezed his eyes shut and pressed the bulb. Time stopped for him and the whole of Imram seemed to lie hushed.

A man's voice from the wall of strips, which now looked like the joyful dance of summer insects, burst on Thomas's ears like the sound of an iron hammer on an anvil:

"Blessing?" it said. "This is Tain. Good!"

Looking up at the high ceiling, his heart pounding, Thomas thought he felt the end of the Falling.